C000174190

NOTHING
BUT
SMILES

A female detective guns for a total creep

LINDA HAGAN

Published by The Book Folks

London, 2023

ISBN 978-1-80462-100-4

www.thebookfolks.com

*Nothing but Smiles is the seventh novel in a series of
standalone murder mysteries set in Belfast and beyond.*

Prologue

He had chosen well. The car park was deserted, as he had known it would be at this time of night. It wasn't really a car park at all, just a piece of rough ground beside the channel where port workers would be arriving in a few hours' time to leave their cars for the day free of charge. But no one was about now. Even ardent couples hoping for a bit of privacy to share their hurried fumbles were gone. He was safe. He had it to himself. Well, almost to himself.

He could hear the water lapping against the bank but nothing was moving on the sea, or the land. Everything seemed asleep. It was still. Dead still.

A fast-food van with 'Dabby's' emblazoned on the side in garish writing stood shuttered, waiting for its owner to open for business once again. He knew it provided early morning breakfast baps for the office workers and staff from the cavernous buildings nearby. It was a favourite with some of the people at the new film studios, he'd read. It served coffee all day too, although he'd never been down there in daylight. It was his night-time place.

The bright lights illuminating the car park and ramps at the Stena terminal shone out brightly but they couldn't bridge the expanse of land and sea between the two channels. Their brightness only made his darkness more intense. He knew loading would begin soon for the early ferry. Then tiny figures would appear on the ship's deck but no one would notice him.

A single streetlight on the roadway behind him was fighting a losing battle against the blackness all around, enveloping him in its welcome shroud. An unexpected blast of wind off the water whipped up a pile of rubbish – wrinkled chip papers and yellow polystyrene packaging, lids gaping open, contents long gone. The mini whirlwind swirled the detritus up into the air and dropped it back down, scattering it like a petulant giant child demonstrating his power.

The figure had watched in the rear-view mirror as he drove while her eyes had grown heavier and heavier until finally her eyelids had slowly closed and her head had slumped forward onto her chest. Then her whole body had slipped gently to the side out of his view. Only when he was sure she was unconscious did he stop the car and begin his routine.

The figure took a pair of thick black neoprene gloves out of the briefcase sitting on the seat beside him and put them on like a surgeon donning his protective gloves before an operation. He was fastidious as he imagined surgeons would be too. He eased them over each finger, making sure the fit was exactly right, not rushing, taking his time, enjoying the sensation as his own hand disappeared, finger by finger, until it looked as if the new black hands were part of him or he was part of them.

His breathing was quickening now as he thought of what was only moments away for him. His excitement was mounting. His legs were tingling. He couldn't keep his feet still. He had waited all day anticipating tonight; anticipating what she would be like; anticipating what he would do to her. He turned on the car radio. Not too loud. There was no one around to hear but he wanted some background sound, something to create a mood. The stillness was unsettling him now as he prepared for what he was going to do. He once again felt that almost crippling fear of being discovered wash over him. They must never catch him. He couldn't go to that place. But they would never catch him. They didn't even know he existed. He was too clever for them. He smiled to himself.

Another cheesy Christmas song about love and family began to play on the radio. Slowly, carefully, he climbed over into the back beside the comatose woman; climbed on top of her. One black hand, shaking now, reached under her skirt and he let out a low moan as he made his first contact with her inner thigh. The sound of his own voice shocked him as if someone else had made the noise. Not him. He took a bottle out of his pocket and flicked the top open with practiced skill.

Soon he would have her. Soon she would be his. Forever.

Chapter 1

Monday

'Have you seen this, Chief Inspector?'

It was a wet and windy Monday morning, not quite cold enough for snow but heading that way; the sort of day when it's hard to get out of bed, even for a confirmed workaholic like DCI Gawn Girvin. Assistant Chief Constable Anne Wilkinson pushed a copy of the local newspaper across the desk towards her.

Gawn had been surprised to be summoned to the ACC's office and hadn't known what to expect. What greeted her when she walked in was Wilkinson looking even more serious than usual. A sour-faced Chief Superintendent Reid hovered beside her. Whatever was wrong was serious and Gawn didn't know how it might involve her. There was nothing she could think of that she had done recently which might have incurred her superiors' wrath or drawn the attention of the newspapers.

Gawn glanced down. The headline jumped out at her, 'Serial rapist on the loose', and her eyes widened as she read the sub-heading: 'No woman safe on Belfast streets'. The by-line caught her attention too. Donna Nixon, her nemesis, a journalist who more than once had interfered in her cases.

'Ma'am, I've heard nothing about this.'

'Yes, well, I've just been asking Chief Superintendent Reid how come I've heard nothing about a serial rapist either, and he informs me he didn't know. So how is it that this journalist does? And where did she get her information?'

Wilkinson's finger stabbed the paper to emphasise each word of her last question.

Gawn felt she was being accused of feeding information to Nixon. Nothing could be further from the truth. She always did her best to keep well away from all journalists, and especially Donna Nixon. As far as she was concerned, the woman was nothing but trouble.

'Not from me, ma'am. I haven't been investigating any rape cases.'

She realised Wilkinson would have known that. Nothing happened in the Crime Department that she didn't know about. Until now, it seemed.

'I know that, Chief Inspector. I'm not accusing you. But you do know this woman, don't you?'

'We're not friends or anything.'

'Don't be so bloody defensive, Chief Inspector. We need to know where she's getting her information. That's all.' It was Reid who had interrupted, his outburst a sure indication he had been on the receiving end of Wilkinson's anger before Gawn had arrived.

'Is she right?' Gawn asked. 'Is there a serial rapist?'

Gawn looked from Wilkinson to Reid and back again. She realised from their expressions they thought Nixon was.

'Unfortunately, it seems she might be,' Wilkinson conceded. She blew out her cheeks in a gesture of exasperation. 'The newspaper's lawyers would hardly let them make a claim like that if they didn't have *some* evidence to back it up. But we have no idea what it is.

'The cases she mentions aren't specific enough for us to identify. But, according to this' – she lifted the paper as if it was a rotten fish and then let it drop back down onto her desk with a sigh – 'there's a big feature coming at the weekend. In the meantime, she probably intends to drip-feed information all week to build up interest until her big reveal. It will stoke up fear in the community. We need to get ahead of this.'

Wilkinson had been looking at Reid as she spoke and he looked decidedly uncomfortable under her glare.

'According to District Command there have been no more than the usual number of sexual assaults reported,' she continued. 'But there was a rape on Saturday night which must have been what triggered this article, I presume. That investigation is ongoing. The Rape Crime Unit is handling it.

'The other incidents were all over the city. Different Local Policing Response Teams dealt with them and no one at District Command seems to have realised there might be any sort of a pattern. There's no obvious link. But there must be *something* to connect them and this woman bloody well knows what it is. I want to know where she got her information and how she managed to join the dots when we didn't.'

Gawn thought her boss seemed more concerned that someone was leaking information to the press than by the fact they might be dealing with a serial rapist.

Wilkinson had stood up while she was speaking. She was pacing backwards and forwards in front of the window. Gawn had never seen her so angry before.

'The chief constable wants an update from me and District Command tomorrow morning. The chairman of the Policing Board has been in his ear already. And the press office is clamouring for a statement. So, we have one day to establish whether there's anything to this or not. This is very serious. I'm sure I don't need to tell you that, Chief Inspector.'

Gawn didn't need to be told that rape was a serious offence and then, suddenly, she realised it wasn't the rapes Wilkinson was referring to. Bad publicity would hit the Christmas trade. And it could hurt tourism too. But, worst of all, it looked bad for the PSNI that they'd missed the connection between the cases and had a serial rapist operating right under their noses without noticing. It made them look incompetent. Gawn understood why Wilkinson was so annoyed.

'I can't call this woman and demand she tells me her source. And I don't think her editor would be particularly cooperative either,' Wilkinson said as she slumped back down into her chair. 'But you seem to have a relationship with her, Chief Inspector. You could meet her and talk to her. See what she'll tell you.'

Gawn blinked hard at Wilkinson's words. She didn't think she had any sort of a relationship with Donna Nixon and she doubted she would get very far if she tried asking for information. The only reason the woman had cooperated in the past was because Gawn had made some deals with her. But Wilkinson would have worked that out, of course. She would have realised that Nixon must have been passed information during her investigation and been given access to interview a key witness. The ACC couldn't be seen to be offering any kind of a deal. She was depending on Gawn doing it for her, without ordering her to. What did they call it? Plausible deniability? She could end up the fall guy if it all went wrong.

'If we find she's right and we do have a serial rapist, we'll be setting up a special task force. You would head it,

Chief Inspector, at the rank of acting superintendent based out of District Command. We need to include them and that's the neatest way to do it.'

So, this wasn't an invitation or even a suggestion. And the acting superintendent rank was the carrot. Do a deal with Nixon to get what they needed and she could have the leadership of a high-profile investigation and the next super's job when it came up. That was the inference. They must really be panicking to have a knee-jerk reaction like this, Gawn thought.

'This is the kind of job that gets you noticed,' Reid added.

Gawn wasn't particularly keen to be noticed. And she wasn't really interested in any promotion, but she was interested in catching criminals and rapists were high on her list of scum, just below murderers and child molesters. She would talk to Nixon but not for what it might mean for her career.

'I'll see if Donna Nixon will meet me and if I can get anything out of her. But she mightn't cooperate with me either, you know. I can't promise anything, ma'am.'

'I understand, Chief Inspector. But I know you'll do your best.'

Chapter 2

The Observatory cocktail lounge wasn't overly busy. It was still early. Later it would fill up with hotel guests after dinner in the restaurant or groups of colleagues choosing a special venue for their Christmas do. Gawn was waiting for Donna Nixon to arrive. She had been surprised when the journalist had phoned and asked to meet her. She had played right into Gawn's hands.

The subdued lighting made the view from the bar out over Belfast from its twenty-third floor vantage point even more spectacular. Gawn had selected her seat carefully. She could see all the comings and goings from her quiet corner.

Gawn sat, sipping her drink. Soon the concierge would begin restricting newcomers to those with a reservation. She hoped Nixon had realised that when she'd chosen the venue. No doubt she would order the most expensive cocktail on the menu courtesy of the PSNI when she arrived. Gawn had checked the menu. She was drinking soda water and lime. She was on duty. This was not a social meeting for her. It was business.

Gawn gazed out of the panoramic window at City Hall below with its colourful Christmas tree. Her attention was drawn to the door opening and she watched as a young couple walked in. Another figure entered behind them. It was the journalist. She paused on the threshold looking around until she spotted Gawn.

'Sorry I'm late. I got caught up with my editor.'

Nixon smiled, her lips forming a thin line.

'No problem. Would you like a drink?'

The woman didn't even glance at the cocktail menu lying on the table between them. Instead, without a moment's hesitation, she answered, 'I'll have a Smith 75, thanks.'

Gawn smiled to herself. She had been right. It was the most expensive cocktail on the menu. She signalled to the waiter and gave the order. While he fetched the drink, Gawn examined Nixon more closely as she struggled out of her black duvet coat, discarded her multi-coloured wool bobble beanie and stuffed her matching fingerless gloves in her pocket.

The first time they had met, Nixon had almost got herself killed sticking her nose into Gawn's investigation. Tonight, she looked not only older but more anxious than their first meeting when her enthusiasm and Nancy Drew attitude had really irked the policewoman.

Nixon had picked up a coaster from the table and was fiddling with it, passing it between her fingers. She couldn't seem to keep her hands still. And her eyes were darting around the room too as if she was looking for someone or something. Gawn realised Nixon was nervous but couldn't think why. Maybe she was worried that Gawn wouldn't help her.

'I suppose you know why I asked you to meet me,' Nixon began.

Her plain grey two-piece skirt suit with a bright pink silk blouse looked business-like and, no doubt, would be appropriate for an unexpected piece-to-camera for local TV if some news broke.

'I'd have to be really thick not to have worked that one out.'

The waiter arrived with Nixon's cocktail in a tall crystal champagne flute and set it down on the table along with a small dish of nibbles.

'I was surprised you agreed,' Nixon said, looking at the DCI from under lowered eyelids. Then, sounding more like her chirpy self, she added, 'I'm starving. I didn't have any lunch today. Too busy chasing up a lead for my story.' She sneaked another look at the policewoman as she took a handful of nuts.

Gawn was going to play a waiting game only for so long. Either Nixon would cooperate and tell her what she wanted to know or the ACC would have to get her information some other way. She tapped her foot against the leg of the table while Nixon insisted on finishing her drink and making conversation as if they were old friends catching up.

Nixon asked about Sebastian, Gawn's husband. Girly chitchat. Nixon didn't know Sebastian, had never met him, but she knew enough about Gawn to be aware of him and where he was now – on the other side of the world.

Gawn's answers to her questions were terse. Her private life was no one's business and certainly not this journalist's. Enough was enough. She needed to get whatever information she could for Wilkinson or stop wasting her time.

'I'll have another one of these,' Nixon said holding the empty cocktail glass out in front of her and examining it, turning it around as if she was appraising its value like an auctioneer on some antiques programme.

'When you've told me where you got the information for your story.'

Gawn's voice had hardened. They both knew why they were there so why waste any more time? But she did catch a waiter's eye and signalled with a slight movement of her hand that he should bring the same again.

Nixon realised she'd pushed her luck as far as it would go.

'Just some good old-fashioned research and lots of slog and the odd twenty quid for a cocktail to loosen tongues,' she said. She smiled and sank back in her seat looking pleased with herself. She lifted the now-empty snack bowl and was running her wetted fingers around inside it, gathering up the dusty residue and licking it off her fingers one by one.

'You expect me to believe you just happened to be researching rapes for no reason at all and you managed to put this all together? By yourself?'

'Uh-huh.' A smug look crossed Nixon's face as she ran her tongue across her lips.

Before Gawn could ask anything else, the waiter arrived back and exchanged their empty glasses for full ones. Gawn waited until he had moved away again before she asked her next question.

'But why were you researching rapes in the first place, Donna?'

She was not expecting the answer she got.

'Because I was frickin' raped.'

Chapter 3

Of all the things Nixon might have said, this was the last Gawn would have anticipated. Some clever quip about a tip-off she would have taken in her stride. But this? Nixon was raped? As she looked closely at the journalist she could see tears welling in her eyes.

'At least I think I was.' There was a tremor in her voice.

'You think? How? I don't mean how. I don't need those details.'

Gawn was flustered. Someone would need all those details. Later. But not now, not here and, hopefully, not her.

'I mean when? Where?'

'I think I was the third victim because I found two others before me and that got me thinking – maybe there could be more. I started asking around. There were at least a couple after me, I think, and then the girl at the weekend and some more women contacted the paper this morning.'

At least six rapes and no one had noticed? A loud burst of laughter from some men sitting nearby made Nixon turn her head sharply. There were only a few vacant tables left now.

'I don't think I can talk here,' she said, her eyes darting around the room, flicking from table to table.

'Where then? Do you want to come with me to a police station?'

A look of horror flashed across the woman's face.

'God, no. You're joking, aren't you? Definitely not.'

'Then where, Donna?'

'Could you come to mine?' She must have noticed Gawn's hesitation for she added, 'I only live five minutes away. We could talk there.'

It was unorthodox but then everything about what she was doing was unorthodox.

Gawn agreed.

Chapter 4

Gawn hadn't expected the night to turn out like this. She had faced down armed killers but this was different. This would bring back so many bad memories. Memories she had kept buried from everyone, even herself.

She was walking down a dimly lit street edging the Sandy Row area of Belfast at one end but convenient for the restaurant and theatre strip known locally as the Golden Mile at the other. She had spent nearly half an hour driving around trying to find a parking space in the area. She was vaguely aware of the noise of passing traffic on Great Victoria Street and groups of young people walking towards the city centre or out to the bars in the university quarter.

Nixon's apartment was on the fourth floor of a modern brick and glass building but the elevator journey barely gave Gawn any time to prepare herself. She missed having her inspector, Paul Maxwell, by her side. She had almost phoned him and asked him to join her but she didn't know how Nixon would react if she'd appeared at her door with him in tow. People talked to him. They trusted him. Gawn had worked very briefly in the Met's Child Abuse and Sexual Offences Command but she had been only too glad to escape to the Diplomatic Protection Unit. That was potentially more dangerous but much less demanding emotionally.

The door opened immediately at her knock. Nixon must have been waiting just behind it. She had changed into ripped jeans and a multi-coloured jumper which made her look younger and her voice, when she spoke, was falsely upbeat, an attempt to be cheery and confident-sounding which was fooling neither of them.

'Come in. Excuse the mess. I wasn't expecting visitors tonight.'

Nixon led her into an open-plan lounge-kitchen-diner. It was tiny but cosy. It had a lived-in feel. An oversized purple velvet sofa and a huge wall-mounted TV dominated the space. The blank screen reminded Gawn of the two-way mirrors of some of the older police interview rooms. A drying rack sat in front of a sliding door opening onto a miniscule balcony. Gawn noticed a jumper and some underwear hanging there to dry. Nixon gestured her to the sofa while she took a bar stool from in front of the kitchen counter and turned it around to face Gawn.

Nixon was perched like a mischievous garden gnome, her legs dangling mid-air. But it was her hands that fascinated Gawn. Now there was no handy bar coaster to fiddle with, she was plucking at a loose strand of wool on the sleeve of her jumper, threatening to rip it into a hole.

'Would you like coffee or something?' Nixon said but she made no move to match her offer.

'Take it easy, Donna. I don't need anything. Take your time and tell me what happened to you.'

Gawn was prepared to wait this time but she didn't have to wait long. Nixon must have been bottling everything up, letting it ferment inside her. Now it gushed out like a fizzy pop bottle shaken before opening. The journalist didn't look at her as she spoke, careful not to make eye contact. Instead, she was focusing on a picture over the sofa. It was the ubiquitous scene of workers high on the girder of a skyscraper under construction in New York, their legs dangling too, like hers.

'It was at the end of November.' Nixon swallowed hard. 'I was out for a drink with friends. They were for making a night of it. I was tired. I'd been busy all week and I'd only gone because I'd promised them I would. I remember them mocking me for being a party pooper.'

She almost laughed at the memory. But not quite.

'So, you left them?'

'We split up. Yeh. And that's pretty much all I remember until my neighbours found me propped up in the street outside about midnight. They brought me in. I have a vague memory of that bit and I asked them about it when I went to thank them the next day. Anyway, they left me on the sofa here and that's where I woke up with the mother of all hangovers.'

Nixon put her hand up to her temple almost as if she still had that headache now.

'And what makes you think you were raped if you can't remember anything?' Gawn asked and waited.

There was a quiver in the woman's voice as she answered.

'Because when I went to have a shower, I wasn't wearing any underwear. I hadn't even noticed. I was too far through myself. My head was pounding and I felt sick. But as soon as I started to undress, I realised I'd no knickers on. Someone had taken them.'

'Are you sure? Could you not have forgotten to put any on? Maybe you were rushing out late for work that morning? Or maybe you'd lost them somewhere?'

Gawn's suggestions sounded stupid, even to her. Of course, you wouldn't make a mistake like that. You didn't just casually lose your underwear, unless you were too drunk or drugged to know what was going on. And Nixon's face showed exactly what she thought of Gawn's suggestions.

'Of course, I'm frickin' sure,' she sparked back. 'I'm not in the habit of going commando – especially at work, especially that day.' Nixon almost spat the words out at her. 'And anyway, there was the drawing too.'

'Drawing? What drawing?'

'On my stomach.'

Nixon was already on her feet and running from the room as she answered.

Chapter 5

Gawn was mulling over what Nixon had told her so far. Did it prove there was a serial rapist roaming the streets? No. It only proved that something had happened to Nixon. Maybe. And maybe to a few others, although she couldn't be sure until she heard more details. But was it rape? And was it even the same man?

Gawn was in the little kitchen area, searching for some mugs. The kettle was just coming to the boil. She'd already found a jar of instant coffee so now she spooned some into the mugs. She took an opened bottle of milk from the fridge, removed the top and sniffed. It seemed OK. The kettle clicked off and she poured some of the boiling water into the mugs and waited.

Nixon had rushed to the bathroom after her outburst and Gawn had listened to the sound of her crying through the thin walls of the apartment. Eventually the noise had subsided and then stopped. She would be back soon and Gawn would need to ask her more questions. She would have to be sensitive. But she knew herself well enough to know that that wasn't exactly her forte.

If Maxwell had been here, he would have reassured Nixon that everything was going to be alright. But he wasn't. It was just her. The Ice Queen. Her nickname. She'd deserved it. She'd always found emotions and relationships too challenging. She had kept everyone at arm's length until Sebastian York had parachuted most unexpectedly into her life during an investigation and changed everything for her. Changed her.

Maybe sympathy or a shoulder to cry on was not what Nixon needed or wanted. She had chosen to speak to Gawn rather than someone from the Rape Crime Unit with all their expertise in dealing with sex crimes. Suddenly Gawn realised it was not sympathy Nixon was seeking. It was justice.

Just then the young woman reappeared. She had splashed some water on her face but there were black smudges where her mascara had run down her cheeks and her eyes were red and puffy. She looked young and vulnerable. Gawn had never thought of her like that before.

'Sorry about rushing off. It was very unprofessional of me.'

Nixon plonked herself down on the sofa.

'Nothing unprofessional about it. You're not the professional here. I am. You're the victim.'

Gawn's voice was full of sympathy now. She believed Nixon's story. Something had happened to her. She just wasn't sure yet exactly what. But she was sure Nixon wasn't making it up to sell more papers. Sometimes in the past she had suspected the journalist had massaged the truth or exaggerated facts to spin a story but not tonight.

'Did you report what happened to you, Donna?'

'No. I was too embarrassed and I wasn't even sure what had happened. And I think the whole drawing thing just seemed so weird. Who'd believe it? That's what this man depends on, I think.'

'Tell me what you do remember. And take your time.'

The two were side by side on the sofa, clutching their mugs of coffee. Gawn had half turned so she could watch Nixon's face as she spoke. The journalist was sitting right back into the far corner of the sofa as far away from her as she could get, almost enveloped in the huge squishy cushions. Her legs were drawn up under her as if she was trying to disappear completely, swallowed into the sofa's soft embrace. Her hands were clutching the mug like a lifesaver.

'It was the last Friday in November. End of the week and it had been one of those weeks, if you know what I mean. I meet up with my friends most Fridays.'

'Always the same place?' Gawn asked. She wondered if Nixon had been stalked or was it just a case of wrong time, wrong place.

'No. We meet up at different bars but always somewhere in the Cathedral Quarter. There's plenty to choose from down there. One of my friends texts or calls me and lets me know which one.'

'So, you got the text and then what?'

Gawn wanted to know the route Nixon had taken. The newspaper offices were at Clarendon Dock on the edge of Sailortown. Gawn knew the area a little. She had driven it but never walked it. It was one of those dusty through routes which carried traffic between the motorways and the city centre during the daytime but was little used after dark. There were no houses, just a dockers' pub and hostel at one end and a disused church and car parks servicing the riverside office buildings at the other. Few people ever walked there and certainly not at night.

'I walked up Corporation Street to Waring Street.'

'Could you have been followed?'

Nixon paused before answering.

'I don't think so. I didn't notice anyone. But I wasn't thinking about that. There are some darker bits on that street, under the flyover and at the skateboard park, but I'm always careful to keep in the light as much as possible. But someone could have been there, behind the concrete pillars, watching me, I suppose.'

17

'So, you got to the bar and met up with your friends. Which bar?' Gawn asked.

'Spud's.'

'Then what?'

Nixon blew across the top of her coffee and took a tentative sip before she answered.

'It was just your typical Friday night in Belfast. The craic was ninety. But I could feel the beginnings of one of my migraines. When my friends decided to head to a club on Dublin Road, I said I'd give it a miss.'

'Where did you split up with them?'

'At Spud's.'

'You didn't all leave together?' Gawn's surprise must have shown in her voice for the journalist seemed to feel the need to defend her friends.

'I hadn't finished my drink. They were all ready to go. I told them to go on without me. I said I'd finish my wine and then get a taxi home.'

'And did you get a taxi?'

'I don't know. I can't remember. After that it's all just a blank.'

'You don't remember anything at all?' Gawn asked.

It was Gawn's turn to take a sip of her coffee and wait. If Nixon had been roofied, she might remember nothing.

'Just snippets. Just like wee bits of a dream you remember when you wake up in the morning. They're all jumbled up and they don't make sense.'

'Tell me anyway.'

'They don't make sense. Not proper sense. And I don't even know if they're real or I just made them up afterwards.'

Gawn didn't ask again. She just sat and waited, cradling her now almost-empty mug between her hands.

'OK. There was a car. It wasn't mine. At least I don't think it was, but I don't know who it belonged to. Maybe I did call a taxi. Maybe that was it. I remember the back seat. I was lying down. I remember being tired. I could hardly keep my eyes open. It was nice lying there. And I had a fleecy blanket or something over me.'

'Something happened to you in the car?'

'I don't know. I told you.'

Nixon's voice was rising. She was getting agitated.

'OK. What else do you remember, Donna?'

'I think I remember music.'

'In the car? On the car radio?'

'Maybe.'

'Did you recognise it?' Gawn asked.

'I think it was Christmas music. You know, like carol singers or something. But maybe I'm making that up too.'

'Anything else?'

Nixon hesitated but eventually she said, 'This sounds really crazy but I think I remember sunglasses.'

'Sunglasses?'

'Yes. But I don't know if someone was wearing them or they were sitting somewhere and I saw them.' Donna's voice trailed off.

Sunglasses in Belfast in late November? Gawn suspected the sunglasses were some side-effect of whatever drug the woman had been slipped. Her face must have revealed her scepticism for Donna hastily added, 'I told you it was mad.'

'Do you remember anything about who was there with you? Was there a man? Did he speak to you? Do you remember his voice?'

Nixon shook her head from side to side.

'A smell? Maybe he was wearing a particular aftershave?'

A shake of the head again.

'I don't remember any man.'

'OK. Next morning, when you realised something had happened to you, what did you do?'

'I had the longest, hottest shower I've ever taken in my life.'

Gawn realised, without evidence collected at the time, it would be very difficult to identify a perpetrator unless someone had seen Nixon being abducted. And, if they had, why hadn't they come forward before now?

'So, you're not really sure you were raped at all.' It was as much a question as a statement.

'I'm sure something happened to me. Maybe I wasn't raped but I was assaulted. I wouldn't just have abandoned my knickers somewhere in the street. And the drawing. I saw it when I got in the shower.'

'I don't suppose you took a photograph?'

'Of the drawing?' Donna interrupted. 'Are you frickin' joking me? I couldn't wait to get the thing off me. And before you ask, I've taken two pregnancy tests just to be sure and I've been checked over at the STI clinic. One thing I know, I would not have let some stranger draw on me to get his jollies. I'm not into kinky sex with strangers. That's not me.'

The two women didn't really know each other well. From Nixon's questions in the Observatory bar about Sebastian, it seemed she knew more about Gawn than Gawn did about her.

'If you can't remember, how can you be sure it wasn't someone you know who brought you home? Or maybe someone you met after you'd left the bar?'

'I suppose it could have been but that wouldn't make it any better, would it?'

'No. It wouldn't. If you were drunk, you couldn't have given your consent,' Gawn said.

'I was not drunk.' Nixon's voice had risen in annoyance.

'You're sure you only had one drink?'

'Yes. One glass of white wine.'

'Well maybe you were drugged then. Could someone have slipped something into your glass? You said it was busy in the bar.'

'It was but I don't think anyone could have spiked my drink. I'm always really careful.'

'What about your friends? Could one of them have slipped you something? Maybe as a joke.'

'No. I've known them for years. They wouldn't do anything like that.'

'Have you talked to them about what happened to you?'

'I asked them how I'd seemed when they left me. I told them I couldn't remember how I'd got home. They told me I'd seemed OK but then Paula mentioned about a girl she works with whose sister was grabbed and ended up in an alley with her underwear missing. And then Susan chimed in that that was funny because she'd heard about a girl being roofied and she'd had something drawn on her stomach. They laughed about it. The idea that some perv was going around Belfast collecting women's knickers and drawing on them to get his rocks off seemed a big joke to them so I couldn't really tell them about me then, could I?'

There was a catch in her voice.

'I got them to put me in touch with the girls. We talked and what had happened to them seemed a bit like what had happened to me. Someone drawing on them seemed too much of a coincidence. It got me thinking, so I started asking around.'

'And you found more victims?'

'Yes. I had to do a lot of digging. It was all just word of mouth. Most hadn't reported what happened to them.'

'But some did. Were the complaints investigated?' Gawn asked.

'Well, someone took the details. How well they were investigated I don't know. Nothing much seems to have happened since. You'd be able to access the records. I couldn't.'

Gawn still wasn't convinced there was a serial sexual predator. Once stories like these started, they spread with others adding their own imagined experiences too, becoming urban myths.

'But I do know in all the cases after me' – Nixon looked at Gawn – 'the women had a drawing of a face on them. Just like me. Explain that.'

Nixon was challenging her.

She rushed out then and came back carrying a bulging box file. She flicked through it and produced a map. Gawn could see it was a street plan of Greater Belfast. She saw a series of dots, some red and some green with a number beside each one.

'The red dots are the last place the women can remember and the green ones are where they ended up. Most are near where they live. Like me. I've given each woman a number. No names,' she explained.

Gawn could see all the incidents had started in the city centre. The green dots were scattered over the plan, east to west, north to south. At a glance, it seemed there were nearly a dozen of them.

'Can I take this?'

'No. I'm not handing it over. I need it. I'm in the middle of writing my article for Sunday. A couple of the women have agreed to be interviewed so long as I don't use their names and Jonah's promised me a double-page spread.'

Gawn knew, being their Sunday edition, it would be even more sensational than the original. A story like this would sell a lot of papers.

'I want to help. I'll scan this for you. But I'm not prepared to give you any of the women's details. I had a hard enough time getting some of them to talk to me.'

Gawn thought she could make a case to Wilkinson for someone to look into the claims. But not her team. And, hopefully, not her.

'Thanks for this. Just one more thing, Donna. Could you draw the face for me?'

Nixon hesitated but then fetched a pen and drew a heart and a crude smiley emoji face with spectacles on the back of the scanned map.

'This is what two of the women said it looked like.'

'You didn't say there were glasses,' Gawn said.

'Sorry. I suppose that's where I got the idea he was wearing sunglasses. He probably wasn't at all.' There was a pause. 'You'll look into this?'

'I'll make sure someone checks.'

'But I thought you'd—'

Gawn interrupted her. 'I'm not in the Rape Crime Unit or District Command. You know that. And I don't allocate cases in the PSNI either. If you want this investigated properly it can't just be me going off on some private crusade like one of my husband's shows.'

Gawn was referring to the American TV cop show *Darrow*, based on her husband's books, which he was working on in Hollywood and was the reason he was 6,000 miles away.

'I'll pass it on. I think there's enough to warrant further investigation but whether I'll be involved, I can't say.'

Gawn felt only slightly guilty that secretly she hoped she wouldn't be.

Chapter 6

Tuesday

Jimmy Sutton was tired. Really, really tired. He was getting too old for all this malarky. What was it they called it? Dog-tired? He didn't really know what that even meant. He'd heard people saying it but do dogs get especially tired? Why? Most dogs he knew did nothing but lie around all day, barking too much like that mutt down his street. His chest was starting to hurt now too. And he'd forgotten his inhaler so his breathing was becoming a little more difficult.

It had been freezing cold tonight and he'd nothing to show for it. He'd been chilled to the bone and even the ride home now wasn't warming him up. He longed for a large Scotch. He could imagine the smooth heat of the single malt filtering down his gullet. And his favourite armchair, beside the electric fire toasting his toes, was calling to him. Not too long now until he'd be home. Every muscle in his body seemed to be aching. He'd had pneumonia last winter. He hoped it wasn't that again. He could barely keep his eyes open.

Jimmy was always careful. It paid to be in his line of work. You needed to plan ahead. He never used his car when he was going out on a job unless it was somewhere outside Belfast. Instead he used his rusty old bike. It meant he could nip in and out of all kinds of places, alleyways and back entries, if anyone was trying to follow him. And no one ever suspected an old bloke on a bike. No one gave him a second look. They barely even noticed him in daylight never mind after dark. He was one of the elderly invisible now, only noticed when they got in someone's way.

Recently he had taken to using the cycle path on his wee outings, as he thought of them. Better than the main road with all the traffic cameras. It was safer too, although there wasn't much traffic about anywhere at this time of the morning, even on the Shore Road. It was still the middle of the night to most people. They would be safely tucked up in their warm beds. He thought of his own bed again and that made him feel even more tired. His knees were aching now too. He wasn't getting any younger.

To add to his woes, it was foggy. He could barely see six feet in front of him but the pathway was ideal for his purposes. No traffic. Nothing would come looming out at him through the wall of fog. The only sound was the water lapping on the shoreline and once the blast of a foghorn from a passing ship.

He veered off the coastal path as the grassy banks of his local park appeared in front of him. He was nearly home now. He would take a shortcut through here. It wasn't open to the public yet. No chance of meeting some early morning dog walker arriving with their mutt.

And it was because of the fog that he missed the body until he almost ran over it lying in the longer grass. He glimpsed something red at the last minute, and realised it was a shoe. He swerved trying to avoid it and tumbled off his bike when its front wheel hit a large rock. He landed beside the shoe with a thud and a curse as the pain shot up his leg. His first thought was that he'd broken it but when he tried to move, it seemed OK. Then he thought about the shoe. it must have been left behind by one of the couples who liked to use the park for their romantic adventures. Sometimes he watched them when they didn't know he was there.

He had found some interesting stuff left behind after they'd gone. Empty beer cans and bottles of course. Prosecco seemed to be very popular these days. And used condoms too. Plenty of those but he'd found a pretty lace bra once. He'd given it to his lady friend as a present. It hadn't fitted her but he'd been fed up with her anyway so it didn't matter that she'd turned her nose up at it and told him what he could do with his gift.

He supposed the park seemed romantic to the young lovers sitting looking out over the lough watching the ships going up and down, the big cruise liners especially, heading off to all those exotic places. Not that they spent too much time looking out. It would be tricky pretending to care about a spectacular sunset when your car windows were all steamed up and you were only interested in getting your leg over. He couldn't help chuckling as he thought about some of the things he had seen. But the laugh turned into a cough which raked his body. His chest felt tight. He longed to get home.

Then he saw the rest of the body that went with the red shoe. His first thought was it must be one of those couples enjoying a bit of sex al fresco. But where was her partner then? He didn't want someone coming at him from out of the fog and giving him a beating for being a Peeping Tom.

Then his eyes moved up the still figure and he saw the blood. Her blond hair was stained with red streaks and her skin was alabaster-white, reminding him of some haloed plaster saint. The girl's eyes were open, staring at him accusingly. He jumped up. He felt a lurch in his stomach and puked, a stream of brown bile splashing down his trouser leg before it hit the ground beside her, releasing the smell of the Guinness he had drunk earlier. She was so pretty and so young and so dead. So very, very dead. Somehow he knew she had not died an easy death for all her peaceful repose.

He noticed her earrings and her pretty silver necklace and reached out to pull at the chain. But it was heavy. It wouldn't give way to his tug. The necklace would only get him a few pounds if he tried to sell it. Not worth the effort. Her skin was icy to his touch. He gave up and let go. All he wanted was to get away.

Jimmy grabbed his bicycle and was beginning to move off when something on the ground caught his eye. It was only a cheap badge. He picked it up and stuffed it in his pocket almost without thinking, a visceral reaction. 'Waste not, want not,' his mother had always told him. He scurried up the bank pushing the bike in front of him and rode off, careering from side to side in his haste. He just wanted to get as far away as he could.

Chapter 7

Loud Christmas music blared out and sunglasses floated through the air coming to within inches of her face but staying just out of reach.

Gawn woke with a start and sat straight up in bed. Beads of sweat were sitting on her forehead and her hands were damp. She held them out in front of her and looked at them. They were shaking. She recognised the noise that had broken into her nightmare. Her mobile phone. It was ringing.

'Girvin.'

'Boss, we've got a body.'

The voice belonged to Paul Maxwell, her inspector. He sounded almost matter of fact. But not quite. He had never become desensitised to the loss of life they encountered. He'd never developed the flippant approach that some of their colleagues employed to help them deal with the more harrowing aspects of their work. He never joked about their victims, especially women, or spoke disparagingly of them no matter what they had done. Gawn admired him for that, even if it sometimes meant he was too sympathetic. He could sometimes be a little gullible.

He didn't apologise for phoning so early.

'Where?' she asked.

'The cycle path beside the M2. In the park.'

She knew exactly where he meant. It was part of her weekend running route from her home in Carrickfergus along the shoreline to the outskirts of Belfast. A route with no access for motor vehicles, used only by walkers, runners and cyclists.

'I'll meet you there in thirty minutes.'

She was already out of bed and halfway across the room before she had cut the connection, fully awake already. Reporting to Wilkinson would just have to wait. Someone else would have to follow up on the rapes. If they were rapes. And if there was a link between them. Wilkinson could find someone else to lead her task force. It wouldn't be her problem anymore.

What did it say about her that she preferred to have a murder to investigate?

Chapter 8

Although she was in a hurry, Gawn had taken time to check under her car before getting inside. The threat level was at High and a notification had come round last week reminding them to be careful about their personal safety.

As she pulled out of the car park under her building, she was surprised to find herself facing a wall of fog. She hadn't heard last night's weather forecast and hadn't opened her curtains that morning in her rush after the phone call. Now she could barely make out the battlements of the hulking Norman castle which had dominated the old town for a thousand years.

The main road was there, she knew, but ahead she could see nothing but greyness – none of the familiar sights of her daily journey to Belfast. It was as if she was alone, the last survivor in a post-apocalyptic world.

Gawn had showered, dressed and was on her way in less than twenty minutes from Maxwell's call. Her clothes had been sitting ready in case of a call-out. Her coffee had brewed while she was dressing. She was trying a new blend, a robusta coffee bean which promised a strong hit of caffeine. Her first sip hadn't disappointed but she'd had no time to savour it. Now the dark liquid was in a to-go cup in a holder fixed to her dashboard. She would need her caffeine fix this morning. She didn't know what she might face at the park.

Belfast Lough was a mysterious, inky sheet of darkness alongside her, disappearing into that grey nothingness. The lights of the County Down coast, which she knew were there, were invisible, hidden in the enveloping grey blanket as if its inhabitants had been spirited away overnight.

Gawn kept her speed low. Their victim wasn't going anywhere. She didn't need to rush. And the drive was giving her time to think. She had allowed her attention to wander as she considered Nixon's story. Suddenly a woman's smiling face, larger than life but complete with sunglasses, loomed out of the mist at her. Gawn swore and swerved. She realised she had almost mounted the pavement. She exhaled noisily. It was only an illuminated advertisement on a bus shelter by the side of the road. She must pass it every day. The figure was offering a discount for early booking on summer holidays but the sunglasses had reminded her of Nixon's attacker.

The roundabout at Whiteabbey appeared then as if by magic. But the fog was beginning to thin here. She could make out the gates of the local police station flung wide open and lights blazing from every window. The road ahead was blocked by a police car. They would be redirecting traffic, keeping it away from the park. A lone policeman waved at her as she approached. She slowed and brought the car to a halt.

The officer was scowling as he walked over to her, making no attempt to disguise his annoyance. She lowered her window. He yawned noisily before speaking.

'You can't get through here, love. You need to go that way,' he stated flatly and offered no further explanation or apology, simply pointing her to move on with a casual flick of his thumb.

Gawn held up her ID.

'DCI Girvin, Serious Crime squad. I need to get through. I'm SIO, Constable.'

He reacted quickly.

She took the first exit and drove slowly down the laneway between the hedges and overhanging trees, their denuded branches like skeletal arms with bony fingers reaching out of the darkness to grab at her. An officer clutching a clipboard and pen was standing by the raised barrier, stamping her feet to keep warm. The crime scene log was thrust towards her. She signed.

Now her day was really beginning.

Chapter 9

Gawn had been here many times before. But only in daylight. This morning it had lost its familiarity. The area had once had a poor reputation in the evenings until local police had stepped up patrols and locked the barrier to stop cars after dark.

The fog was dispersing quickly now, making strange shapes recognisable. The sky was lightening too. She could make out the bowling green and the public toilets to one side and the outline of the swings and slide in the children's playpark to the other. Today there'd be no elderly men enjoying a quiet game nor any squealing toddlers on the swings. Today's visitors would be the white-suited CSIs.

Police vehicles lined the narrow roadway and filled the parking bays, some with their headlights blazing to provide extra illumination. Gawn could see an ambulance and more flashing lights ahead near where the exercise equipment stood. Beyond that, hidden by the slope down to the water's edge, a ghostly glow from the arc lighting erected around the crime scene reached up into the sky.

Gawn pulled her car tightly into the side of the roadway, careful to leave room for vehicles to pass. She climbed out and stood. Just stood. Her team expected this. She was giving herself time to sense the crime although they didn't know that. She wasn't superstitious or overly fanciful, she didn't think, but she believed all crimes left traces. Some you could see and the CSIs would find, and others you could only feel.

'Morning, boss.'

Maxwell. She could see his breath hanging on the still air as he greeted her. He was just extricating himself from a scene suit, after viewing the body.

'What have we got? Male or female, Paul?'

'A girl… a young woman.'

'Any idea who she is?'

The first hours were crucial. They both knew that. If this was a murder, a quick identification could be vital. But she mustn't let her mind run ahead. It could be suicide or even natural causes. Sebastian sometimes accused her of being disappointed if she didn't have a murder to investigate.

'Yes. Her bag was lying beside her. Her student pass was in it with her photo on it. Her name's Orla Maguire. She's nineteen.'

'Local?'

'No. There was a letter from the Student Loans Company in her bag, addressed to her in Strabane. But she was probably living somewhere around here for the university. We can't get that information until their offices open at nine, boss. I've arranged for someone to go out and inform the next of kin,' Maxwell answered.

'Any chance it was an accident or suicide? Had she been in the water?'

'No.' He shook his head. 'The body was well above the waterline. And it's definitely not suicide.'

'Who found her?'

'A guy cycling along the path. He was on his way home from his night shift in Belfast. Billy took his statement and let him go. We have his contact details.'

'No chance he could have killed her?'

'She's been dead about four to eight hours according to the doc and he only left work twenty minutes before he found her and phoned it in so, no. His alibi will be easy enough to check. He was working with a cleaning crew all night. He has witnesses to the time he left at the end of his shift.'

She didn't ask if he would check the alibi. She knew he would. Instead she asked, 'Who pronounced her?'

'Jenny.'

Jenny was Dr Jennifer Norris, the assistant chief pathologist and Gawn's best friend.

'Is she still here?' Gawn asked. 'I don't suppose she's making any guesses about cause of death, is she?'

'No and no. But at least she offered a time of death, 10pm to 2am. Blunt force trauma would be my guess, boss, as far as cause goes. There was blood on the back of the head. But she could maybe have hit it falling or something. They haven't found a weapon but they've only just started looking.'

'Was there any sign of a struggle?'

'The ground's hard. There were no marks I could see of a struggle or where she might have slipped and fallen. But Mark Ferguson's down there now so if there's anything to find, he'll find it,' Maxwell told her.

Mark Ferguson was Gawn's favourite crime scene manager. They had worked together many times.

'Anything to indicate what she was doing here in the middle of the night?'

'No, but there was one thing,' Maxwell said.

'Yes?'

'I guess there must be a sexual element to it.'

'Did Jenny say that?' Gawn asked.

'No. But she didn't need to. I could see for myself. The victim's clothing was disturbed, pulled up. Her pants were missing. And they weren't lying about anywhere. So, either she wasn't wearing any or–'

'Someone had taken them,' Gawn said.

Chapter 10

Maxwell didn't mention any drawing and Gawn didn't either. She wanted to keep that piece of information to herself for now. The rest of the MO didn't fit the few details Nixon had provided.

Gawn knew the CSIs would be working there for the rest of the day. Photographs would be taken from every possible angle and they would use a drone to get an overview of the crime scene once it was fully light. Maxwell had already given permission to begin the process of removing the body. She'd only risk Ferguson's ire at another detective tramping through his crime scene if she tried to go down to see it for herself. It seemed Maxwell had everything in hand. There was nothing for her to do here. And she had somewhere more pressing to be now.

As they stood, still talking, figures swathed in white emerged up the incline out of the mist walking slowly towards them. Hoods covered their heads. Masks gave them slits for eyes which made them look like characters from some alien abduction movie. They were illuminated from behind by the forensic arc lights, and the almost-ghostly glow of the rising sun, and with the backdrop of the twinkling lights of the city, they looked weird and threatening. All that was needed for the perfect horror setting was a bank of fog rolling in from the sea. But the thick fog had gone now.

The men were manoeuvring a gurney with a black body bag on it. Gawn and Maxwell watched in silence. The world was waking up. Traffic was increasing on the motorway just yards away from them on the other side of a stand of trees planted as a barrier. The road had been re-opened to traffic. The woosh of cars was almost relentless, almost hypnotic. The daily commute had begun for the inhabitants of East Antrim.

When the silent figures came level with them, Gawn stepped forward. She would see the victim later, of course, when Orla Maguire took her place on Norris's unforgiving steel table. Nothing hidden. Her body uncovered and washed down to retrieve any evidence of her attacker. Prepped ready for the indignity of a post-mortem examination. She would be like a wax figurine, only less lifelike than the ones in Madame Tussauds. There would be no spark of life or personality left.

Gawn would see lots of photographs of the woman, caught in snippets of time. Pictures would already have been taken from every angle at the scene and there would be more taken during the PM. Their harsh reality would only emphasise the loss of a young life. They wouldn't help Gawn get a sense of the living, breathing woman. But Gawn wanted to be aware of the person behind the images, behind the stories she would hear told and re-told over the next few days by the woman's friends and family.

Without speaking, Gawn signalled she wanted to see the body. One of the men partially unzipped the body bag, just enough to reveal the girl's pretty features and part of her upper torso. Her face was unmarked. There were no obvious signs of violence. She could have been asleep but for the matted mass of red behind her head.

Gawn would have liked to examine the body for a drawing but she couldn't do that without breaching protocol and drawing attention to anything she might find, so she paused only for a second or two. It was long enough for her to take in the carefully applied make-up, the row of ear piercings and the silver chain, with a Claddagh symbol hanging from it, around her throat. She noted the red sparkly top the girl had been wearing. Orla Maguire had not been casually dressed. She'd been going somewhere worth dressing up for. Someone.

Then, as the men moved towards a private ambulance parked just beyond her car, Gawn had taken her leave of Maxwell too. She knew he could handle everything here and she would catch up with him later. She still hadn't asked him if anything had been drawn on the victim's body. If he knew, she expected he would have told her. She would attend the PM or, if Norris worked quickly, she could read the report. She didn't want word of the macabre drawings to leak out.

She hadn't told Maxwell anything about her evening with Donna Nixon nor her suspicion now that there might be a serial rapist at large and that this death could be his handiwork. She would do that later. First, she needed to report to Wilkinson.

Gawn drove towards Belfast keeping just under the speed limit. She needed to speak to the ACC urgently now. They could be looking for a serial rapist who might now have a taste for murder as well. And now she did want to lead the task force.

Chapter 11

While Gawn was en route to Belfast, her sergeant, Erin McKeown, had phoned with a message from Wilkinson. Gawn was to meet the ACC at the Stormont Hotel.

So now she was waiting for a break in an unrelenting line of traffic. The hotel's modern extension fronted the main Upper Newtownards Road and it was rush hour.

Purple glider buses were plying their trade, the designated bus lane funnelling all other traffic into a single outer lane.

When someone eventually signalled for Gawn to cross in front of him into the hotel grounds, she found the car park already full. She had to use the lower overflow area and walk up the hill, using the time to rehearse what she was going to say to the assistant chief constable. At the revolving doorway she paused and stood looking around, trying to figure out where she would find the woman in the unexpectedly busy scene that lay before her.

There was a buzz of chatter overlying the cheery Christmas Muzak. A huge Christmas tree, brightly decorated and sparkling with tinsel and baubles, filled one corner of the foyer to the side of the lift. To her right a sunken area with sofas and armchairs and a roaring fire was fully occupied. To her left a reception desk was manned by two efficient-looking young women in smart corporate uniforms dealing with a line of people waiting to check out.

Just then the ACC – not in uniform – exited the lift accompanied by two women and three men. All civilians. Then she recognised one of them. She'd seen him in headquarters. He must be Wilkinson's personal bodyguard. The ACC stopped and said her goodbyes. There were handshakes all round, some smiles and some serious looks too.

Wilkinson was still looking serious as Gawn approached her.

'You got my message then, Chief Inspector. Of course you did or you wouldn't be here. Sorry. I can barely think straight after that meeting. They have my head turned. Questions, questions and more questions. And I didn't have any answers for them. I think I need a drink. Some coffee should do the trick,' Wilkinson added and sighed loudly but she smiled too.

Gawn had no doubt Wilkinson had been more than able to deal with these people, whoever they were and whatever they had been asking.

Gawn realised she could do with more coffee too. Her to-go cup hadn't lasted beyond the park. With what she suspected Wilkinson's reaction was going to be to her news, she thought another hit of caffeine would be a good idea.

Two middle-aged women, dressed in smart business attire and carrying folders, stood up and vacated the seats beside the stone fireplace. Wilkinson made off at speed to lay claim to them. Gawn followed and they settled themselves into the comfy armchairs, pulling them slightly closer together so they could talk without being overheard. Gawn noticed Wilkinson's bodyguard finding a quiet corner where he could watch the whole room.

'A pot of coffee for two, please,' Wilkinson said to a waiter who had appeared beside them and then added, 'Is that alright for you, Gawn?'

'Yes, ma'am. Fine.'

Wilkinson pulled her chair even closer to Gawn's. Their knees were almost touching.

'That was my quarterly meeting with local business representatives. Normally it's just a formality really; a rather pleasant breakfast meeting with the bacon butties here, which I can recommend by the way. Unfortunately, today's meeting was already in the diary and, of course, there was only one topic on their agenda.' She rolled her eyes. 'Yesterday's front-page story.'

Gawn said nothing.

'Well, put me out of my misery. Did you manage to contact Nixon?'

'Yes. I did, ma'am.'

'And was she forthcoming? Did she tell you anything useful? I have a meeting with the chief in less than two hours and I'd like to have something positive to tell him.'

'She was willing to talk to me but whether you think what she told me is positive or not I don't know,' Gawn said.

The waiter was already back, carrying a tray. He set its contents on a low table between them.

'Can I get you anything else, ladies?' he asked.

'No. Thank you,' Wilkinson said and, as he moved away, she added, 'Shall I be mother?'

Gawn couldn't help smiling. She didn't know whether the ACC knew it or not but she had once overhead a couple of junior PCs referring to Wilkinson by a nickname – Mother Superior – no doubt because her home was in an apartment complex built on the site of a former convent in South Belfast.

Wilkinson poured the coffee.

'Well?'

She wanted answers.

'Nixon told me enough to make me think there's something in her claim. The incidents all involved women who ended up somewhere near their home but they couldn't remember how they got there, so they were probably drugged.'

'You believe her?'

'Yes. I do. All the victims turned up minus their underwear, not just that it had been removed to make life easier for the rapist but he'd taken it away with him. And–' she paused a beat '–one of the victims was Nixon.'

Wilkinson's face had been getting more and more serious. Her brows had knitted together, almost forming a continuous line above her eyes, but they disappeared under her fringe when Gawn mentioned that Nixon had been a victim too.

'*She* was attacked?'

'Yes. It's personal, ma'am. She doesn't know whether she was raped. But she was assaulted and she had something drawn on her lower abdomen.' Gawn looked around to make sure no one was listening before she added in a whisper, 'A smiley face.'

A look of shock passed across Wilkinson's features.

'God almighty. The press will have a bloody field day with that piece of information. It's the stuff of horror movies. Some pervert roaming round Belfast drawing smiley faces on women and raping or assaulting them,' Wilkinson said. She looked around quickly then, realising she had raised her voice and checking no one had heard and reacted.

'That's how she got started looking into this, ma'am. It's not just another story for her. It's her way of coping with what happened to her.'

'Well, we all have to find our own ways to cope with trauma, don't we, Gawn?' Wilkinson said.

Gawn flinched. Wilkinson knew of her episodes of PTSD, of course. She only hoped she didn't also know about some of the methods she had used to cope with it.

'So, you think we do have a serial rapist. At Christmas. Great,' Wilkinson continued.

Gawn didn't think the time of year had any relevance. Not to her, anyway. For criminals there was no such thing as a season of goodwill.

Gawn took a gulp of her coffee. It was hot, not as strong as she would have liked, but it gave her thinking time before she spoke again.

'There's something else.'

Wilkinson cocked her head to one side, reminding Gawn of a tiny inquisitive bird.

'There's more?'

'I thought I was going to have to tell you someone else would need to lead the investigation into this rapist. But my team had a call-out to a suspicious death this morning and I've just come from the scene – a young woman's body was found on the edge of North Belfast. A young woman minus her underwear.'

Gawn didn't need to spell out what she was thinking. Wilkinson was ahead of her.

'Was there a drawing?'

'I don't know yet, ma'am.'

'So, he might have escalated to murder?'

'Possibly. I know we shouldn't jump to conclusions and this doesn't exactly fit the pattern. At least as far as we know what the pattern is. And the death could have been accidental so I won't be assuming it's the same man, but it is a possibility. And, if it is him, he's speeding up. An attack on Saturday night and another on Monday.'

'Then it's all one case and you can lead the investigation,' Wilkinson stated. 'I'll be able to tell the chief that at least. Some positive news, but…' Wilkinson took a sip of her coffee and Gawn waited for what was coming next. 'This needs to be a task force, not just your team. When we announce it, the idea of a dedicated task force will increase public confidence that we're doing something. The optics are all important on this one, Gawn. We have to be seen to be responding quickly.

'And you'll need to include some of the detectives who've been working on the other cases once you've confirmed them. They have the local knowledge and the local contacts. It can't just be your team charging in like the 7th Cavalry to take over, tramping all over everything they've been doing… or not doing. District Command wouldn't take it well,' she added with a twist of her mouth.

Gawn stifled a sigh. She didn't want to get stuck in the middle of a clash between Wilkinson and the ACC in charge of District Command. She had hoped the murder would mean her team could simply take over. Involving new detectives, ones who might feel under scrutiny, wouldn't be easy, and liaising with District Command, when the original oversight had been theirs, could be a nightmare. Wilkinson had her faults, but she usually took a back seat and gave Gawn a free hand to run things her way.

'Maxwell can take charge of your current cases while you're dealing with this. You can use an inspector from one of the stations already involved.'

It would be good experience for Maxwell to lead the Serious Crime unit but Gawn knew she would miss him by her side. Without acknowledging it, even to herself, she had come to depend on him. He was a steadying influence on her and the thought of working closely with some stranger, who she didn't know and wouldn't trust, did not appeal.

'You'll be working under ACC O'Brien at District Command, reporting directly to him. You'll be able to use your own office and you can set up an ops room with the additional personnel in the conference suite.'

Gawn was surprised. She would have expected a task force to work out of one of the other stations in Belfast. The top brass must want to keep a close eye on it. It would be like working in a goldfish bowl, every move scrutinised.

'I need Inspector Maxwell, ma'am.'

Gawn didn't need Maxwell. But she wanted him. His down-to-earth attitude anchored her flights of intuition and sometimes she needed him to curb some of her crazier ideas. She trusted his judgement. She trusted him.

Gawn looked directly at Wilkinson. It wasn't often she felt she had the upper hand with the top brass. But this time she did. They were obviously panicking and she had the insider contact with Nixon.

'He can manage the Serious Crime cases and I'll use another inspector for the task force but I want Maxwell involved too. As an advisor, if you want to give him a title. He knows how I work. If you want this rapist caught, having him working with the team will make that more likely.'

Gawn's eyes hadn't left Wilkinson's face all the time she was speaking. It was a clash of wills. For five seconds neither blinked, then Wilkinson looked away. If she refused, what would Gawn do? She knew the answer to that. She would involve him anyway without permission. But she didn't want to put him in an invidious position.

'It just means more work for Maxwell,' Wilkinson eventually said.

'He can handle it,' Gawn said with relief. 'Thank you, ma'am.'

'Don't thank me, Gawn. For any of this. Not yet. And Maxwell mightn't thank me or you either. You'll have officers with their noses seriously put out on this one. Especially the more senior ones. They'll take this as a personal criticism. I'll fob them off as much as I can but don't expect any of them to be pleased to be handing everything over to a task force.'

Gawn could imagine. She had finished her coffee and was preparing to leave when Wilkinson's words stopped her.

'And don't expect ACC O'Brien to welcome you with open arms either. He'll be looking to find fault. You'll need to be on your toes with him. His officers should have spotted the link. And the buck stops with him. If you can't get this man he'll try to pin the blame on you to save himself from any fallout.'

Gawn was surprised that Wilkinson had so openly criticised her counterpart. If they were rivals, it would make her job that much more difficult.

'And you'll have the press to contend with too. They'll be all over it, trying to outdo themselves. And I'm afraid I'll be breathing down your neck as well. Obviously, you'll report in the first instance to O'Brien. He's in charge of the DPC but you'll keep me in the loop. I expect that, Gawn. I'm depending on you. Good luck, Acting Superintendent.' Wilkinson smiled and raised her coffee cup as if it was a glass of champagne and she was offering a toast of congratulations.

Gawn had no illusions. She suspected it was much less of a glass of celebratory bubbly and more of a poisoned chalice she had just been handed.

Chapter 12

Gawn sat in her car for a long time after the ACC's black unmarked Range Rover had swept out of the car park. She waited, her mind fizzing. What had she taken on? A rapist or murderer she could deal with but all the publicity and the inter-departmental politics she could be facing was something else. She felt a tightness in her chest; her heart was fluttering.

She didn't know ACC Aidan O'Brien but she did know a bit about him. He'd reached the rank of commander at the Met before returning to his roots in Belfast. Their paths had never crossed in London but she was sure they would have had colleagues in common. Thinking that didn't make her feel any better. He was now the ACC in charge of District Policing, a powerful man, talked of as a future chief constable, and she didn't want to have him as an enemy.

She needed to talk to Maxwell. Urgently. They had worked together, with one short break, for nearly three years. They had developed an understanding and what for Gawn amounted almost to a friendship although she doubted Maxwell would define it like that.

She was surprised to see someone standing at her office door when she reached the Serious Crime suite. A workman was changing the nameplate. There it was in black and silver: 'Supt. G. Girvin'. Wilkinson had wasted no time. She must have arranged for this to be done before they had even spoken this morning.

'Admiring your new nameplate, *Superintendent*.'

It was Maxwell. She hadn't heard him come up behind her.

'Paul! No. I'm just surprised, that's all. I didn't expect it.'

'You mean you didn't expect you'd get a new nameplate before you'd told anybody?'

He meant before she had told him, of course. He would have expected a heads-up if she was being promoted. It would affect him too. He would have to work with a new DCI.

'Jamie told me,' Maxwell said.

Jamie Grant was the most junior detective on the Serious Crime team and an inveterate gossip.

'He noticed the workman changing the name when he was coming back from the canteen. It would have been nice to know about it before he announced it to everybody in the incident room.'

'Come in,' Gawn said and pulled him into her office by the sleeve. She closed the door behind him.

'It's just an acting role. That's all. I didn't go for a promotion. I'm leading a special task force for one investigation only. It's not permanent and I don't expect it to be. I don't want it to be.'

They were facing each other in the centre of her office standing almost toe to toe, like a pair of boxers at a weigh-in. Maxwell was making no attempt to disguise his annoyance.

'Wilkinson only told me about it this morning before anything was decided.' That wasn't wholly true. She hadn't decided but Wilkinson obviously had. 'I was coming back here to tell you. I wasn't keeping it a secret.'

His body suddenly relaxed, his hunched shoulders fell and the rigidity eased from his jawline. He dropped down without invitation into the armchair in front of her desk.

'Well, give us all the info then, boss. What are we investigating?'

'About that,' she began, 'Wilkinson wants you running the team here.'

He didn't say anything.

'Don't go into sulky teenager mode, for God's sake, Paul. I think I'll need all the friends I can get on this one.'

'I don't do sulky teenager. That's Molly's tactic.' He was talking about his daughter but a slight smile had formed on his lips.

'Good, because I need your help. I convinced Wilkinson I need you on the case as an advisor.'

'An advisor, eh? I like the sound of that. No work, just talk.'

'You wish. I'll need all you've got on the Maguire case updated by tomorrow morning so we can brief the task force together. That'll be the earliest I can pull this mishmash group together. God, it feels like I'll be running some sort of A-Team or something.'

'Is that what you're going to call yourselves, the A-Team?' he asked.

She thought he was stifling a laugh.

'More like the Z-Team,' she replied smiling now, glad that he seemed to have got over his annoyance.

She told him about her meeting with Donna Nixon and what they knew so far about the rapist.

'I don't want to get caught up in some pissing competition, Paul. Wilkinson and O'Brien seem to be on different pages, if they're even reading the same book, and I'm caught in the middle. And all the time this man seems to be escalating. He could be on the streets again anytime. Up to now, according to Nixon, he's struck at weekends but we can't assume we have until Friday or Saturday before he goes after another woman.

'Orla Maguire could be one of his victims. If you can identify her attacker by tomorrow and we can find something to link him to the other victims then there'll be no need for a task force.' She finished speaking and folded her arms across her chest in a gesture of finality.

'And no promotion to superintendent either,' he said.

She was sure he was just teasing her now. She hoped.

'Come on, Paul. You know me better than that. I'm not in this for the promotion. I don't want it. It's just not me sitting behind a desk all day telling others what to do, is it?'

'Well, not the sitting behind a desk bit.' He smiled. Now she was sure he was teasing her.

She smiled back at him before saying, 'But I understand Wilkinson's reasoning. If I'm going to be dealing with a lot of disgruntled inspectors and chief inspectors, then I need to be able to play the seniority card. Otherwise, it could be a problem. It probably still will be.'

Chapter 13

Gawn spent the rest of the morning on the phone while Maxwell drove to Strabane to talk to Orla Maguire's parents. She didn't know which job was tougher – talking to the dead girl's relatives or having to explain everything to her colleagues.

Before she started her round of explaining and apologising, she contacted the Rape Crime Unit hoping for some help. A girl had been raped on Saturday night. Perhaps it had been the same man who had attacked Nixon and the other women.

'We've got our man,' DCI Megan Rowe told her. 'He's already been charged.'

'Was it someone she knew?' Gawn asked.

'Yes. An ex-boyfriend. He's confessed. We've had him in custody since Sunday questioning him so I'm afraid he couldn't be anything to do with your victim in the park if she died on Monday night. Good luck anyway. Anything I can do to help, let me know.'

Gawn hadn't mentioned any drawing on the woman's body to Rowe. She still hoped to keep it a secret, for now.

Once it got out, there was the possibility of copycat attacks.

After that she began the phone calls to the inspectors and chief inspectors in stations around Greater Belfast where rape or sexual assaults had been reported in the month of December. When she finally surfaced out of her office and went to the incident room to make herself a cup of coffee, she was surprised to hear Norris had phoned to say she'd already finished Orla Maguire's post-mortem and had left a message inviting Gawn or Maxwell to come for an update.

The pathologist had been unusually speedy. They must have hit a quiet patch for her. Normally she would have just sent her report through, so if she wanted to speak in person, Gawn thought she must have found something important. She hoped. Gawn waited, curbing her impatience, until Maxwell returned and they set out for the hospital complex.

* * *

Jenny Norris's favourite rock music was blasting out when Gawn and Maxwell entered the nondescript building in the grounds of the Royal Victoria Hospital which housed the regional mortuary. They could hear the thumping beat as they walked along the windowless corridor towards her office.

'How does she get away with it?' Maxwell asked. 'I thought Munroe would put a stop to all that when he came back.'

Jenny Norris had been appointed during the chief pathologist's sabbatical. After spending years working in the Medical Examiner's Office in Boston, her way of doing things was very different to his and she was a very different personality to the dour Scot too. Gawn and Maxwell had expected sparks to fly between them when they finally came face to face but they seemed to be able to coexist happily.

'You know Jenny. She could charm… the birds.' Gawn realised she'd been going to say charm the pants off any man.

'Hello. Twofer today, I see.' Norris greeted them, smiling, as they walked in.

'Twofer?' Gawn's puzzled expression made both Norris and Maxwell laugh.

'It's obvious you have someone who does your shopping for you. When was the last time you went to the supermarket?' Maxwell asked.

'Twofer. Two for the price of one, Gawn,' Norris explained.

'Right. OK. Enough fun at my expense. What about Orla Maguire? You've done the PM already? I didn't expect you to work so quickly.'

'Three-line whip,' Norris said and saluted. She noticed their puzzled looks and explained, 'A phone call from your boss. They've really got their knickers in a twist about this one.'

Gawn hadn't heard anyone use that expression for years. It had been a favourite saying of her father's.

'What did you find?' Gawn asked.

Norris turned the music off. She sounded serious now, her voice like the one she used when giving evidence in court.

'Your victim was a fit and healthy young woman. She had an appendectomy scar but no other significant injuries apart from to the back of her head. Cause of death was traumatic brain injury. Her skull was accelerated forward causing internal surface damage and subarachnoid haemorrhage – a classic example of a coup-contrecoup injury from a blow to the back of her head.'

'Could it have been an accident?' Maxwell asked.

'Maybe but I doubt it. Not from the force that would have been required and the fact that she would have had to fall backwards. Just falling backwards by itself wouldn't usually be sufficient unless it was from a height and I would have expected other injuries in that case. And, if it was an accident, wouldn't someone have tried to help her; phoned an ambulance or something? Death wasn't instantaneous. She could have survived for at least a few minutes. I believe it's more likely she was pushed or maybe she was struggling with someone, trying to get away from them. But in that case I would have expected fingermarks where someone was trying to restrain her.'

'Did Ferguson find any signs of a struggle?' Gawn asked.

Norris shook her head.

'What about DNA?' Maxwell asked.

'There was nothing under her nails, Paul. She must have been taken by surprise or been drugged. The tox screen should show us that. But she didn't die where you found her. Her body had been moved. From the pattern of lividity, I would say she was lying on her back on a very hard surface for a time and then moved to the park and dumped on her side.'

'So the park isn't our primary crime scene,' Gawn said.

'No. There was nothing on the body to indicate where she'd died but you might have more luck with her clothes. There could be some residue that would help. I've already sent them to the lab. We found vomit at the scene too. Some of it had landed on the victim's skirt and from the spatter she must have been on her side when the mystery person puked up his dinner... or rather copious amounts of Guinness. So it happened after the body was dumped in that position.'

'Was it your witness who called it in?' Gawn asked looking at Maxwell.

'I don't know. He told Billy he'd felt sick. But if he was working all night I suppose he'd hardly have been drinking. We just assumed it was him when we saw the vomit.'

'Assumptions.' She clicked her tongue. 'We don't assume anything, Paul. Remember. Check it out. But, anyway, she was raped,' Gawn added turning back to Norris.

'Now who's making assumptions?' the pathologist responded.

'But Paul told me her clothes were disturbed and her underwear was missing.'

'Yes, it was but she hadn't been raped. There were no internal or external injuries consistent with a sexual assault and before you ask, there was no seminal fluid found anywhere. Which doesn't discount the use of a condom, of course, but there'd been no forced penetration. There were no needle marks on her body but that doesn't rule out the possibility she was slipped something in a drink or even took something voluntarily. I've run a tox screen, as I said, but you'll just have to wait for the results. And I have to warn you the lab's short-staffed at the minute so it might take a while. Same for her clothing and jewellery. Meantime–' Jenny Norris paused and rotated her computer monitor '–I said there were no other injuries on her body but there was this. It's why I asked you to come over rather than just sending my report as usual. I thought it could be important and it might be why O'Brien was so keen to get the PM done quickly.'

Gawn was surprised. She'd assumed Norris had meant Wilkinson had phoned her, not O'Brien. She'd not even spoken to him yet and here he was meddling in her investigation already.

'It must mean something,' Norris said. 'And I guessed you mightn't want anybody knowing about it.'

A close-up of a smiling emoji face with a pair of sunglasses and a heart filled the screen.

'Freaky,' Maxwell said and pulled a face.

'It was on her lower abdomen,' the pathologist informed them. 'With an arrow pointing down to her genitalia.'

'Have you taken a sample of the... ink, is it?' Gawn asked.

'Not ink. I don't think it was a pen. Lipstick, maybe. I'm not sure. But a sample's already on its way to the lab too. I'll send the report on everything as soon as I have it.'

'That's weird. He drew that on her?' Maxwell was still staring at the screen, his face wrinkled in disbelief.

He had reacted to the picture, Gawn hadn't and Norris had noticed.

'This isn't news to you, is it, Gawn?' Norris asked.

'No,' she said. 'I was expecting it. It's happened before.'

Chapter 14

'You didn't think to warn me?' Maxwell asked.

He and Gawn were sitting in his car outside the mortuary. 'It made me look stupid – not knowing about it.'

'If there'd been no drawing, there was nothing to warn you about. And you'd seen the body and didn't mention anything about a drawing, so I thought there wasn't one. I was hoping there wasn't one.'

'She was lying on her side. I only saw her back,' Maxwell said.

'I really hoped there wasn't a drawing. Honestly, Paul. I knew some of the women who were attacked had been drawn on but I'd hoped to keep word of it under wraps for as long as possible. The fewer people who know, the better. The only person I've told is Wilkinson. Though O'Brien must have heard.'

She paused and sighed.

'It's bound to leak out now one way or another,' she said. 'Probably someone at the mortuary will tell a friend or even sell the info to the papers. They'll absolutely lap it up, of course. They'll have a field day.'

'It's really creepy-looking though, isn't it? A bit like something you'd see on that *CSI* programme. In Las Vegas, not Belfast.'

'What happens in Vegas, no longer stays in Vegas, Paul. Unfortunately. USA today, Magherafelt tomorrow thanks to TV and the internet. We're dealing with a very sick individual who is escalating but we mustn't underestimate him. He's managed to stay under the radar but we need to get him. Now.'

Chapter 15

Gawn had all the incident reports Wilkinson had sent her set out on a sturdy mahogany table which dominated the conference room. The room was already beginning to look more like a workspace, a base for the task force, instead of its normal role as the location for 'hot-air meetings' as Gawn called them.

Alongside the reports was a pile of PSNI personnel files and an unfolded street plan of Belfast. She was moving bits of paper around, glad to have something more productive to do after spending so much time on the phone apologising. Especially when none of it was her fault. It had been hard work smoothing so many ruffled feathers. Diplomacy or grovelling, as she thought of it, was not her thing. If she hadn't known that before, she certainly did now.

Maxwell had just returned from meeting Orla Maguire's parents at the mortuary for Mr Maguire's formal identification of his daughter's body. He had waited there for them, while Gawn had returned to begin the task of selecting her new team.

The meeting with the Maguires had been difficult, he'd told her. She knew from his voice that he'd been upset. He was a family man through and through. They didn't seem to know much about their daughter's life in Belfast and nothing about her friends, especially any new male friend she might have been seeing, he told her.

'This girl lives off Holywood Road. She would have reported the attack at Strandtown,' Maxwell said as he handed one of the incident reports to her.

'Yes. I know. I've already had a look at that one. It seems a likely prospect. Do you know this Sergeant Trimble?' she asked, glancing down at the page in her hand and deciphering the signature.

'Aye. He was a constable when I was there. I heard he got promoted.'

'What did you think of him?' she asked.

'He'd put you in mind of an older Jamie but I'd trust him to get the job done. He's solid.'

'This girl seems to have withdrawn her story the next day according to this follow-up note so I suppose we can't really blame Trimble for not doing anything more about it.'

Maxwell nodded his agreement. 'He would have had plenty to do without chasing after a wee girl who'd decided to change her story. Uniforms are in the middle of a major drink-driving initiative for Christmas, you know.'

Gawn looked down at the map and then lifted another report.

'What about Mike Collins at Lisburn Road?' she asked.

'I've never come across him.'

'Me neither and this woman withdrew her complaint as well,' Gawn added and flopped down into a chair. 'I wonder how many sexual assaults take place that we never even hear about?' she asked but she didn't expect Maxwell to answer. Violence against women, including rape, was a major problem. And growing. She ran her fingers through her hair in exasperation revealing the line of a thin white

53

scar on her temple, a reminder, if she ever needed one, of her time in Afghanistan.

'Here's an interesting one.' Maxwell proffered her another page. 'DI Sam Rainey at Musgrave Street.'

'I don't know him either,' Gawn said.

'Her,' Maxwell corrected her. 'Samantha. The poor man's Gawn Girvin, they call her.'

'What did you just say?' Her voice was sharp. She had never heard anyone using that phrase.

'It's just a bit of fun, boss. No one means anything by it. She's a redhead, like you, and tall. Sam knows about the nickname and she doesn't mind. She takes it as a compliment, she told me.'

'You know her?'

'Not well. She only moved to Belfast from Fermanagh a couple of months ago but our paths have crossed. At those training days you keep sending me to "for my own good".'

Gawn gathered up the pages into two neat piles and sighed. She would really have preferred to be working with her own team and she did intend to use some of them, but to keep Wilkinson and O'Brien happy she knew she had to use a few other officers. The three she had picked out would do.

'That's enough, I think. You need to talk to your team. I hope they've found something useful with all their inquiries today. I think I have my task force selected. I'll send for Trimble, Collins and Rainey and have them here first thing tomorrow morning and I'll have another word with Nixon tomorrow too. We need her to identify the other victims. She's messed us around long enough.'

Gawn expected Maxwell to take the opportunity to leave but she was surprised when he hung back at the door.

'There's something you should know about Sam Rainey, boss. It won't be in her file.'

Gawn looked up.

'You're reporting to O'Brien at District Command, aren't you?'

'Yes.'

'Then you should know, O'Brien's her uncle. As I said, that won't be in her file. He's her mother's brother. She insists he's had nothing to do with any promotion she's had, but she's had a fairly meteoric rise through the ranks and people talk.'

'People always talk, Paul. I know that only too well.'

Gawn dismissed his information with a shrug but when he closed the door behind him, she didn't move out of her chair. She bit her lip and steepled her fingers. Another complication. Was she starting with a mole on her team?

Chapter 16

'Did they find anything useful yesterday, Paul?'

Maxwell had joined Gawn in her office as she waited for the three new officers to arrive. He was drinking a cup of tea. She was sipping from her extra-large coffee cup emblazoned with the word 'Boss', a birthday present from Maxwell.

'We've traced Orla's boyfriend. His name's Jarlath Magennis. He's a student on the same course as she was. Billy and Jack talked to him yesterday. He says he didn't see her at the weekend. Only on Friday night. The two of them went to the cinema at Yorkgate. He'd expected them to meet up again on Saturday but she rang him on Saturday morning and told him something had come up and she'd be busy for the rest of the weekend, so she couldn't see him. He says she didn't explain why. Billy got the impression they'd had a falling-out when she put him off. Anyway, his story is he hadn't expected to hear from her after that and hadn't tried to contact her. So he says.'

'Have you checked her phone?' Gawn asked.

'It's missing. It wasn't in her bag and they didn't find it in the park. It could have been thrown in the lough when her body was dumped. We're waiting to hear from her service provider.'

'What about her computer? I presume she had one.'

'Doesn't everybody? Yes, we collected it from her room. They're working on it.'

'Does her boyfriend live in Whiteabbey?' she asked.

'No. He's in that new student accommodation in the Cathedral Quarter. Fancy serviced rooms. All mod cons. No student hovels these days.'

Gawn ignored Maxwell's sarcastic tone. She knew he had a thing about students. He'd never been to university but he had been stationed near the Holylands as a young officer straight out of training and had plenty of experience dealing with their anti-social behaviour, especially around St Patrick's Day.

'Does he have an alibi?' she asked.

'Yep. He was in classes during the day on Monday. We've checked. He was there alright and then he'd taken on some extra hours at the bar in the students' union on Monday evening. When he'd finished his shift, he met up with some mates who live in the same halls and he was with them until after midnight. He's given us their names.'

He would have checked the alibi, she didn't need to ask.

'And he'd no idea what she was doing or who she was doing it with on Saturday and Sunday?' Gawn asked.

Maxwell shook his head. 'So he says.'

'So what happened on Saturday that made Orla change her plans? Who did she meet instead?' Gawn asked. 'Because from the way she was dressed, she was definitely meeting someone. And was it the same person she was with on Sunday?'

'We're questioning her friends this morning. Jo and Erin were headed there first thing. Hopefully she'll have told them what she was doing.'

He had been standing looking out the window while he sipped his tea.

'That looks like your man Collins from his personnel photo.' He was watching a tall, lean figure walking purposefully across the car park. 'He looks as if he spent all night polishing his shoes.'

'He wants to make a good impression. Nothing wrong with that, Paul. I remember you arriving for the first time, *Sergeant* Maxwell,' Gawn said. 'If you'd have had any more gel on your hair that day, it could have walked in by itself.'

They both laughed at the memory.

'I didn't know you'd noticed. I guess Collins wants to impress you or maybe he's got wind of what this is about and he wants to justify his lack of action.'

'I've not signed on with Professional Standards, Paul. This is an investigation to find a sexual predator at the very least and maybe a murderer now, and I want results. Quickly.'

Next to appear was Sandy Trimble. He was walking along the corridor towards them as Gawn and Maxwell were making their way to the conference room. It was just coming up to nine o'clock.

Trimble spotted Maxwell and there was a momentary hesitation as he seemed to be calculating whether he should greet his former colleague or keep his eyes down and pretend he hadn't noticed him. Maxwell made the decision for him.

'Sandy, how are you? Long time, no see.'

Maxwell reached out a hand and Trimble shook it vigorously. 'This is Superintendent Girvin, Sandy.'

'Ma'am.' Trimble nodded but this time he offered no handshake taking his cue from her.

'Good morning, Sergeant.'

The two men followed her into the room. It looked different this morning. Half a dozen desks had been set up around the walls since yesterday, some with computers switched on ready for use. There was just about space left for the heavy mahogany conference table which stood in its usual position in the centre of the room. A whiteboard had been wheeled in near the window, partly blocking the view. It waited blankly to be filled with notes and photographs of their victims and eventually, hopefully, their suspects.

'Nearly everyone's here, I see.' Gawn met Maxwell's eye.

Collins jumped up from his seat. 'Constable Collins, ma'am. Mike, Michael,' he added.

Another round of introductions but still no sign of Sam Rainey. She was late.

'I think the final member of our group must have been held up in traffic,' Gawn said to explain why she wasn't making a start to their meeting. She was just going to suggest coffee, when there was a tentative knock on the door.

'Come.'

Gawn could see from only a cursory glance how Sam Rainey had earned her nickname. Of course, the two women were very different but superficially they could be sisters and, at a distance they could be mistaken for each other. Rainey was probably an inch shorter but her hair was the same rich shade of auburn and cut in almost the same short style. Her eyes were green too. She was dressed in a black midi pencil skirt, a crisp-looking white blouse and a grey tweed jacket with mandarin collar. It gave her a suitably business-like vibe. It was not unlike the outfits Gawn chose for herself.

'I'm so sorry I'm late, ma'am.' Rainey's expression matched her words. 'ACC O'Brien called me into his office when I was on my way here. Otherwise, I would have been on time.'

Gawn and Maxwell exchanged a look. So, this was how it was going to be, it said.

Chapter 17

'I'm sure you all saw the newspaper headlines on Monday about a rapist in Belfast. Perhaps you've already put two and two together and remembered the sexual assault complaints you dealt with recently,' Gawn began, then paused.

She was watching their faces closely. She registered their reactions as she explained about the task force. It was news to Collins and Trimble but Gawn was sure Rainey had already heard all about it. From Uncle Aidan, no doubt.

'The complaints reported to you are likely to be some of the ones in the article although we won't be sure until next Sunday or if Nixon gives us the names and contact details of the women she's spoken to. But let's start with what we do know. Constable Collins.' She swivelled to face him as she spoke. He swallowed hard under her stare.

And so it started. She may have told Maxwell that she wasn't doing Professional Standards' job for them, but he wasn't sure the three officers would have agreed. She spent over an hour going over their cases. Every detail. Her questions left nowhere for them to hide. Maxwell knew her interviewing technique well. He had watched her breaking down hardened criminals. These three didn't stand a chance.

Suddenly Gawn said, 'You seem to have done as much as you could under the circumstances. All of you. If the women didn't want to pursue their complaints it wasn't your fault. Now we need to re-contact them and get the names from Donna Nixon of all the others she claims to have found and then interview them too.'

'You say "we", ma'am. Does that mean you want us on the task force?' Rainey asked. The two men may have been thinking that but only Rainey had the nerve to ask.

'See it as your chance to redeem yourselves or just see it as me using your local knowledge and the connection you already have with the victims. Either way, yes, Inspector. I want you on the task force. At least until you let me down. I don't do failure. There'll be no third chances.'

Chapter 18

Gawn didn't know what to expect when she faced Aidan O'Brien for the first time. She had always believed the saying 'better the devil you know' and she was used to working for Wilkinson.

'Superintendent, we meet at last.'

She couldn't help noticing his long thick eyelashes, almost as if he had applied mascara. His eyes held hers. Was he flirting with her or was that just her imagination? Wilkinson had warned her about him. Is this what she'd meant?

O'Brien had risen from his seat and walked around his desk to face her. She realised he was even more intimidating in person than she'd expected. He was taller and his deep brown eyes were penetrating, seeming to see through her. His handshake was firm but not overly firm.

'Take a seat.'

He pointed to one of the armchairs in the corner of his office, not the uncomfortable-looking modern upright metal and black leather chairs in front of his desk that she had begun moving towards.

Gawn looked him over as he joined her. He was so thin he looked as if a simple push would knock him down. His face looked gaunt too, his cheeks concave, and there were touches of grey in his neatly trimmed beard. But Gawn knew he was a fitness fanatic and held a black belt in judo. He would be no pushover.

'I've read your initial report. Very succinct. Now, tell me what you plan to do to catch this bastard.'

She was shocked at his question. He had seated himself opposite her. Gawn could feel her mouth go dry under his stare. It was an unusual reaction for her. She wasn't normally intimidated by authority figures but there was something almost fierce about O'Brien, especially his eyes. He had the look of a zealot and she could imagine him in pilgrim garb leading the questioning at the Salem witch trials.

'I've selected the officers for the task force, sir.'

She deliberately made no mention of Rainey. If he didn't mention their relationship, then she wouldn't either. Let him think she didn't know about it. If she had to watch her back she would need all the advantages she could muster, and having knowledge of that without him realising might be one of them.

'They've already begun looking through all the rape and sexual assault reports in the past four weeks in the Greater Belfast area.'

'You think this only goes back four weeks?'

'Honest answer, sir?'

He nodded.

'I don't know. I hope so but we'll start there and work back.'

'I've heard I should expect honest answers from you, Superintendent. No bullshit, as one of my colleagues put it.'

'I don't have time for any bullshit, sir. I believe this man is a serious threat and he appears to be escalating. I won't be wasting any time and I don't expect to be held back by bureaucracy or any macho games.'

O'Brien seemed slightly taken aback, regardless of what he had just said about her bluntness. He gathered his thoughts and then continued, ignoring her last comments, 'You'll be having another word with the journalist as a matter of priority then, of course?'

'Of course, sir. We need to get all the information she has. I've arranged a meeting for Inspector Rainey and myself with her.'

She paused and waited again for his reaction. Would he mention their relationship this time? He still said nothing. She wondered if he assumed she already knew about it or whether he was hoping to keep it secret from her.

'We need to convince Nixon to give us all the details, not just hints so we have to waste our time guessing or re-interviewing every assault case in Belfast. We need her to identify the other victims so we can speak to them, today if possible,' Gawn told him.

'And you think she won't give you the names?'

'It's a possibility, sir. She's worried we'll scare the women off and they'll refuse to let her use their stories if we question them. She promised them anonymity. She'll not be keen to give up their names.'

'I presume you'll be playing the sisterhood card then.' He saw her raised eyebrow and went on, 'I guessed that was why you were taking Samantha Rainey with you. All girls together, eh?'

'I'm taking Inspector Rainey because she's my number two on the team, sir. My usual inspector is on other duties for ACC Wilkinson. Otherwise *he* would be with me.'

Gawn didn't regard herself as a feminist. Male and female members of the Serious Crime unit were held to the same standard. She made no allowances. She expected total commitment. She was leading this case, as far as she was concerned anyway, not because she was a woman worried for the safety of other women but because she was a police officer concerned with law and order.

Chapter 19

'May I ask why we're meeting at Belfast Castle, ma'am?'

'It wasn't my idea, Inspector. It was Nixon's.'

Gawn had explained, as they drove along, about Nixon's personal involvement in the case. Rainey had been shocked that the journalist wasn't just investigating the story but she'd been a victim too.

'How did you get her to agree to set up a meeting?'

How indeed? Gawn wasn't going to reveal to Rainey the promise she had made. Better no one else knew. Especially her.

'Let's just be glad she did agree. You and the others have been wasting your time this morning trying to identify the victims. We need her to give us the names.'

Just then the winding road up to the impressive grey stone castle, its baronial architecture a reminder of Belfast's close links with Scotland, widened out and the trees thinned giving them their first view over the city down below. It lay spread out, its industrial past glories reflected now in the shiny silver form of the Titanic Museum dominating the shoreline at the harbour just as its namesake had once done over a hundred years ago.

Gawn was surprised to find the car park full. She spotted a gleaming vintage white Rolls Royce bedecked with white satin ribbons. Smartly dressed men and women were milling around despite the chill in the air and the lightest touch of frost still lingering on the grass. A photographer was fussing around, corralling them onto an exterior spiral staircase reminding Gawn of a sheepdog and a herd of recalcitrant sheep. A wedding party. Of course.

Gawn recognised Nixon's battered Fiat. She pulled in beside it. She and Rainey got out of the car. Just then the journalist walked out of the building clutching a champagne glass and approached them.

'Chief Inspector. Oh, sorry, I hear congratulations are in order. *Superintendent.*' Gawn was reminded of Maxwell's scathing tones when he had first noticed her new nameplate.

'A wee glass of champers seems very appropriate under the circumstances. To celebrate your promotion.' She held the glass up in a toast.

'Never mind my rank. It's not important. I'm investigating these rapes which is what you wanted, isn't it?' She sounded fiercer than she'd intended.

'Yes,' the grudging response came.

'This is Inspector Rainey, Donna. She's part of the task force. We want to get started on finding this man, but we need your help. You want him off the streets. So do we.'

Nixon didn't respond at first. She took a sip of her drink to fill the hiatus.

Gawn's voice softened.

'Look, Donna, we've already talked about this. We can't investigate in the dark. You need to help us. We need names. We need to interview the women. I thought you understood that now. You agreed. Please.'

Gawn wasn't going to plead in front of Rainey and she wasn't going to reveal what she had agreed with the journalist earlier. And she thought threatening would be counterproductive, making Nixon more determined to hold out on them, so she just waited.

At last Nixon spoke. 'The first victim has agreed to speak to you.'

Gawn realised she had been holding her breath. She released it now in a sigh.

'Great! When?'

'Now,' Nixon replied. She looked around. 'That's why I told you to meet me here.'

Her gaze had come to rest on the giggling bridal party making their way across the grass towards them.

'Her name's Kylie Renfrew. She's one of the bridesmaids.'

* * *

'This is the policewoman I told you about, Kylie.'

Nixon had walked across and spoken to a teenage girl dressed in a full-length, dark green velvet bridesmaid's dress, and brought her to where Gawn and Rainey were waiting. Gawn had noticed the girl earlier when they'd first arrived. Then she had been laughing and joking in the bridal party; now there was a very different look on her face.

'You can't come to my house,' she began, holding her hands up palms outward as if to physically hold them back. 'Nobody knows about… it. My dad would kill me.' She glanced round and shouted to the others, 'I'll be over in a minute. I've met some of my old schoolteachers.' She waved to them to go ahead.

'Kylie, we need to talk to you,' Gawn began.

'Donna's promised me I only have to tell you what happened. That's all. This isn't official or anything. I'm not being interviewed. I'm not making a complaint or a statement or whatever you call it. I never went near a police station. I wasn't that daft. I know what everyone would think. Just a stupid wee bitch, drunk, up an alley. I wish I'd never gone to that party.'

'This is off the record. I promise. Now, what party are you talking about?' Gawn asked.

'It was a sort of hen party. The rest of them had all gone to Magaluf but my dad said I was too young and I couldn't take the time off school.'

'What age are you, Kylie?' Rainey asked.

65

'I'll be sixteen in a couple of months.'

'So, they had a party in Belfast for you instead?'

Rainey had taken over the questions after exchanging a look with Gawn, silently asking for permission. Gawn was happy for her to do it. She wanted to see her in action.

'Kinda. Shannon, she's the bride, she's my sister. She knew I'd been disappointed that I didn't get to go with them. She'd tried to convince my dad to let me go but he wouldn't budge. So she arranged the night out instead. It wasn't really a party. Just a bit of craic. We all went into town in a big, stretched limo with pink wigs and pink sashes on. We had a wee look round. We got some fancy cocktails and had a bit of a rake through the Christmas market and a few beers. Then we went back to Shannon's for a while.'

'And a few more drinks?' Rainey suggested.

'Aye.'

Kylie dropped her eyes, not wanting to meet Rainey's look.

'And then what?'

'I was on my way home. My folks are strict, you see. Well, my dad is anyway. I had to be home by midnight otherwise he said he would come for me and I didn't want that. I'd be scundered; being picked up like a wee kid from primary school or something.'

Kylie glanced round to make sure her friends weren't within hearing distance.

'And then?' Rainey prompted.

'Shannon offered to get Troy to walk me home but he'd already gone to bed and I didn't want to be a bother.'

'Troy?' Rainey asked.

'Her boyfriend.' She giggled. 'Her husband now. I walked home myself. It was only down the road. A few streets. Not far. I didn't notice anybody behind me. He must have come out of one of the alleys. I didn't hear him. He just grabbed me from behind and put his hand over my mouth to stop me screaming and pulled me down the alley. He had me up against the wall. My face was against the bricks. He said if I looked round at him or made a noise he'd cut my throat.'

'Did he have a knife?' Rainey asked.

'I didn't see one but I wasn't going to chance it. I just sort of froze.'

She paused and they all waited.

'He put his hand up my skirt then and the dirty old bugger was pulling my pants down. He had something – I don't know what it was – and he was digging it into my stomach. I was scared it was a knife. Then I heard some fellas coming along the street. He musta heard them too. He ran away and I ran home.'

'You didn't say anything to these fellas?' Rainey asked.

'No. I didn't say anything to anybody until the next day. My dad would have gone ballistic. He'd blame me and Shannon. I didn't want to get her into trouble or spoil her big day if there was a row. I told my best mate, Julie, and she said I should report it. But I didn't want to.

'Then big mouth Julie went about telling everybody anyway. Look, nothing really happened to me. I've had boys do nearly as much before. It was nothing. He didn't cut me and I didn't want to make a fuss. I still don't and I have to go now. They'll be looking for me. They'll be cutting the cake.'

She had already started to move away.

'Just a minute, Kylie.' Gawn's authoritative voice stopped her. 'Did you see this man's face even for just a second?'

The girl shook her head.

'Would you recognise his voice if you heard it again?'

'No. It could have been anybody.'

She rushed off then and they didn't try to stop her.

Gawn turned to Nixon.

'There's nothing much to go on there, Donna. Some man having a quick grope of a wee girl too tipsy to put up much resistance.'

'So that makes it alright, does it?' Nixon said angrily.

'No, of course not. But I have to be pragmatic. I can't waste resources if this is all you have. You can't even be sure this is the same man who attacked you or any of the other women you claim were attacked.'

Nixon pounced on Gawn's words.

'Claim! You mean you don't believe me now?'

Gawn's neck was on the block. She'd told Wilkinson she believed there was a serial rapist. She'd convinced her there was a case to be investigated. The task force had been set up. Now it could all disappear into a few unrelated assaults, and Orla Maguire's death that Maxwell was already investigating. The one rapist they had been sure about was already charged and he hadn't drawn on his victim. She knew that now. Nixon would crucify her in the press for taking a promotion, even only an acting one. She'd want revenge for losing her scoop.

'How do you explain this then?'

Nixon held out her closed hand. She opened it slowly to reveal a lipstick.

Chapter 20

The three women were sitting in Gawn's car, sheltering out of the wind. Gawn and Nixon were side by side in the front, Rainey in the back leaning forward, her head poking between the seats. Gawn was wearing blue forensics gloves and holding the lipstick container in her hand, letting it roll round on her palm.

'I don't suppose I really need the gloves, do I?'

'Probably not. I've touched it and God knows how many others. It must have been lying up the back alley for over three weeks,' Nixon admitted. 'I only got it yesterday.

Kylie told me which alley it was. I went and had a look around and found it.'

Gawn was holding it up to the light trying to read the torn label on it.

'So, it might have absolutely nothing to do with what happened to her? It could have been dropped any time, by anybody,' Gawn said.

Reluctantly Nixon agreed. 'I suppose so. It just seemed a coincidence. With the drawing on me. He'd used lipstick on me, I think.'

Gawn bit her lip as she considered what to do.

'Do you think it would be worthwhile taking a look at the alley, ma'am?' Rainey asked.

'I doubt very much you'd find anything else after all this time and I don't think it's worth wasting a CSI team's time but knock yourself out, Inspector.' Gawn realised she had sounded dismissive but she was annoyed. She had really hoped they were going to hear something useful.

'You don't believe there is a serial rapist now, do you?' Nixon asked.

'If Kylie's the best you have, then probably no. If you'd kept a sample of the lipstick used on you and we could have identified it as being the same type as this, then that would be different.'

'Christ, Gawn, you really expected me to start taking samples of the lipstick off my stomach? I just wanted it off me. I scrubbed myself raw. I could barely hold myself together that morning. We're not all cold bitches like you, you know.'

For a split second Gawn looked as if she had been slapped across the face. She caught Rainey's reaction in the rear-view mirror. She wasn't sure if it was sympathy or a smirk. Rainey would know of her Ice Queen nickname, of course.

'What about the other women? Can't you get one of them to speak to us?' Gawn continued, ignoring the journalist's outburst.

'Would it be any use?' Nixon asked.

'Look, I'm not convinced yet but I'm willing to let the evidence convince me. It's just that we don't have a lot. I need more.'

'I'll be in touch,' Nixon said and jumped out of the car slamming the door behind her.

'I hope she doesn't do anything stupid,' Gawn said, watching the retreating figure hurrying away.

'Like what?' Rainey asked.

'I've no idea but she's put herself in danger in the past.'

Chapter 21

It was the first briefing for the task force. They were all gathered in their new temporary ops room. Jamie Grant, Jo Hill, 'Jack' Dee and Erin McKeown from Serious Crime had joined the three seconded officers as well as Gary Erskine from IT support and a couple of uniformed constables from District Command. Gawn wasn't sure whether they had been sent to offer more manpower for searches and interviews or if they were keeping an eye on what was happening and reporting back to O'Brien. She thought she was in danger of becoming paranoid.

Maxwell was there too but he was standing apart, watching. The others were all seated around the heavy central table like guests at some bizarre feast. The table was strewn with half-empty cups and flattened yellow Tayto crisps bags revealing how the team had been fuelling themselves as they worked. Rainey was collecting up the detritus.

Someone had started populating the rollerboard. There was a line of square white sheets of paper numbered one to five and what details they had or suspected about each victim. A plan of the Greater Belfast area with colour-coded string leading from each numbered square to points on the map was in the centre of the board. Gawn suspected this was Rainey's work. Almost in spite of herself she was beginning to be impressed by the woman's enthusiasm.

Now Gawn wanted answers.

'I know you haven't had very long but any luck with the lipstick, Jo?'

Despite what she'd said about the lipstick, she wasn't going to overlook it. She had given it to DC Jo Hill to send to the lab but she had asked her to find out what she could about it too.

'Yes, ma'am. I thought the price label might give us something. It's in zlotys.' Seeing puzzled looks passing between some of her colleagues, she added, 'That's the currency in Poland.'

'It came from Poland?' McKeown asked.

'It must have originally. Yes, Sarge. The double Z on the base refers to the company that made it. Zofia Zuzanna in Warsaw. I found it on the internet but it's out of business now. This shade is called Salome, I think.'

'Like the character in the Bible? That one that did the Dance of the Seven Veils?' Dee asked.

'Yes,' Hill agreed.

Gawn noticed a look pass between them. Grant seemed about to make some remark but instead glanced towards Gawn and kept his mouth firmly shut.

'I don't suppose you've had any luck tracing where it came from or how it ended up in an alley in East Belfast?' Gawn asked.

'We've a big Eastern European population now, ma'am. Someone could have brought it with them from Poland. The brand was never imported into the UK.'

'It could mean something and it could mean nothing. We don't have enough yet to link it to our investigation. Anyone could have dropped it. We could be wasting our time trying to chase it up.'

Gawn's mobile buzzed in her pocket. She answered it.

The others sat silent, listening to her side of the conversation.

'That was quick … Right … I see … OK. You'll let me know as soon as you have anything more? … Thanks.'

She turned to face the team.

'The drawing on Orla Maguire's body was not a match for the lipstick found in the alley,' Gawn said. 'Dr Norris was able to rule it out immediately.'

'It just means he has more than one lipstick. He must have because he'd lost this one before Maguire was killed,' Rainey said.

'It's not quite that simple, I'm afraid, Inspector. Apparently, it wasn't lipstick at all that was used on Orla Maguire. They're trying to identify exactly what it was but they've discounted lipstick now. They're thinking maybe body paint of some kind. So until we hear back from the lab we'll leave it.'

Gawn turned to face Maxwell. 'Any updates on the Orla Maguire, investigation, Inspector?'

'Mr Maguire did the formal identification of his daughter's body and her housemates have been interviewed. She was living in a rented house in Whiteabbey, sharing with three other girls. Erin and Jo talked to them.'

He nodded to the two women and that was McKeown's cue to speak.

'They're very upset,' McKeown told her. 'They all got on well enough though they did tell us Orla was a bit secretive and a bit of a dreamer. She had big ideas, big plans for her future.'

'What sort of plans?' Gawn asked.

'They didn't know. She'd been a bit of a star in her own wee world back home at her school in Strabane and they thought she might have hoped for a career on the stage or modelling or something like that. But apparently her parents weren't keen. They wanted her to get a nice safe job when she finished her degree so she never told them.

In the real world she'd a part-time job in a wee bric-a-brac shop in Carrickfergus and she'd just got an extra weekend job for Christmas in a café in Belfast too,' McKeown said.

'Was she working last weekend?' Gawn asked.

'Yes. She was doing an extra shift on Saturday. She'd worked in Belfast, came back to the house and got changed to go out. She left about nine, they said.'

'Where was she going?'

'They don't know. She didn't tell them. All they know is she was meeting a man. But she didn't tell them who he was.'

'But one of them told us she seemed very excited about it and she'd gone to a lot of trouble getting ready,' Hill added.

Gawn remembered the make-up and the jewellery she'd noted on the body at the park. Maguire had been going on a date.

'Do they know where she'd met this mystery man?' she asked.

'No,' McKeown replied. 'They told us she'd come in on Saturday evening after work and then when she came downstairs she was all dressed up. She told them she'd got some good news and she'd be going away for a few days. She had an overnight bag with her. But she wouldn't tell them where she was going. They said she'd got a letter that morning so it might be something to do with that. We searched her room but there was no trace of a letter.'

'Was there a letter in her handbag?' Gawn asked directing her question to Maxwell.

'Just the one from the Student Loans Company,' he told her.

'I wonder why she didn't share her good news with her housemates,' Gawn said. 'Can you get some of your team to put together a timeline for Maguire's movements over the weekend and see if you can pick up any sightings of her on Monday? I take it she wasn't at her university classes that day?' Gawn had directed her question to Maxwell.

'She didn't have any classes on a Monday so nobody noticed she was missing.'

'Did Norris give you a definitive time of death?'

'She suggested midnight at the latest,' he answered.

'So where was she all day Sunday and Monday? And who was she with? Let's concentrate on tracing Maguire's movements. At least until we have something definite to follow up on the drawing. Now what about her phone and computer?'

'Still no sign of her phone. It hasn't shown up anywhere and we're still waiting to hear back from her service provider,' Maxwell said.

'I've started looking at her computer, ma'am. The only interesting thing I've noticed so far is in her search history,' Erskine said.

Gawn turned her famous stare on him.

'She'd been researching a lot about fashion over the last few weeks. I mean a lot. London and New York Fashion Weeks. She must have spent hours at it. I've just begun going through her emails. She got a lot of spam.'

'OK. Keep at it. Meanwhile, you and I are going to have another chat with Ms Nixon,' Gawn said and looked at Rainey. 'I'm tired of playing games.'

Chapter 22

Gawn was struggling to keep the battered Punto in sight as Nixon manoeuvred it along the narrow streets of North Belfast.

'Where's she going?' Rainey asked, looking around, unable to identify any familiar landmarks.

'Your guess is as good as mine. She's obviously got something arranged. She must have organised it after we spoke to her at the castle and she just wanted me to beg before she agreed.'

Suddenly Nixon swung off the main road without signalling. Gawn had to break sharply to make the turn after her. The little Punto was stopped in front of a row of three-storey terrace houses. They had seen better days. They looked almost derelict. Nixon was waiting at the front door of one of them. The garden was a riot of tall grass and weeds, which also poked out between the paving slabs forming a pathway to the front door.

Gawn and Rainey joined Nixon. They heard a series of bolts being pulled back and the door swung open but only to the extent of a security chain.

'It's me, Tilly,' Nixon said to an unseen figure.

The door closed and then opened fully. A woman stepped out, a huge grin on her face.

'Gawn Girvin! Ach, it's lovely to see you again! Donna told me you were the policewoman she was bringing.'

'Tilly?'

Before she realised what was happening, Gawn found herself being pulled into a bear hug by the diminutive woman she had identified as Tilly.

'Come in. Come in. All of you.'

Tilly ushered them inside and carefully locked the door behind them making sure to slide each bolt into place before she led them down a narrow corridor to the back of the house. Two women were sitting waiting in a dreary room. The expressions on their faces wouldn't have been out of place in a dentist's waiting room. They looked up at the new arrivals.

'How do you know Tilly?' Rainey whispered as they followed her and Nixon along the hall.

'Long story,' Gawn replied.

'You've already met victim one. Here's victim two, the one before me and victim four, the one after,' Nixon announced and stood back.

'This is Carla,' Tilly added and patted the younger of the two women, identified as victim two, on the shoulder.

'Thanks for agreeing to speak to us,' Gawn began. She smiled, hoping to put them at ease.

Gawn reckoned Carla was in her late teens. She suspected she must be the Carla who had reported her assault at Musgrave Street station. The look that had passed between the girl and Rainey seemed to confirm this.

'Can you tell us what happened to you, Carla?' Gawn asked.

Rainey had moved into the shadows at the back of the room. Rather than tower over the two women, Gawn sat down, perching on another sofa directly across from them. Tilly was in motherly defensive mode, hovering behind the young women, ready to intervene.

'I was supposed to go clubbing with my mates but I'd been held back at work… for late-night stocktaking… for Christmas.'

'Where do you work, Carla?' Gawn asked.

'In CastleCourt. I'm a sales assistant.'

Gawn nodded. She hoped encouragingly.

'We were going to The Garage. I'd been looking forward to it for weeks. My favourite DJ was doing a set. My mates had texted and said they'd gone inside because it was raining and they were getting wet. I remember rushing up Royal Avenue and past the front of City Hall. I was getting wet too. I turned down Patterson's Place and then someone came up behind me and knocked against me. I thought it was an accident. He'd tripped or something but I felt like a pin jabbing into my arm and the next thing I knew I was on the ground down the alley at the side of the club and a man was helping me sit up.'

'You'd lost consciousness?' Gawn asked.

'I think I must have.'

'Who was the man?' Rainey asked stepping forward.

'He said his name was Davey. He's a Street Angel.'

'A what? You never mentioned any Street Angel to me. I've never heard of any Street Angels,' Rainey said.

It was Tilly who explained.

'They're volunteers, love. They patrol the city centre at weekends helping people in trouble, drunk or drugged-up, or just needing help to make their way home safely. But I haven't heard them called Street Angels in Belfast. I thought they called themselves Street Pastors. Some of the churches run the scheme, you see.'

'Well, Davey told me he was a Street Angel,' Carla said truculently.

'What happened then?' Gawn took up the questioning again.

'He offered to help me get home, but I was beginning to feel a bit better and I didn't want to miss my night out with my mates. I'd paid for my ticket and I'd been looking forward to it so I went into the club. I just thought I must have fainted because I hadn't eaten very much all day.'

'What made you suspect something had happened to you?' Gawn asked.

'Well, when we came out after two o'clock, Davey was still hanging around. Just him. By himself. Me and my mates got a taxi home together but he watched me until I got into it. I thought it was nice of him to make sure I was OK. I told my friend that but she said it was weird. Why would he do that? There must have been other people needing help. Why had he stood around for hours in the cold waiting for me to come out? And then, when I got home, I found something on my stomach.'

'A face? You never mentioned that either,' Rainey said accusingly.

'No. Not a face. Just a red line.'

'You never mentioned any red line to me,' Rainey repeated and looked at Gawn.

'No. I didn't. I'm sorry. I just wanted to forget it by the time I was talking to you. I'd only come to report it because my friend wouldn't give over. She kept on at me. But I chickened out. I told her' – Carla nodded towards Rainey while looking at Gawn – 'that something had happened to me but I couldn't remember what.'

'He must have been interrupted when he was drawing on you. He didn't have time to draw a face, just a line. The drug must have worn off more quickly than he expected. Did you tell her you might have been drugged?' Gawn asked, looking over at Rainey.

Carla kept her head down.

'No. I just said something had happened. I told her I'd had too much to drink. I told her I was sorry for wasting her time. I thought I'd get into trouble.'

Gawn didn't quite sigh aloud but she couldn't help exchanging a look with Tilly and then Rainey. If this girl had come forward at the time with all her information perhaps Orla Maguire would still be alive.

'Would you recognise this Davey if you saw him again?' Gawn asked.

'Maybe. I'm not sure. It was nearly a month ago. It was dark and I only saw him for a minute or two. I was more worried about my coat getting wet and my new top being ruined and missing my night out.'

'What do you remember about him, Carla? Anything at all that might help us identify him?'

'He was old. Like about the same age as my mum and dad. His hair was cut short, not a skinhead or anything, but short and he had a moustache. I think. Although it was a bit funny-looking, a bit like that French detective on TV.'

'Poirot?' suggested Rainey.

'Yeh, I think that's his name. My mum loves him but it looked a bit fakey like that to me.'

'It might have been a false moustache?' Gawn asked.

'God, I don't know. Maybe. But he was really old-fashioned looking. His clothes smelt funny. Fusty, if you know what I mean. Like the stuff my mum brings down from the attic sometimes when she's looking for a fancy-dress costume or something. Oh, and he was wearing glasses,' the girl added.

'Sunglasses?' asked Gawn.

'I don't know if they were sunglasses. I just thought they were those ones like my dad's that get darker when it's bright.'

'But it wouldn't have been bright down an alley at night, would it, Carla?'

'No. I suppose not. I was lucky, wasn't I? I could have ended up like that girl in Whiteabbey.'

The expression on her face said more than her words.

Chapter 23

The second woman had sat impatiently through Carla's recital of her experience, fidgeting as if she would have preferred to be anywhere but where she was. Now she spoke up without prompting.

'I suppose I was friggin' lucky too then.'

No one responded.

'You'll want all the details of what happened to me,' she said. 'Well, I don't remember much either.'

'I don't know your name,' Gawn said.

'Call me Hermione. You know like *Harry Potter*.'

Hermione smiled but there was a bitterness to the line of her mouth and Gawn was sure that was not her real name. She didn't care. All she was concerned with, for now, was hearing her story. They needed to know where and how this man operated.

'I'd been visiting a friend. He lives off Dublin Road. I suppose I'd better confess all. We'd been out and had a few drinks in town and… Look, Tilly says we can trust you. Is that right?' She stared at Gawn and waited for some sign before she went on.

Gawn gave an almost imperceptible nod of her head.

'OK. Here's my story, for what it's worth. Steve and I had smoked a few spliffs.' She paused and Gawn waited. She knew there was more to come. 'And done a line of coke.'

Gawn's face remained impassive. But she couldn't see, from where she was sitting, how Rainey had reacted. She hoped she wouldn't put Hermione off speaking to them.

'By the time I left his place I was still a bit spaced out. I called an Uber and I vaguely remember standing out waiting until it arrived but that's more or less all I can remember until I came round propped up against the front door of my house off Tates Avenue.'

Gawn wondered how many of the women might have called a taxi. Could that be a link between them?

'What time did you leave your friend's flat?'

'About 2am. I think.'

Gawn could see Hermione was considering whether she should add something to what she had told them so far.

'Look. I'm a teacher. So's Steve. I don't want to get into trouble or get him into any trouble either. It wouldn't look good if all the drug stuff came out. I'd probably lose my job. But I was angry when I'd had a couple of hours sleep and found a face and a heart drawn on my stomach. Your man must have painted on me like Donna and Carla. It freaked me out. I phoned a friend and she went with me to report it.

'But afterwards, when I thought about it, I realised all the details would come out. The drugs and all. And I hadn't been raped. I was on my monthly and I reckon that must have put him off. I hadn't even lost my pants like the others either though I didn't know about that then. I went back to the station and withdrew my complaint more or less straight away.'

'Did you get a good look at the driver who picked you up?' Rainey asked.

'No. He was out of the car and standing behind me to open the door.'

'Very gallant. They don't usually budge from the driving seat unless you have luggage to go in the boot,' Rainey commented.

'I just thought he'd reckoned I needed some help cos I was a bit the worse for wear and he was being nice.'

Tilly snorted. 'Nice! Huh!'

'Do you remember anything about him? Anything that could help us identify him?' Gawn asked.

'His voice. He was very quietly spoken. I almost didn't hear what he said to me.'

'What did he say?' Gawn asked.

'How lovely my top was. His girlfriend had one just like it.'

'Was it special?' Gawn asked.

'Not really. It was just new for Christmas. Here. I'm wearing it tonight.'

Hermione opened her coat and Gawn could see a bright sparkly red top. Her eyes widened. It was the same top Orla Maguire had been wearing.

Chapter 24

Carla and Hermione had left. They couldn't get away quickly enough when Gawn said she didn't need to ask them any more questions that night.

Now Donna, Tilly and the two police officers were sitting, waiting. The tick of the clock on the mantelpiece above the unlit fire was loud. No one had spoken for several minutes.

'Well, at least we know a little more,' Gawn said trying to be upbeat. 'And there does seem to be a connection between the attacks.'

'Are you sure number five will turn up?' Rainey asked.

'She's a busy woman. She said she could be held up at work,' Nixon assured her.

Gawn noticed a smirk on Nixon's face and wondered what it meant. She had been surprised when the journalist had told her on the phone that another victim had agreed to meet them and there was no way they'd not believe her.

Gawn was aware Rainey kept glancing at her sideways and at Tilly too, watching them both. When Tilly offered to make some coffee, Rainey volunteered to help. While they were waiting for the kettle to boil and Tilly had set Rainey to spooning coffee granules into mugs, the inspector asked, 'Do you know Gawn well, Tilly?'

'Not really. We met a wee while ago. She was looking for her friend. I was running a refuge in Newcastle for abused and trafficked women at the time and she came to check if her friend was hiding there.'

'Hiding? Her friend had been abused?'

'No. Her friend was missing. They were looking for her. Something to do with a murder. It was all nonsense of course. Jenny could never have killed that woman. Gawn knew that.'

'Oh, so she was there officially with her inspector to question you,' Rainey said.

'No. It was all unofficial. She was by herself. She was looking for her friend. I told you.'

Tilly seemed to be going to add to what she had said and then suddenly stopped.

'Anyway, she's a good policewoman and a good friend. You remember that, dear.'

Before Rainey could comment, they both heard a light knock on the front door.

'You take the coffee through. I'll get the door.'

Tilly watched Rainey walk out carrying the tray. She looked worried.

Chapter 25

There were voices coming from the hallway. Gawn recognised Tilly's but there was something vaguely familiar about the other female voice too. She'd heard it before. Somewhere.

The door opened and Tilly walked in followed by a figure in a long camel-coloured trench coat which flapped open to reveal a uniform underneath. Gawn instantly recognised Chief Superintendent Susannah McDonald.

The two policewomen sprang to their feet.

'Ma'am,' Rainey said but Gawn heard the whispered 'shit' that followed it.

McDonald nodded in acknowledgement but didn't speak until she had sat down heavily on the sofa between Nixon and Tilly and adjusted her skirt, flattening it down over her knees and picking a piece of fluff off it.

'You wanted to question me?' she asked looking up directly at Gawn.

'You're number five!' Rainey blurted out.

'I believe that is how Donna refers to me. Yes, Inspector.'

Gawn could see McDonald was upset but trying not to show it.

'Ma'am, thank you for talking to us. I know it can't be easy. If you could take us through what happened to you,' Gawn began and then stopped. She sounded uncertain. She was uncertain. McDonald was a victim but Gawn was shocked that, if the woman had been attacked, she hadn't reported it. She headed the Drugs Squad and there was no way she should have kept this secret. It could put her in a difficult position, open her up to blackmail.

'Let's forget the "ma'am" bit. For tonight. Just call me Sue and I don't expect my name to appear anywhere in your report – even my first name. If it does, I'll just deny everything. Understood?'

McDonald looked from Gawn to Rainey and waited until both had nodded.

'Understood, ma'am… Sue,' Gawn said.

McDonald took a deep breath and, making sure to maintain eye contact, began her story.

'That night, the night it happened, I'd been… playing away, as men euphemistically call it. It's not something that had ever happened before. And it won't happen again. I can assure you of that.' She held Gawn's eye as she spoke. 'My husband was in New York on business and I'd had a very pleasant dinner with an old friend. An ex-boyfriend who I'd met a few weeks ago when he moved back to Belfast. He suggested prolonging our evening so we ended up taking a room in a hotel.'

'Which hotel?' Gawn asked.

'At the back of City Hall. Ten Square. Anyhow the hotel doesn't matter. I wasn't attacked there. We'd eaten at The Muddlers Club and then walked through the Christmas market on our way to the hotel. We stopped for a beer in the market but it was so busy and so noisy, we only had one. But it had been a very pleasant evening remembering old times as students and then it became a little bit more.'

Now McDonald dropped her eyes and seemed to study the pattern on the almost threadbare carpet under her feet. No one broke the silence. The ticking of the clock seemed to grow louder. The siren of a passing emergency vehicle, maybe an ambulance, maybe a fire engine, sounded in the distance and then faded away.

'Believe it or not, I am happily married but my husband works abroad a lot. He travels for business and I'm busy too. Sometimes it can get lonely. You understand, Superintendent?'

Gawn thought of her long weeks of separation from Sebastian. Had she ever been tempted to 'play away'? Not really. So far. But she wasn't going to be a hypocrite. She wasn't going to sit in judgement on the woman. It happened; she knew.

'We spent a pleasant time together. What I can remember of it anyway. I'd had a little too much to drink, which is probably why it happened in the first place. I'm not a great drinker.' Her voice grew stronger and she added, 'Anyway, we did nothing illegal. We were consenting adults. My conduct might have been morally questionable but there was nothing that could affect my work.'

Gawn wondered if she was trying to convince them, or herself.

'My friend had an early meeting next day so he left and I slept on. I woke around seven and called down to reception to get a taxi. I wasn't feeling great between the hangover and the guilt, so I wasn't at my best. My friend had already settled the bill. I went out to the taxi and that's it.'

'That's it?' Gawn said.

'That's it. Next thing I remember I was propped up at my front gate between the rubbish bins and the recycling boxes. They were due to be emptied that morning. Thank God the lorry hadn't been round. Your man hadn't brought me right to my front door as Donna tells me he did with the others. If he had, I'd have got him on my home security camera.'

'You didn't question any of your neighbours? One of them might have caught something on their cameras,' Gawn suggested.

'I did not.' Her tone seemed to bring an end to that line of questioning. For now.

'I see,' Gawn said and wondered if she would be able to question them. She thought not. At least not yet. Later, she might need to insist.

'When I went to shower and change, I found I wasn't wearing any knickers. I thought maybe I'd left them at the hotel in my rush to get away but I didn't phone to inquire. I didn't want to draw attention to myself. I assumed, if the housekeeping staff found them, they'd just throw them away. I'm sure they find all sorts of things left behind which aren't valuable and they just dispose of them. Now I realise, of course, he'd taken them. A trophy for the pervert.'

McDonald took a deep breath and sighed.

'And, of course, there was a grotesque drawing on my stomach too.'

'You didn't by any chance take a photograph of the drawing?'

McDonald looked at Gawn, her face a picture.

'No. I did not. My husband was due home and I wanted to get rid of any trace of my… lapse. I just wanted the damn thing off me.'

It was the first time McDonald had shown a flash of anger.

'Can you tell us anything at all about the man who attacked you?' Gawn asked, changing the subject and keen to try to establish if it was the same man who had attacked the others.

'Very little. He was already out of the taxi and standing round the back with the boot lid open when I came out of the hotel as if he was expecting to have to load luggage for me. I didn't get a proper look at his face. I think he was tall, taller than me but that's just an impression.'

'What about the vehicle?'

'Dark. Black, I think. Or very dark blue. A Mercedes. I think.'

She sounded anything but confident.

'Anything distinctive about it?' Gawn asked.

'It smelt nice. I remember that. Clean. Like it was brand new or it had been valeted recently.' She paused and Gawn waited, hoping the woman would be able to remember more. From the look on her face it seemed she might be going to add something to her description.

'There was something, I think, but I can't remember what it was. Something I must have noticed.' Her brow was furrowed as she concentrated, trying to remember.

Gawn waited, but when it was obvious McDonald was not going to be able to remember anything else, she asked, 'Did the driver speak to you?'

'Only to ask my address, but by that time I was feeling woozy.'

'Did you feel a jab or a prick? The other women were drugged. Do you think you were?' Rainey interrupted.

'I don't remember feeling anything but it's possible he drugged me. It's all I can suggest. I must have been drugged. I shouldn't have been that hungover on a few glasses of wine and some champagne. And a beer,' she added.

'And you didn't get tested afterwards?' Gawn asked.

'For drugs?' McDonald asked in return.

'Yes.'

'I could hardly do that without raising red flags somewhere, could I? A chief superintendent in the Drugs Squad getting tested for drugs. Can you imagine the headlines?'

Gawn didn't respond.

'Anything else you can tell us, Sue?'

'No.'

'You didn't by any chance get a rape kit done either, did you?' Gawn asked. She got the answer she expected.

'No. I did not, Superintendent. No matter where I might have had it done, word would have got out. You know what this place is like. It would have been all around headquarters before I'd left the hospital.'

Gawn knew she was right. Someone would have found out about it.

'Did you get anything useful from the other two women? I saw them leaving,' McDonald added, very decidedly changing the subject. She'd obviously been waiting outside until the others had gone and she'd worked herself up to coming in to talk to them. Now she stood up, readying herself to leave.

'Very little,' Gawn admitted with a shrug.

'Your man seems to have a type though, doesn't he? Tilly told me about the others. We're all about the same height. We all have blond hair, cut short. And we must have similar tastes in clothes.'

With a flash of intuition, Gawn asked, 'A red top?'

'Yes.'

'Were you wearing it that night?'

'No, not that night,' responded McDonald.

'But I was,' said Nixon.

Chapter 26

McDonald and Nixon had left and Rainey was already halfway to the car when Tilly called Gawn back.

'I think I might have opened my big mouth and landed you in trouble,' she whispered. She looked worried.

'What do you mean, Tilly?'

'Your sidekick.'

'Inspector Rainey?'

'Yes. She was asking questions.'

'About what?'

'About you. She was asking how I knew you and I told her about us meeting when you were looking for Jenny. I hope I haven't got you into any trouble. Watch your back, Gawn. I don't know why but I don't trust that one. She's hiding something.'

Tilly was referring to a suspicious death case where Gawn's best friend, Jenny Norris, the pathologist, had been the chief suspect for a time. Gawn had bent rules to protect her friend and find the real killer. If Rainey suspected and poked around, she could make trouble.

'Don't worry, Tilly. If I had to do it again to save Jenny, I'd do it without a thought, no matter if it got me into trouble,' she reassured the older woman but she looked pensive as she joined Rainey in the car.

'That was a bit of a surprise, wasn't it? I wasn't expecting McDonald to show up like that. Were you?' Rainey asked.

'Not McDonald specifically but I thought it had to be someone important or somebody with connections. I thought maybe a politician or someone from the media. If it was just a few women worried about their boyfriends finding out, Donna would have been able to talk them around or pay them enough to get their cooperation for interviews. And whoever it was, it had to be someone she knew we couldn't ignore.'

'Like a chief superintendent in the Drugs Squad. Wow!'

Rainey blew out her cheeks. Her eyes were sparkling.

'We'll continue to refer to her as victim five. No names. No identifying details. She's a victim just like all the others and she deserves anonymity, if that's what she wants. We're trying to catch a sexual predator. That's our priority. We haven't suddenly signed up to sit in judgement on our fellow officers. We tell no one. Is that understood, Inspector?'

'Of course, ma'am.'

Gawn wondered if she should add 'not even your uncle' but she didn't.

Still nothing had been said of Rainey's relationship to Aidan O'Brien. Gawn couldn't be sure whether this was because the woman really did want to make her own way in the force or whether she was working for her uncle and didn't want Gawn to know of the connection. Anyway, if O'Brien suddenly knew about McDonald's involvement in the case, she would know who had leaked it.

'We need to get back and set up interviews for tomorrow now we have details of where the attacks took place and when. We can ask some questions at the hotel and see which taxi firm they called for victim five that morning and if they have CCTV covering the outside of the hotel that might have caught something useful. And we'll need to get any footage we can from that nightclub Carla was in and find Davey, the Street Angel. That's top priority. He could be our man. But he might be just what he said he was and he could have seen what happened to her. He could be a witness and the only one we've heard of so far who wasn't drugged.'

Chapter 27

Gawn had been surprised to be summoned to O'Brien's office again. And annoyed. She had better things to do. It was late. What did he want now? She wasn't used to having her every move questioned like this.

'Come in.'

When she stepped into his office, she was amazed to see O'Brien, jacket off, tie loosened, not behind his desk, but leaning against it, a cup and saucer in his hands.

He smiled at her and she was surprised at how that changed his features. Some of the gauntness and severity seemed to disappear from his face and his eyes, instead of being almost threatening in their intensity of stare, suggesting something more gentle lurking under his façade of authority.

'Coffee?'

He beckoned to her to sit and poured a cup for her before sitting down beside her and settling into the armchair making himself comfortable.

'I wanted to discuss your little problem,' he said with no hint of irony in his voice.

She bit her lip to stop herself reacting to his choice of phrase. That isn't exactly how she would describe it. And it wasn't just hers, was it?

She was suspicious. Gawn remembered Wilkinson's warning about the ACC. What was he up to? Why this change of character? Outwardly, at least. She didn't trust him.

'Now, what would Lieutenant Darrow do in these circumstances if it was her case?' he asked and turned his full gaze, his soulful brown eyes, on her.

For a second Gawn thought she had misheard him.

'Pardon, sir?'

'The famous Lieutenant Darrow of the LAPD. What would she do? I'm a great fan of your husband's work, you know. I find it a good way to relax after a day in here. I never miss an episode if I can help it. Do you discuss cases with him?'

She knew it was common knowledge that Sebastian was involved with an American TV series and that he'd written a number of books about a female detective but her colleagues knew better than to question her about it. It wasn't that she was ashamed of what he did. He was clever and talented and she was proud of him. The books had sold well, very well, and the TV series had won awards but she never expected that the ACC would watch it and she certainly never expected him to bring it up now. Why now? What was his motive? Because she was sure he must have one.

'No. Of course not, sir. I would never discuss any cases with an outsider. Anyway, it's all just his imagination.'

'But aren't you his model for the eponymous cop?' O'Brien said and gave her a look which made her squirm with embarrassment. What sort of mind game was he playing with her?

'No. No way. He'd already written some of the books before we even met.' She knew she sounded too vehement.

O'Brien tutted and a smile played around his lips again. He was enjoying her discomfort.

'You disappoint me, Gawn.'

It was the first time he had called her by name. It made her feel even more uncertain about what was going on.

'I was looking forward to hearing how you were going to identify this maniac and take him down all inside forty minutes, not counting commercials of course.'

A grin spread across his face now, making him look positively boyish, and she realised he was teasing her. She just didn't know why or how to react to this new version of the ACC.

'Very funny, sir.'

'We need to be more proactive, Gawn,' O'Brien said, suddenly more serious again. The smile, which had softened his features, had gone. He stood up and set his empty cup down on his desk. 'There's been no progress. And you'll have heard about the latest attack, of course.'

Had their culprit struck again?

'I haven't heard about any attack, sir. I've been interviewing some of the victims. Was the woman raped?'

'It wasn't a woman.'

'He's started assaulting men now!' Her voice had risen half an octave.

'No. It was a group of vigilantes. They attacked a young man near the Waterworks in North Belfast and beat him up.'

'But why? What had he done?' she asked.

'That's just it – nothing. He's autistic and I suppose his behaviour must be a bit unusual sometimes. Some girl told her brother that the boy had been bothering her, "looking at her funny", as she put it, and that was enough for him and his friends to mete out their own brand of justice.'

'Is he badly hurt?' Gawn asked.

'Badly enough. He's had to have his jaw wired. The story will be in all the papers tomorrow morning.'

'It's a mess, sir.'

'Indeed it is. So what are you going to do to get ahead of it and stop it happening again? When are you going to have a suspect or at least some details to give the press to keep them happy? We need to be able to show some progress.'

'We have made progress today, sir.'

She had finished her coffee now, so she stood up wanting to face him, not to be at the disadvantage of having him tower over her. She already felt at a disadvantage enough. She didn't know what he hoped to gain from this new more casual approach. It was unsettling her.

'I've talked to several of the victims now and we have some idea of how our man operates. With at least two of them he posed as a taxi driver.'

'You haven't found any similar cases anywhere else?'

'No. Nothing like it anywhere in the UK or Ireland.' It was the first thing she had checked. 'We're checking with Interpol but we have to wait for them to get back to us.'

'Well, tell me what you suspect so far.'

He sat down behind his desk and pointed to the chair opposite him. She sat.

Chapter 28

O'Brien turned out to be a good listener.

'You still haven't found any attacks further back than four weeks?'

'We've been concentrating on getting the details of the cases Nixon has already found. Then we'll check further back,' Gawn replied. 'But one of the things I have learned is that most sexual assaults aren't reported. What we hear about is only the tip of the iceberg. Calls to anonymous helplines are going up week on week, sir, but there's still a stigma associated with reporting rape. It's hard to get over the victim blaming. "She was wearing a short skirt", "she had too much to drink", "she brought it on herself". A lot of the women who do come forward feel like they're the ones on trial, if it even gets to court.'

O'Brien nodded.

'From cases I've come across in the Met, I would guess something must have happened to your offender to trigger this spree. Something must have changed in his life to set him off.'

'Like what?' she asked.

'Who knows? Don't expect it to be something rational. It could be anything – the loss of his job, the death of someone important to him, some slight from a female co-worker. Who knows? He's a maniac. But something must have triggered him.'

Gawn suddenly became aware of rain beating against O'Brien's office window. It was pitch black outside.

'Maybe the cold and rain will keep him off the streets, sir,' she suggested.

'Will it keep young women off the streets?' O'Brien asked. 'No.' He answered his own question. 'And, if there are victims out there, he'll be out there too looking for his opportunity. He's got a taste for it now, Gawn. And with Orla Maguire he might have got a taste for a bit more.'

She looked directly at him. His face was serious now, no hint of his earlier good humour.

'You mean murder, sir?'

'Your offender could have found he enjoyed the extra thrill it gave him being able to do whatever he wanted to his victim when she was dead. Total power. Because this is what it's all about for him. It's not really about sex, Gawn. It's about power. We all know that about sexual assaults. It's about having power over women and with him it seems to be about humiliating them, making them suffer; perhaps the way he was made to suffer by someone. I'm afraid violence seems like the natural progression to me. If you can call anything he's doing "natural".'

'Do you think he stalks his victims?' Gawn asked keen to hear his ideas.

'He might. But you know he has a car or at least access to a car to pose as an Uber.'

'Maybe he's a driver,' Gawn suggested.

'Maybe. But he could just lurk about the city centre and swoop in before a real Uber arrives. It would probably be worth your while asking around to see if any drivers have been complaining about someone poaching their clients. They may even have confronted him or have him on their dashcams.

'The women must assume he's the car they were expecting, if they even think about it at all. It seems most of them were drunk or hungover. I'm not blaming them,' he added quickly in reaction to her look. 'Or maybe they just assume he's some kind man offering them a ride home.'

'I thought women were sensible enough these days not to accept lifts from strangers, sir,' Gawn said.

'Who says he has to be a stranger? He might be known to some of the women and, anyway, your man is clever and plausible. He must be. I don't think you should expect him to be some weird-looking monster when you catch him. I've come face to face with some sex offenders in my career. Not all of them looked weird. Some of them were outwardly very charming. He can charm these women. They trust him.'

Gawn thought immediately of Orla Maguire, a pretty girl, who had met a man who charmed her. She ran her hand through her hair and noticed O'Brien reacting to the scar on her temple but he said nothing.

'But don't discount the possibility it could be a woman you're looking for, Gawn.'

She looked up at him sharply. She had never considered they could be looking for a woman.

'But the victims described being picked up by a man,' she said.

'They were drugged. Maybe it was a woman disguised. I know of some high-profile cases of females involved in abuse and murder, don't you?'

'I can think of a few,' she agreed.

'And your victims were sexually assaulted, not necessarily raped.'

'Yes.'

'Which could suggest an impotent male or a female taking out her anger on other women.' He saw Gawn's disbelieving look and added, 'It happens. I know. I've come across it. Your offender, if it's a male, is probably outwardly quite successful, quite attractive but with an underlying problem with the opposite sex. If it's a woman you're looking for, she must have issues with other women but she probably manages to hide it most of the time. Something happened within the last few weeks to set him or her off. I would guess the original grievance is against a woman who resembles the victims in some way.'

Gawn yawned.

'You're tired,' he said.

'I'm sorry. That was very rude. I don't sleep well when I'm on a case. There's always so many ideas swirling round inside my head. And now I've got this press conference tomorrow to worry about too, sir.'

O'Brien had insisted there would be a press conference the next day and she would make a statement and answer questions at it. He wouldn't let her defer it even for a day or two until they knew more. They had only a partial description of their culprit and she wasn't happy giving out too much information to the press yet.

'It needs to be done and you need to do it, Superintendent. I thought you realised your role is as much PR on this one as finding the culprit. You're the face of the task force. We need to restore public confidence. It's not enough that we're doing the job. We need to be seen to be doing the job.'

Chapter 29

Thursday

Gawn had taken part in press briefings before but she'd never felt so unprepared doing it. O'Brien had told her the press office had suggested it would increase public confidence if she appeared. She didn't know whether she believed him or not. She remembered Wilkinson's warning that he would try to put the blame on her if they didn't catch their man. She suspected putting her out front would make that easier.

Gawn was glad Maxwell was with her. She was glad of his support. He gave her arm a squeeze of encouragement as she opened the door and walked into the room. A wall of sound of cameras whirring hit her. She walked straight ahead, ignoring them. Noel Christie, the director of Strategic Communications, was already sitting behind a table at the front of the room. So was O'Brien. There was an empty chair between them. For her.

As soon as she sat down, Christie launched into his introduction ending with, 'Superintendent Girvin will now make a short statement and, if she has time, take some questions.'

Gawn cleared her throat. 'Good morning.'

She was surprised her voice sounded so normal. She had expected everyone would be able to hear her anxiety.

'In response to the recent spate of sexual assaults in the Greater Belfast area, as you've heard, a special task force has been set up and I want to take this opportunity to assure the public that we have the officers and all the resources we need to carry out a speedy investigation to identify and apprehend the assailant.'

She heard her own voice drone on almost as if it was a stranger speaking, reading the prepared statement that O'Brien had approved. Now, she was nearly finished.

'For operational reasons, as you will understand, it's not possible for me to give details of our investigation but we have provided what we can for you in your handout. And I want to assure the public again that we are confident of making an early arrest.'

O'Brien had given her that last line and told her he expected her to say it. She knew the handout was unhelpful, giving little away and probably only serving to annoy the journalists by its lack of transparency.

As soon as she finished speaking, Gawn found herself looking out over a sea of raised hands.

The first few questions were benign and she began to relax a little, hopeful she would be able to get through the session without a major problem; without being pressed too hard about what they had learned that made her confident of an early arrest. Christie was acting as gatekeeper. He was studiously avoiding some of the older, more experienced hacks and she suspected he might have primed some of the younger journalists in advance to ask straightforward questions.

Eventually however, he had to take a question from the back of the room. A man's hand had been raised throughout the Q&A but Gawn had not been able to see his face. He was hidden behind a TV camera. When he stood up to ask his question she realised it was Jonah Lunn, Donna Nixon's editor.

'Chief Inspector… sorry, *Acting Superintendent* Girvin, can you confirm that the attacker is drawing on his victims?'

For a second, she thought she had misheard him; she hoped she had misheard him but the muttered reaction in the room convinced her otherwise. She focused on Lunn's face. Details of the emoji drawing had leaked or, rather, Nixon had told her boss now. Gawn had known it was only a matter of time but she had hoped to keep it under wraps for a little longer.

'I'm not prepared to confirm or deny any details about the attacks at the present time, Mr Lunn.'

'I guess I can take that as a "yes" then, Superintendent. Well, can you explain to the public why we should have confidence in your task force to protect our womenfolk and find this man when you're withholding information and you failed to even identify that there was a serial rapist until it was pointed out to you, and you haven't arrested anyone or have any credible suspects?'

O'Brien should be stepping in here taking the heat for that, not her. But he didn't speak. Gawn swallowed hard and looked straight at Lunn as she answered. She couldn't mention that they hadn't investigated some of the attacks because the allegations were withdrawn almost immediately and others had not been reported at all. That would make it sound as if she was blaming the victims and she would never do that.

'As one of the womenfolk I can assure you, Mr Lunn, that the dedicated officers in the task force are determined to identify and arrest whoever is responsible for these attacks. And to do so as quickly as possible.'

Gawn paused. She could stop there. She should stop there but she needed to say more. Not just to promote community confidence, but to provoke the perp, force him into action when he mightn't be so well prepared, when he might make a mistake.

'We are using every resource available to us. This predator is a pathetic individual who thinks he is clever but in fact he has just been lucky and his luck is running out. We are closing in on him. He is no longer able to attack women at will. We will not stop until we have him in custody. That is my promise to *our womenfolk*, Mr Lunn.'

'Did you intend to provoke him? Or do you just have a death wish, Gawn?' Maxwell asked her as she swept out of the room with him at her side.

'Lunn provoked me, Paul. And we have to do something to try to get this man to make a mistake. We have no useful description. He has a moustache. He doesn't have a moustache. He's old to one of his young victims and middle-aged to another. He's taller than average. He's not very tall at all. I could walk past him in the street and I wouldn't even know. We need to try to force him into making a move when he isn't ready and we are. Then he'll make a mistake.'

'It's a dangerous tactic, Gawn, and it could backfire on you spectacularly.'

Chapter 30

Emoji Man. That's what they had started calling him. The report on the lunchtime local TV news had used the name. It was catchy. Gawn would have preferred no one knew about the drawings. They were too reminiscent of a Hollywood horror film.

Some of the online newspapers had even mocked up a drawing of the face. One had filled the entire page with a huge emoji. One had him smiling, another with a string of red hearts. Gawn was looking at one now as she sat at her desk. There were no sunglasses on it. So, they didn't have all the details.

Her phone rang. It was O'Brien. He didn't introduce himself but she had no difficulty recognising his gruff voice.

'My office. Now.'

She had spoken to him only briefly after the press conference. He had been livid and given her a rollicking. Whatever it was he wanted to say now, she didn't think she wanted to hear it.

'Come in!'

Was it only yesterday she had stood outside this door for the first time?

'You've seen the news reports online?' he began, no sign of their friendly conversation of the previous evening in his voice.

For a split second she had a déjà vu sensation of Wilkinson's office on Monday morning.

'Look what it's started.'

He flung a printout across the desk at her.

She picked it up and saw a picture of an emoji face on a brick wall.

'Where's this?'

'On a wall beside a school in East Belfast.' He paused and then added, 'An all-girls school,' enunciating each word slowly.

'Are they sure it's new? I mean lots of graffiti features emojis. This might have been there a while.'

'Not according to the headmistress.'

'Did she phone you, sir?'

'No. Her local member of the Legislative Assembly did, who just happens to be on the Board of Governors and on the Policing Board. He's concerned.'

'We're all concerned, sir, but this is just someone's idea of a joke.'

'Can you be sure?' he asked, staring at her.

'Yes. It's not exactly like the drawings on the women. It's just some random person, probably a teenager, trying to scare the girls. It'll be his idea of fun.'

'I'm glad you can dismiss it so lightly, Superintendent.' O'Brien's voice was full of sarcasm. 'I've arranged for you to meet Joshua Mullholland in his constituency office at 3pm. Convince him.'

Chapter 31

Gawn was on time. In fact, she was early. Mullholland had a reputation for being difficult. But his constituents loved him, apparently. He was known as a man who got things done for them.

'I have an appointment to see Mr Mullholland,' she informed a middle-aged woman behind a desk in the vestibule to his constituency office. The politician's face glared down at her from every side in election posters decorating the walls. It was a bit overwhelming, reminding Gawn of some Hitchcock nightmare sequence. No matter where she turned, she could see his stern face looking at her.

'I'll let Mr Mullholland know you're here. Take a seat, please.'

A Scottish lilt to the words reminded Gawn that Mullholland had married recently in Edinburgh. Perhaps this was his wife. She knew many of the MLAs employed family and friends.

Gawn was waiting on a hard upright chair trying to avoid meeting Mullholland's eyes on the posters. But it was difficult. They were everywhere. She almost jumped when the inner door was flung open and the man himself appeared, seeming to fill most of the doorway. He gave the impression of being a huge man, not only tall but wide too. She knew he was only in his late forties, not so very much older than Sebastian, but he could have passed for her husband's father. He looked much older and that impression was emphasised by his fashion choices.

The MLA's clothes seemed far too big for him. His suit hung shapelessly on his body. Even his shirt collar was gaping. Today he was wearing a three-piece suit in a bold stripe with a watch and chain on his waistcoat like men in old sepia prints she had seen. All he needed was a bowler hat to fit right in with those images of 1920s Belfast.

Mullholland's haircut was not exactly trendy either. He was clean-shaven with heavy jowls and he had a ruddy complexion which suggested an outdoor life, perhaps farming, but he had had a successful career in business before getting involved in politics.

'Superintendent Girvin,' he boomed at her.

'Sir, nice to meet you.' She tried to muster a sincere smile. She must have managed it, for Mullholland broke into a smile too.

'Come in. Fiona, get us some tea.'

He moved slightly but he was still filling most of the space in the doorway and she had to brush past him. She noticed there seemed to be no 'pleases' in his vocabulary.

Gawn was relieved to find there were no posters in Mullholland's inner office. In fact, she was surprised at the no-frills decoration. There were no bookshelves stuffed with legal tomes to impress visitors, no elegant sofa, no comfortable armchairs nor coffee table for entertaining.

But there were photographs on the wall behind Mullholland's desk. Gawn ran her gaze along the line of pictures while sitting down opposite him. One was of the MLA with a former Prime Minister. Next to it was a picture of a golfing foursome. Gawn was shocked to see a familiar figure in the group – ACC O'Brien. Were the two friends? He hadn't mentioned that to her. There were older pictures too – school groups. But there were no family photos and no wedding photograph anywhere.

Gawn had sat down in response to Mullholland's casual gesture to her, and she was about to launch into a prepared speech explaining her belief that the graffiti was the work of some adolescent with a twisted sense of humour, nothing more sinister, when there was a timid knock on the door. Mullholland's secretary hurried in with two cups and a small plate of biscuits balanced on a tray. She handed one cup to Gawn and set the other down on the desk.

Mullholland didn't quite dismiss her with a swipe of his hand but he didn't acknowledge the tea either. Instead, he gazed steadily at Gawn making her feel uncomfortable. It was no doubt a tactic he had perfected in dealing with opponents on committees.

'O'Brien assures me you're the best person to be chasing this maniac. He tells me you have quite the track record, Superintendent. I thought he might be flannelling me.'

Gawn didn't know quite how to respond to this comment. She couldn't agree without seeming to praise herself, something she was not in the habit of doing, but to deny it would suggest she shouldn't be leading the task force and she couldn't do that either. She said nothing, just smiled and took a sip of the rather insipid tea.

'Mr Mullholland,' she began, 'I understand perfectly that Ms Holstead, the principal, is worried about the emoji graffiti outside her school. It's unsettling for the pupils and parents but I'd be happy to speak to her, to reassure her.'

She wouldn't really be happy – another waste of her time.

'It's unpleasant and unsettling and, no doubt, designed to be frightening. Some people think it's funny to scare others. But there's absolutely no indication that the person carrying out these attacks has taken to drawing on walls. I imagine this is just some local youths. They're probably known to some of the pupils in the school.'

She had been looking at him all the time she was speaking and was pleased that he seemed to be nodding in agreement.

'But you can't actually tell me for certain that it wasn't the man you're looking for, can you?' he challenged her.

'Well, no. Of course not, sir. But my instinct and my experience tell me it isn't.'

'I understand, but you must understand my position too. There's very real concern out in the community. Fear. Especially among women. People look to me and I've promised them they'll get the protection they need. I expect you to make officers available to watch the girls at the beginning and end of the schoolday and regular patrols to ensure there is no reoccurrence of the drawing. The school has arranged for it to be painted over. We wouldn't like it to reappear overnight, would we?'

Gawn didn't have men to spare to sit outside a school morning and afternoon, nor to divert patrols to watch the school overnight. And for how long? And just this school or would others expect the same protection? Well, O'Brien would just have to step up. That was something for uniform to do. He could get the local station to provide an obvious presence, at least for a day or two. Her team had better things to fill their time.

Chapter 32

'How'd you get on, boss? What's the great man like?'

'Surprisingly reasonable, Paul. A bit pompous but I've never come across a politician who isn't full of himself,' Gawn responded. 'Anyhow, that's that done. Got him out of our hair. Now, back to more important matters.'

She had sent Rainey to speak to the headmistress as soon as she got back. It would keep her busy and hopefully keep O'Brien and Mullholland off her back too.

Now she was with the rest of the team hearing what they had found.

'You were right, ma'am,' Trimble said. 'Driving seems to be a cut-throat occupation these days. They're all trying to poach each other's customers. The taxi firms complain about the Uber drivers and about the pirates.'

'Pirates?' Maxwell queried.

'Unofficial cabs. No PSV licences. No proper insurance. Undercutting the taxi guys,' he explained to Maxwell. 'They just lurk about the place at night and nip in to pinch their fares.'

'Sounds like something our man could do to grab his victims,' Gawn said. 'Have you managed to speak to any of them?' she asked.

'Not yet, ma'am. They're not exactly sitting out at a taxi rank with a light on their roof. They trawl around in the evenings and nip in when someone's standing out looking for a taxi,' Trimble told her.

'Spot of overtime then, gentlemen. Tonight. You two hit the town and see who you can find.'

Trimble and Collins exchanged looks. Gawn noticed but ignored them. She was fighting the clock as much as their perp. Tomorrow he could be picking up another young woman and attacking her.

'But if he usually attacks on Friday and Saturday nights, he might not even be out tonight, ma'am.'

Collins sounded a little plaintive. He must have had something special planned for that evening. Too bad. Social lives wouldn't exist as far as Gawn was concerned until they had this man in custody.

'He could be out looking for locations or potential victims tonight. But even if he isn't out, you can speak to some more drivers, the ones you didn't get to today, and see if they can identify any of the pirates for you. You might get lucky. They might have dashcam footage of altercations they've had or be able to give you some car registrations.'

As she and Maxwell left the room she heard Grant saying, 'Aye, aye, Captain,' in a mock pirate accent followed by a burst of laughter from the others.

Chapter 33

Gawn was tired.

She wasn't sure they were any closer to identifying Emoji Man. And the press conference had been an ordeal for her. She had lost her cool and O'Brien had been livid. The rollicking he had given her afterwards brought back memories of her army days. All she was thinking of now was a hot bath and then bed. Maybe she would sleep better tonight, but she didn't really think so.

She opened her front door and stepped from the brightly lit communal corridor into her darkened hallway. Her hand was raised to flip the switch when she spotted a sliver of light coming from underneath her bedroom door. She was sure she hadn't left it on that morning. Someone had been inside her apartment and then, as she watched, a shadow blocked the thin line of light as someone passed noiselessly behind the door. They were still here.

Gawn felt a surge of outrage. She stepped back into the corridor. One quick call and all she had to do was wait. But she couldn't, of course. Someone had invaded her privacy. He was still here and she wasn't going to stand around waiting for the cavalry, in the form of uniformed officers, to come to her rescue. Who knew how long that could take? Or what he could be doing in her bedroom in the meantime?

She imagined someone going through her possessions. She didn't have anything particularly valuable, but the thought of someone trawling through her belongings made her angry. And he could be in her bed doing God knows what. Her sense of violation was rising. He could be long gone before help arrived.

After talking to despatch, Gawn slipped her feet out of her shoes and moved silently back into the apartment and that was when she saw them, the sunglasses, sitting out on the kitchen countertop. She hadn't noticed them before. It was him. Emoji Man. He had come after her.

Maxwell had warned her she could provoke a backlash. Emoji Man hadn't gone after a woman in her own home before, that they knew of. That would be a major escalation. All she could think was that, if he got away with it, it would bring an even greater hysterical reaction from the press and encourage vigilante groups who didn't need much in the way of an excuse to play judge and jury.

She unclipped her personal weapon and checked the safety catch. She was glad to feel the Glock's solid bulk in her hand. The metal was cold and hard against her palm. Reassuring. She realised she was shaking slightly. Not from fear, but anticipation. She was ready for him.

She raised the gun as the bedroom door slowly opened and bright light flooded out into the living room. A man, a nearly naked man, with only a towel wrapped loosely around his waist, stood framed in the doorway illuminated from behind; just a silhouette.

'Police. Put your hands up! Now!'

The figure reacted instantly. He let go of the towel which dropped to the floor and raised his hands.

'Don't shoot! Don't shoot, for God's sake. It's me, Gawn.'

Sebastian. Her husband. She recognised his voice with its tinge of an American accent. He wasn't due home for Christmas until next week. But here he was, standing in front of her. Naked. He reached down to retrieve the towel.

'Stand still. I said put your hands up and keep them up!'

'It's me. Sebastian. What are you playing at for God's sake, babe?'

She switched on the light and lowered the gun.

'I know it's you. I can see that.' She smiled as her eyes moved slowly down his body. 'I just like looking at you.'

'You witch! You think that's funny. You scared the daylights out of me. Come here.'

She had frightened him. She had frightened herself too. She'd overreacted.

Gawn set the gun down carefully on the countertop, making sure the safety catch was on and then threw herself into his open arms.

'I've missed you, babe,' he said as he hugged her.

She didn't get a chance to respond, her mouth already covered by his. They kissed with a fierceness born of a frisson of fear of what might have happened, and their long, lonely nights apart. He was nuzzling at her throat, his lips soft and moist, his teeth nipping gently at her skin as he moved her back until she was pressed tightly against the kitchen counter. She felt his hands moving over her body, sending thrills of pleasure through her. She whimpered in anticipation of what was to come as he unbuttoned her shirt. So much for the Ice Queen, she thought to herself.

Then, suddenly, she pushed him away.

'No! No! Stop! They'll be here. Any minute. They can't find us like this.'

'Like what? Who'll be here?' he asked, moving in closer again and pressing her body into his.

'I called for backup,' she managed to say as he kissed her again. With an effort, she pushed him back, disentangling herself from his hold.

'They mustn't find us like this. Please, Seb.'

She was almost crying torn between desire and panic.

For a second a look of anger flashed across his face. Gawn didn't blame him for being angry. She was frustrated too. She was tempted to ignore any consequences but then an image popped into her head of officers breaking down the door, thinking she was being attacked and finding them like this. Sebastian laughed.

'Jeez, Gawn, you're killing me, babe. I think you're more than enough for me without any backup.'

'It's not funny. Go. Please. Get dressed or something. At least stay in the bedroom where they won't see you.' She was pushing him back across the room. 'I'll get rid of them. As soon as I can. I promise.'

Gawn turned to await the arrival of the patrol officers. She had just finished rebuttoning her shirt and was tucking it into the waistband of her trousers and smoothing it down to disguise what had been going on when she heard the bedroom door opening again behind her. She turned to see her husband's mischievous face.

'I'm going to have another shower. A cold one this time. But they better be quick, babe. We need to finish what you started,' he said and closed the door.

Chapter 34

Gawn was lying awake. Sebastian was asleep, snoring gently. Jetlag had kicked in.

Her mobile rang. He had insisted she turn it off – it was their time, he had said – no phones, no work, just the two of them. But once he had nodded off, she had switched it back on again.

She sat up and looked at the screen. She didn't recognise the number. But it could never be good news when a call came at night.

'Girvin.'

'Superintendent.' O'Brien's voice exploded in her ear. He sounded worried, not angry. He hadn't phoned at this time to give her another rollicking, had he?

'Sir? Is something wrong?'

'Samantha... Inspector Rainey has been attacked,' he said.

'Is she alright?'

'She will be. I think. Just bruised. That's what she says anyway. She managed to fight him off.'

'Did they get her attacker?' Gawn asked.

'No. He got away.'

Gawn sensed Sebastian moving in the bed behind her. She felt the touch of his fingertips lightly tracing the line of her spine, moving slowly down her back, sending tingles through her body. She turned and smiled at him but then wriggled out of reach.

'Where is she now, sir?'

'They're checking her over. I presume they'll take her to hospital as a precaution but if you look out your window now you can probably see them.'

'My window? This happened in Carrick?'

'Yes. She was on her way to see you.'

'I'll go and check on her now, sir.'

'I want you in my office at 0700, Girvin. I want to hear what you intend to do to get this Emoji bastard and whoever attacked Rainey. No woman seems to be safe now. Anywhere.'

'Yes, sir.'

But he hadn't heard her. He had already rung off.

'Who was that?' Sebastian asked in a sleepy voice.

'My boss.'

'Wilkinson?'

'No. O'Brien. I've been seconded to a special task force.'

She had told him nothing about her latest case. She had asked him about the sunglasses, which had spooked her, and he had explained he'd been wearing them when he left LA. He had never queried why she was asking. He'd had other things on his mind at the time.

'Not another one of those sad old guys who has no life outside work and expects everyone else to be the same,'

Sebastian said as he struggled to sit up and watched her collecting her clothes from the floor where she'd discarded them in her haste to join him in bed.

'One of my colleagues has been attacked, Seb.'

'Oh, is he alright?'

'She. Yes. I think so. But she's O'Brien's niece so he's on the warpath. I need to check on her.'

She was almost dressed already, not her usual immaculate self but it would do. She was stepping into her shoes when Sebastian reached out and took her hand. He turned it over and kissed the inside of her wrist.

'I hope your friend's OK, babe.'

'She's not my friend, Seb. Just a colleague.'

But she didn't tell him the attack had happened in Carrickfergus.

'I might not be back for a while. I'm going to see how she is and then I might need to check what they've done so far to find her attacker.'

She leaned over and kissed him lightly on the forehead. She could see he was worried. So was she but for different reasons. Was this her fault? Had someone attacked Rainey because of what she had said at the press conference? Or was there a copycat out there now?

Chapter 35

Gawn didn't bother retrieving her car. O'Brien had said she would be able to see the activity from her window. He was right.

As soon as she stepped onto the walkway at the marina, she could see the flashing lights of an ambulance in the car park of the nearby hotel. Police vehicles were lined up either side of it like a guard of honour.

The car park was in darkness. But not total darkness. There was one light high on a pole at the roadside and moonlight reflected off the water of the inner harbour providing extra illumination. There were lights too, escaping from a few of the hotel bedroom windows where guests were watching what was happening. A sheet of light spilled out of the opened front door of the hotel bar as some punters, having checked out what the excitement was all about, made their way back inside.

As the moon emerged from behind a cloud Gawn could see the outlines of the vessels stored in the boatyard beside the car park. They looked like lurking monsters. The jangling of their rigging and the flapping of the tarpaulins added an ominous soundtrack to the scene. Anyone could be hiding there. She imagined eyes watching her from deep within that darkness.

Gawn jogged over. She had so many questions. Had Rainey really been coming to see her or had she been spying on her? Why had she been attacked? Was it just random? Surely not. Carrickfergus was outside Emoji Man's normal hunting ground and Rainey didn't fit the profile of his victims.

Yes, she didn't fit the profile but Gawn realised she did resemble her. Only superficially, of course. But from a distance or in poor light they could be mistaken for each other. Rainey's sobriquet of the poor man's Gawn Girvin might have got her into trouble.

Before she had reached the ambulance Gawn was convinced that she had been the intended target, not Rainey. She had anticipated that their quarry might react to her comments at the press conference but by attacking another woman in central Belfast, not someone fifteen miles away and not her. She had arranged with O'Brien to double patrols in the city centre, making a police presence very obvious to reassure the public and hopefully deter their predator, and she had called in favours to put plainclothes officers in some of the most popular bars to keep an eye out for anything suspicious.

Targeting a police officer was audacious. Or maybe it wasn't him at all. They might have a copycat. That was an even more chilling thought.

The back doors of the ambulance were lying open. Gawn could see two paramedics and Rainey inside. She was sitting up but she looked pale and she was holding her left arm tightly to her side. Two police officers were with a small group of onlookers standing nearby. One officer was waiting beside the ambulance. He made no move to prevent Gawn climbing in. He recognised her and she recognised him too as one of the men who had responded to her earlier call to the apartment.

'How are you, Sam?' Gawn asked as she climbed inside, fearful of what she might hear. What had he done to her?

'I'll live,' the woman replied with a smile and a shrug which brought a wince with it. 'I banged my arm when I fell.'

'What happened?'

'We need to get you to hospital now, Sam,' one of the paramedics interrupted in a cheery voice. 'We'll get you checked out in A&E, eh? And get that arm of yours X-rayed. You'll be as right as rain in no time.'

The other paramedic sounded less friendly. He directed his comment to Gawn.

'You'll have to get out now unless you're coming with your friend.'

'Just a couple of minutes, please. I need to ask some questions.' As she spoke, Gawn delved into her pocket and withdrew her ID. 'This is part of a police investigation. I won't keep her long.'

'Two minutes,' he agreed as he walked past her and stood just at the threshold of the ambulance.

Gawn waited, pointedly staring at him until he moved further away. She didn't want anyone overhearing them.

'Can you remember exactly what happened, Sam?' Gawn feared, if it was their predator, that Rainey might have been drugged.

'I wanted to speak to you. I tried ringing but your phone was going straight to voicemail.'

Gawn remembered how Sebastian had insisted she turn her phone off for a couple of hours. She had thought it would do no harm and she had turned it back on again as soon as she could.

'Sorry.'

She felt so guilty. She never turned her phone off. If Rainey had been able to speak to her none of this would have happened and the woman wouldn't be facing a trip to hospital.

'It's OK. You weren't to know I'd phone. I drove down when I couldn't reach you. I wasn't sure what the parking's like outside your building so I parked over here. I started to walk over. I wasn't on my guard. I'm sorry.'

'Don't apologise, Sam. It's not your fault. You'd no reason to think you'd be attacked.'

Rainey smiled bravely but Gawn could see she was in pain.

'I was passing that line of vans parked over there.'

Rainey nodded across to the far side of the car park close into the boatyard's chain-link fence and buried in its deep shadow. Four white vans sat in a row. Gawn knew the hotel offered special rates for business users working in the area. She'd noticed vans parked there before.

'He must have been waiting for me. He grabbed me from behind. He had something in his hand. I thought it was a knife but the more I think about it now, I believe it was a syringe.'

The policewoman's voice cracked.

'I fought him off.'

'Good for you, Sam.'

'But I couldn't get away from him. He pushed me and that's when I fell and hurt my arm. I banged it against the side of one of the vans. I thought that was it. I'd had it. He was standing over me and I expected to feel a needle but then someone shouted and he ran off.'

'Did you get a good look at him?'

'Not really. It happened so quickly and he was all in black. And he had a balaclava on. I couldn't even tell you what colour his hair was. And I couldn't see his eyes. He was wearing sunglasses.'

Neither spoke. For a second, Gawn didn't react. Then she asked, 'Did he say anything to you?'

'Yes. Just before he ran off.'

Gawn waited.

'He said, "You were lucky this time, Gawn."'

Chapter 36

Friday

Once the ambulance had left, taking Rainey to Antrim hospital, Gawn had spoken to the officers who'd responded to the 999 call. They hadn't been able to get much of a description of Rainey's attacker. He had been dressed all in black and all anyone, even the men who had interrupted the attack, could tell them was he was of medium height and build. It could have been anybody.

Gawn spoke to the local inspector who arrived shortly after the ambulance had pulled away and asked him to get any CCTV footage from around the hotel and the traffic cameras on the Marine Highway. If they were lucky perhaps they'd spot a vehicle they could connect to the investigation. She didn't know how. They didn't have any suspects.

She explained to him the connection between the attack on Rainey and the task force investigation, without going into detail, of course. No syringe had been found so far but they would search again at first light, he had assured her. She knew they would make a special effort for one of their own.

She realised, after the ambulance had pulled away, that she'd not asked Rainey what had been so urgent that she had driven all the way to Carrickfergus when she couldn't get hold of her on the phone.

Gawn had gone back then to the apartment, but Sebastian had been snoring loudly when she checked on him. She didn't disturb him. She knew she wouldn't be able to sleep. She showered and changed, then left him a note explaining she'd be home late, if at all, and not to wait up. It was Friday; she was sure Emoji Man would strike again. Then she drove to Belfast and was at her desk before dawn.

Chapter 37

'Has she no frickin' home to go to? Do you think she lives in that office?' Trimble asked Collins as they walked past Gawn's office door just after 7.30.

They had arrived and judged they had time to nip down to the canteen before heading to the ops room for the briefing. Now they were clutching sausage and egg baps and hoping she wouldn't notice them as they passed.

Gawn liked to work with her door open. It was a habit from her days as an inspector, working in a side office off the main incident room. She had seen the two men walking quickly past trying not to attract her attention. That was her signal to move.

She'd spent a tricky thirty minutes with O'Brien. He wanted results. So did she. She gathered up her jacket from the back of her chair, took a final gulp of her coffee and pulled a face. It had gone cold while she'd been working.

The team was gathered in the ops room, everyone but Rainey. Gawn hadn't expected her to be there, of course. She thought they probably wouldn't see her for several days if the doctors had told her to rest, or longer if they'd found her arm was broken.

Gawn started the briefing by informing the team about the attack on their colleague. She gave them no details about where it had happened. Sympathetic noises were made but they didn't really know each other well. They weren't like her Serious Crime team whom she almost thought of as a surrogate family.

'I'll check how she's doing when we've finished but I don't expect she'll be around for a few days so we'll be one officer down. Our man could be out on the prowl tonight. He won't care if we're short-staffed.'

She swung round and looked directly at Collins and Trimble. They were her best hope for a lead.

'Anything from your taxi hunt last night?'

Trimble had a blob of tomato ketchup by the side of his mouth where he had hastily scoffed down the last bite of his Belfast bap. No one had told him. She didn't mention it either.

'We got talking to lots of the drivers, ma'am. They had plenty to say for themselves. Lots of complaints about drunk punters and finding drug paraphernalia stuffed down between the car seats. Some of them did complain about their fares being poached but they don't know who's doing it.'

'No black Mercedes?' she asked.

'No.'

The door opened and, when Gawn turned around, she was surprised to see Sam Rainey standing there. Her arm wasn't even in a sling. She looked immaculate, dressed in a smart navy trouser suit, hair shiny and neatly styled, her make-up perfectly done.

'Inspector Rainey.' Gawn couldn't help a note of surprise sounding in her voice. 'I wasn't expecting to see you today.'

'They checked me over. It's just a soft tissue injury. I've a bruise on my arm but otherwise I'm good to go.'

Rainey sounded perky and Gawn wondered how much of it was an act. The woman had been in pain last night and she wouldn't be surprised if she was full of painkillers today.

'Great. We need everyone we can get. We're no nearer to finding our man and it's Friday.'

She didn't need to say anything more.

'Any progress tracing where Maguire was on Sunday and Monday?' Gawn directed her question to Maxwell.

'Not yet. She just seems to have disappeared.'

'Who was looking for our Street Angel?' Gawn asked, turning round again to face the others.

'I was, ma'am,' Dee said. 'I spoke to the woman from the church. She says they have teams go out on Friday and Saturday nights. They have regular areas they patrol and they have a special van they park near City Hall where they can give out hot drinks or let anyone sit for a while if they're in trouble. Until they can get picked up.

'She said they don't have a Davey who volunteers with them and she couldn't remember anyone called Davey helping as long as she's been involved and that's nearly five years. And she said they don't go out alone anyway. There's always at least two of them together for their own protection. Whoever this man was, he wasn't anything to do with them.'

Gawn wasn't surprised.

'Has anyone started looking at the footage from around The Garage yet?'

No one spoke.

'OK. Jo, get whatever CCTV footage there is from the street cameras in that area. Start looking for a man on his own hanging around between City Hall and Patterson's Place the night victim two was attacked. I know we don't have much of a description but do your best. If he was by himself, he might stand out.'

'Yes, ma'am.'

'And, Jack, you get down to the club this morning and ask if any of the doormen have noticed a lone man hanging around. And get any CCTV they have. It mightn't just have been that one night. It might be a regular spot for him.'

Jack was about to respond when Gawn continued. 'I know it won't be open yet but there'll probably be someone there setting up or cleaning up or whatever for tonight. Just speak to someone as soon as you can. It's urgent.'

Gawn could feel time running out.

Chapter 38

'You're looking remarkably well after last night, Sam,' Gawn said and meant it. She was glad Rainey seemed to have got off lightly. She felt relieved. It eased her conscience. She blamed herself for the attack.

'It was nothing really. I could have done without going to A&E but they don't like taking any chances, do they?'

'What was it that you wanted to tell me so badly last night?'

'It's probably nothing, ma'am, when I think about it this morning, but it seemed important then.' She looked a little embarrassed. 'I went to the academy to see the headmistress, like you told me to. When I was driving into the school car park, a black Mercedes was just driving out.

There was a Street Pastors sticker on the back window. I recognised it. I didn't see who was driving so I asked the headmistress.'

Gawn waited and hoped for something to help them. A break-through.

'It was the mayor's car with a donation of some books they'd been promised for the school library.'

'The mayor? I suppose it's a bit of a coincidence with the car and the sticker but it's a bit of a leap to make any connection with our case. It's a fairly common car. And a politician showing support for a local charity's not surprising either. Who is our mayor anyway?'

Gawn didn't follow politics. But she wasn't being dismissive. Sometimes she got hunches and often they didn't work out, but sometimes they did.

'It's a woman this year, ma'am. Alanna Lawson.'

'Oh well. That's that then. We're not looking for a woman.'

Then she remembered what O'Brien had said about their predator. She hadn't been convinced but she hadn't totally dismissed the possibility.

'You'd like to do a bit of digging about this, wouldn't you, Sam?'

Gawn recognised the signs. It was the kind of thing she would do herself if their roles were reversed. She didn't dismiss gut instincts. Good police officers had them and she was beginning to think Rainey had the makings of a very good police officer.

'Yes, ma'am. I would. I think the same black Mercedes followed me when I left the school. It was only for a while, and I couldn't see the driver. But I think it was following me.'

* * *

'She thinks the Lord Mayor has something to do with these attacks?' Maxwell sounded incredulous. 'Are you kidding me?'

'She's not saying that, Paul. She thinks there might be some connection. That's all. It is a bit of a coincidence about the car and the Street Pastors. And if it did follow her that would be suspicious, wouldn't it? Anyway, I said she could spend a bit of time following up on it today.'

'Are you sure you're not just letting her run off on a wild goose chase to keep her out of your hair? Big black cars. She could have been imagining it. She's probably jumpy. Lots of women are. Kerri thought some man was following her from the supermarket yesterday. He wasn't, of course.'

Maxwell was referring to his wife and Gawn thought of her own reaction when Sebastian had appeared the night before. She'd been jumpy. Maybe that was all it was with Rainey too.

'We need everyone working flat out, Paul. I wouldn't be wasting anyone on a wild goose chase. I'll let her run with it for now. If she hasn't turned up something useful by this evening's briefing, then we'll forget it.'

'She's as bad as you for jumping to conclusions,' he said under his breath as he walked away.

She heard him but she didn't react.

Chapter 39

'Right. Let's have an update,' Gawn said and looked around the room.

The team was gathered in the ops room. All except Rainey. But before anyone could respond, the door opened and she walked in carrying a box of doughnuts from a local bakery.

'Sorry I'm late, ma'am. I picked this up at reception.'

'Thanks, Inspector. Trying to sweeten us for more work?' asked Grant, ostentatiously licking his lips to show what he thought about the prospect of the sugary treats.

'It wasn't me. I can't claim any credit for it. It was delivered for you, ma'am.' She passed the box to Gawn.

'Me?' Gawn hadn't ordered any doughnuts for them. Not this time, although she had in the past for her own Serious Crime team. Usually when they had cracked a case and made an arrest. She examined the box. It was from a local firm that often delivered to them. Her name was on the order form on the outside, as Rainey had said.

'Did you order them, Inspector?' she asked Maxwell.

'Not me.'

Gawn opened the box and let the lid fall back so the contents were visible to everyone.

'What the hell!' The words were uttered before she had time to think about her reaction.

There was a murmur. Someone sniggered.

'What is it, ma'am?'

If it had been anyone other than Pepper asking that question, Gawn would have suspected he was trying to be funny; asking to embarrass her.

'It's a sex toy, Walter.'

She was referring to a pink object taped to the centre of the box with a ring of doughnuts around it. Gawn closed the lid firmly and handed the box to McKeown. 'Get this checked out, Erin. No one eats any of the doughnuts. Heaven knows what's in them. Get everything checked for prints and find out from reception who delivered it and when.'

'Right, boss.'

The younger woman took the box and scurried out of the room.

'I've got some background info on the Lord Mayor,' Rainey said, bringing them back to the purpose of the briefing.

Gawn could see looks of bemusement on the faces of the rest of the team. They were obviously still thinking about her special delivery and had heard nothing about the mayor being involved with their investigation. She wanted to get them back to thinking about the case.

'Let's hear it then,' she said.

'Her name's Alanna Lawson. She's only been in office for a couple of months but she's a bit of an up-and-coming figure in political circles. So they say.'

While she'd been speaking, Rainey had pinned up a black-and-white headshot of the mayor. It was a posed PR photo, probably used at the last election. Lawson was an attractive youngish blonde.

'Her husband, Taylor Lawson, is an accountant. He was her election agent last year when she stood as a candidate against Joshua Mullholland for his seat in Stormont. She nearly got in and she's tipped to do it at the next election. She's a rising star.'

'All very interesting, Inspector, but it doesn't get us any closer to finding Emoji Man,' Maxwell said.

'Well, I thought it was interesting that Lawson used to volunteer with the Street Pastors. He stopped when his wife became mayor. I suppose he was too busy when she had to take over and he mustn't have time for a regular commitment now. I phoned Mrs Dunmore, the woman from the church Jack spoke to yesterday, and she confirmed that he had been a volunteer.'

Rainey pinned another photograph on the board as she was speaking. It was of a youngish man with a weedy moustache smiling into the camera.

'Taylor Lawson,' she announced. 'I went and showed his picture to victim two. That's why I was late. She says it could be her Street Angel, Davey.'

'Could be or is?' Gawn asked.

'She wasn't definite, ma'am. Just said it could be.'

Chapter 40

Gawn was waiting with Maxwell in his office.

'You think Emoji Man sent the doughnuts, boss?' Maxwell asked.

'Who else? We've no other cases on. He attacked Rainey last night and, keep this to yourself, Paul, he thought it was me he was attacking. I was the target.'

McKeown arrived at his open door just then, preventing Maxwell from commenting on her admission.

'I checked with Harry in reception, boss. It was wee Kevin from Dockers' Doughnuts at Titanic who delivered the box. Same as always. I phoned them and they told me they got the order over the phone late this morning. It was a man's voice but there was nothing distinctive about it. He paid by credit card. I've checked that too. It was a stolen card.'

'Fingerprints?' Gawn asked hopefully.

'One set on the box. I sent Jamie out to Dockers. They were Kevin's.'

'So we've got absolutely nothing,' Gawn said. 'How did he get the–' she paused before going on '–the toy substituted for the doughnuts? Kevin couldn't be involved, could he? Or someone else from the bakery?'

'I'd be surprised, boss. There's only a couple of them and they've all worked there for ages. Kevin told Jamie he had a delivery to an office on Holywood Road right before he came here. The caller said it was urgent – a last-minute thing for a leaving party today – so he did it first. Your box was on the back of his bike while he was inside doing the delivery. All he can think is someone must have swapped it then.'

'Was it the same man who ordered the second delivery?' Maxwell asked.

'According to Kevin the voice didn't sound the same. The second man had a bit of an English accent. But he admitted he wasn't really paying much attention to the voice. It was good business for them. Fifty doughnuts. A big order and they were getting a generous bonus for a quick delivery. It was paid for by a corporate card which checks out and they were expecting the delivery when Kevin got there so it seems genuine enough.'

'In which case our man must have been following Kevin and taken his chance when he stopped,' Gawn said.

'But how could he be sure Kevin was going to stop somewhere?' Maxwell asked.

'Good question, Paul. Look into the people who placed the other order, Erin. Maybe our man works there,' Gawn said.

'There was something else, boss.' McKeown handed her a small business card. 'It was at the bottom of the box under the... toy. I had it fingerprinted. Nothing.' She shook her head.

'That would have been too much to hope for. He's careful. He doesn't make simple mistakes like that,' Gawn said and then began reading the card aloud so Maxwell would know what was on it. 'Just a wee gift to keep you sweet until I can do the job myself.'

Her voice had wavered very slightly as she finished the message. She turned the card around to show him the printed words with an emoji face with sunglasses and a red heart.

'We're getting to him. Good,' Gawn said.

She didn't feel as confident as she hoped she'd sounded. He had come after her last night and then mistaken Rainey for her when she'd shown up in the car park. And it seemed he wasn't finished with her. He intended to come after her again. But she was sure he would be targeting other women as well. They needed to find him. Fast.

'I've been thinking about what Rainey found out,' Maxwell said when McKeown had left. Gawn was glad he was changing the subject. They needed to concentrate on the case, not get sidetracked.

'Victim two would probably say any number of men whose photograph someone showed her might be her Street Angel. And anyway, we don't even know for sure he was the one who attacked her. Maybe he really was just trying to help her,' he added.

'I know, Paul. It's not much. The identification would never stand up in court. But it's something and we've nothing much else, have we?'

Gawn was perching on the edge of his desk now, her long legs crossed at the ankle. She was looking thoughtful.

'And it isn't surprising the mayor has a Street Pastors sticker on her car if her husband volunteered with them, is it?' Maxwell persisted.

'No,' she agreed.

'You'll have to tell them upstairs, you know. If City Hall gets word we're asking questions about the mayor and contacts the chief's office and you haven't forewarned them, they'll chew you up,' Maxwell said.

'And spit me out. I know.'

She was so glad she had insisted he was involved in the task force. He kept her grounded. She always listened to his advice.

She didn't always take it, of course.

Chapter 41

Sebastian had made a casserole which he could warm up no matter how late Gawn appeared home.

And it was late. Nearly midnight. She had hung around the office in case word came of another attack but none had. She wasn't hungry. She was sitting beside him on the sofa pushing her food around on her plate. She set it down on the coffee table, uneaten.

'What's wrong, babe?'

He put his hand on top of hers, stroking the length of her fingers. He seldom asked about her work. When he was away, it only made him worry about what she might be getting up to for he knew there was nothing he could do. It just made him feel helpless. When he was with her, he tried to make their time together work-free.

Production had finished early on his TV show and he had wanted to surprise her. Now he was glad he had. He could see how worried she was. She hadn't told him about the box of doughnuts and the message. And she wasn't going to.

'It's this bloody case, Seb. He's out there somewhere in Belfast tonight looking for his next victim. I know it and I can't stop him.'

'Emoji Man?'

'Don't you start, for goodness' sake. That name makes him sound like some sort of a joke. There's even a meme of him now, apparently. I found two PCs laughing over it on their phone in the canteen. And, according to some smart-ass comic on the radio at lunchtime, we're investigating the case of the knicker nicker. He was making a joke of it; of what the women had gone through. But there's nothing funny about it or him, Seb. It's sinister. And he's evil. Women are afraid.'

'I know, babe. Are you?'

'Of him?' she asked.

'Yes.'

'No.' She hoped he hadn't noticed her slight hesitation before answering. 'I'm only afraid of not catching him. If he just stops, we might never get him.'

'Have you no idea who he is? No clues at all?'

'Not really. We can't get any witnesses. We have one possible identification which would never stand up in court. The women were needle-spiked so they're not sure where they were attacked and we haven't found any useful CCTV images. We've got nothing.'

She ran her fingers through her hair in exasperation.

'When I'm stuck with a storyline—' Sebastian began.

She interrupted him, 'This isn't some silly story, Seb.'

'I know that, babe. I'm not stupid.'

She noticed the hurt look on his face and realised she'd sounded dismissive.

'Hear me out, please. I want to help. If I'm stuck, I find it helps to go back to the beginning and see if there's anything I can change or add to help Lieutenant Darrow solve the crime.'

'Real life doesn't work like that, darling.' She sighed loudly but smiled at him too. 'I can't just magic up clues that don't exist to suit the plot.' She reached across and kissed him tenderly on the cheek. 'But thanks for trying to help.'

'Humour me for one second more, Gawn. We use police and FBI advisors on the show all the time. One of them uses a technique called visualization. You could try it.'

'I've heard of it. I'm not sure if it works.'

'What have you got to lose? Think back, babe. Right to the very beginning of all this. Is there something you could have missed? How did you first hear about these attacks?'

Gawn remembered the night in the Observatory and then in Nixon's apartment when she had been shocked by the journalist's revelations. It hadn't been her best night. She hadn't wanted to be there and when Nixon had blurted out about being raped, she'd been stunned. Could she have missed something?

'Donna Nixon told me.'

'Right. Now close your eyes, babe. Think about where you were when she told you. Look around you. Be there again. What did she say exactly? Visualise the two of you together. Her words, her attitude, how you felt about what she was saying. Is there something you could have missed? Anything at all? Something she said that seemed unimportant then with everything else she was saying?'

Gawn was quiet for a long time. She was thinking, remembering. Then suddenly she sat up a little straighter. Her brow furrowed as she tried to get her memory clear.

'There was something she said, Seb. It was just a throwaway line. I didn't think it was important so I didn't ask her anything about it. I barely registered it.'

'What was it?' he asked eagerly.

'She'd told me she'd woken up the day after the attack with no pants on and I asked if there was any chance she could have decided to go commando.'

He sighed loudly.

'Really? That's what you asked her?'

'It's not as stupid or as crass as it sounds. I thought maybe she'd been wearing leggings or something and mightn't have wanted a panty line to show. She said something about...' She paused again trying to get the memory clear. 'She said she wasn't in the habit of going commando, "especially that day". I never asked her what was so special about that day because she went on to tell me about the drawing and that seemed so much more important. I wonder if it could have any significance?'

'Find out. Ask her.'

'Now?'

'Yes. You're not going to get any sleep tonight otherwise. Which would be fine if you wanted to make love all night instead, but you don't. You'd be too busy thinking about your case,' he said and put his hand on her knee.

She saw the twinkle in his eye and smiled back at him, then removed his hand. She knew he was joking.

'Phone her now,' he urged. 'It's late but she mightn't be asleep and it could be important.'

Nixon wasn't asleep but she took a long time to answer and Gawn was almost ready to hang up.

'Hello?' Nixon sounded annoyed.

'Donna. It's me.'

'Gawn? I was just having a bath. I'm dripping all over my bedroom floor. What do you want? Not more questions. I've told you all I can remember.'

She sounded exasperated.

'You told me that you wouldn't have gone commando the day you were attacked, *especially that day*. That's what you said. What was so special about that day, Donna?'

'I was going to a fancy reception at City Hall. I'd been trying to get an exclusive interview with our new Lord Mayor and then out of the blue she invited me to go to an event she was having for some of her charities. I suppose she was hoping I'd give them some free publicity. Which I did, of course. But it was going to be quite a stylish affair and I'd dressed up a bit for it, my new short black leather skirt and the top I'd bought for Christmas. The red top,' she added slowly, realising its significance.

Gawn did too.

'Nobody came on to you or got too friendly at the reception?'

'No. It was all just polite social stuff. Finger buffet, a few speeches about the charities and a local choir performing the usual *Danny Boy*. I barely knew anyone there except for a couple of other politicos, like the High Sheriff, and someone from the Beeb. And I was

131

introduced to the mayor's husband, Taylor. He's quite the charmer.'

'Could someone have noticed you and followed you from the reception back to your office?'

'They could have seen me. I wasn't hiding. I was circulating, talking to people, making contacts. As you do. But anyone would have had to be some speedy superhero, if he was going to follow me back to my office.' Nixon laughed. 'I was chauffeured back. The reception overran and by the time I'd finished the interview as well I was going to be late, so Alanna offered me a lift.'

'Alanna Lawson? The Lord Mayor? In her car?'

'Not herself. Her official car. I felt like a real VIP, sitting in the back chatting to Dave, her driver. They've sold the old official car off, you know. I was in a brand-new electric Mercedes.'

Chapter 42

Saturday

There had been no reports of attacks overnight on Friday. Gawn didn't know whether to be relieved or disappointed. Perhaps all the extra patrols and the media fuss was getting to him. Or perhaps no one had reported anything – as was the case with some of the previous victims like Donna. She didn't want to think he might simply have moved on. Perhaps there would never be another attack. All the frenzy would die down eventually, the news cycle would move on and someday this would all be just another cold case raked up in some television show for its twentieth anniversary.

Perhaps this was going to be the case she didn't solve. It happened to every detective sometime. That case that stuck with them. The one that would haunt them. She didn't want that to happen to her or to the victims.

Gawn had the whole team on standby all weekend. They needed to be ready. And for Nixon's report in tomorrow's paper too.

'You're seriously suggesting the Lord Mayor is involved in this now?' Maxwell asked again.

'No. Of course I'm not, Paul. But what about her husband or her driver?'

Gawn had been surprised and excited when she had talked to Nixon. Now, she thought she might have jumped to conclusions as Maxwell had accused her of doing so many times in the past. But she couldn't stop that niggly feeling in the pit of her stomach. Coincidences. Too many coincidences.

'Look, victim one had been at the Christmas market on the hen night and victim five was in the beer tent, at least for a few minutes, and then picked up from the hotel just behind the market. Victim two must have passed across the front of the market on her way to Patterson's Place even if she didn't go into it. Now we have Nixon in City Hall on the day she was attacked when the market had just opened for business. City Hall or the market has to be our ground zero or one of them at least. Our man could hang around there looking for victims.'

'Or he could work there,' Maxwell suggested and rubbed his chin as he considered her comments.

'And what do you make of the mayor's driver being called Dave?' she asked.

'A common name.'

Gawn was in Maxwell's office. She had wanted to share her ideas with him before she said anything to anyone else. She could trust him to tell her if he thought she was being fanciful. Instead, he seemed to be coming round to what she was thinking.

Just then her mobile vibrated in her pocket. She looked at it and recognised Nixon's number.

'Donna, have you remembered something more?'

'He phoned me.'

'Who phoned you?'

'Emoji Man. He phoned me. Just now.'

Nixon sounded breathless, scared and excited all at once.

Gawn beckoned Maxwell closer and pushed the button for speakerphone.

'You're sure it was him, Donna, not just some crank or joker who'd read your article and got hold of your phone number?'

'No. He knew I was one of the victims. He knew I was in Spud's that night. It was him alright. I'm sure.'

Gawn saw the shocked look on Maxwell's face and knew her own must look the same.

'Did you recognise his voice?'

'No. He was using one of those distorter things.'

'Why did he phone you, Donna? What did he say?' Gawn asked.

'He was boasting. He said to tell you he *is* clever. You won't stop him. He'll have that little present for you tonight. He didn't explain what it was.'

Gawn knew exactly what he had been talking about.

'Tonight? Is that all?'

'Isn't that enough? He's going to attack some other poor woman tonight.' Nixon was almost shouting down the phone at her.

'I'll send someone to your office to get your phone. We should be able to trace the call.'

'Do you think he would be that stupid, Gawn?' Maxwell asked her when she had finished the call with Nixon.

'No, of course I don't. It's probably a burner he's thrown away by now, but we'll try anyway. And why did he use a voice distorter, Paul?'

Before he could suggest an answer, she said, 'Maybe he's someone she would recognise. Not from the night she was attacked. She doesn't remember anything about her attacker. But maybe he's someone she knows.' She paused. 'Anyway, we've got him reacting to us now which is what I wanted. He'll make a mistake. Maybe this is it.'

Chapter 43

'Check the exact date the Christmas market opened this year, Mike. I think it was within a day or two of the first attack.'

Gawn was in the ops room and standing looking at the plan of Belfast on the board.

'You think the market is where he picks out his victims, ma'am?' Rainey asked.

'Maybe.'

'But Nixon was grabbed somewhere in the Cathedral Quarter.'

'Yes, but I've found out now she'd been in City Hall earlier that day. Erin, I presume all the stallholders would have been criminal records checked,' Gawn called over her shoulder to her sergeant sitting at a desk near the door.

'For what, ma'am? They wouldn't need CR checks to work on the stalls,' McKeown said. 'They're only here for a couple of weeks.'

'Someone in City Hall must have a record of all the stallholders. Get the names and cross-reference with criminal records.'

'Just here, ma'am?' McKeown asked. 'Quite a few of the stallholders are foreign.'

'See what you can get access to. Start with the UK and Ireland. You'll probably not get much joy before Monday but try. And, Inspector, you and I are going to take a wee trip down to the market and have a look around.'

* * *

By the time Gawn and Rainey arrived, the market was already very busy. Christmas was only a few days away now. The stalls were doing a brisk trade.

'Why do you think no one was attacked last night, ma'am?' Rainey asked.

Gawn had been wondering about that too. She had feared that they'd scared him away but now, after Nixon's call, she thought he'd been preparing for a special attack tonight to make them look stupid. Make her look stupid or worse.

'I don't know, Sam. Maybe it just wasn't reported. That's what we're up against.'

They passed the tall gaily painted wooden nutcracker soldiers guarding the entrance to the market. Jolly music was playing to put everyone in the mood for spending money and it seemed to be working. There were crowds milling around all the stalls, some browsers already with bags of shopping and others chomping down on hotdogs.

The sky was leaden. Snow was on its way within the next day or two according to the weather forecast. It was making its way down from the Arctic Circle. Exactly when it would arrive was still uncertain but the inevitability of its arrival was not in question. Gawn could feel the oppression of the heavy sky and the inevitability that their quarry would strike again too. But when? Would it be tonight? And would it be here?

'You go that way. I'll go this way and we'll meet up here again in fifteen minutes.'

'What am I looking for?' Rainey asked.

'Your guess is as good as mine.'

Gawn felt she was clutching at straws. They still had very little. Only suspicions she wasn't going to take to O'Brien or Wilkinson just yet. And the call threatening another attack tonight. She believed it was their culprit who had called Nixon but there was a chance it could just be a crank, someone who had managed to find out the journalist had been a victim too. Belfast was a small place and people talked. It was difficult to keep anything secret for long. But an attack tonight wouldn't be surprising. It was his MO but, if he was reacting in anger to what she had said, he could attack anywhere – deliberately change his MO.

Gawn was wandering through the lanes of stalls trying to get a sense of their quarry. Why here? Was the perpetrator someone associated with the market? It would be closing up in a few days. He could move on. That thought did not console her. She wanted to get him.

She stopped occasionally to pick up a trinket and examine it. There were some interesting pieces of ethnic jewellery on sale and lots of delicious, enticing smells. She stopped in front of a stall selling a selection of continental meats and sausages. The smell of the chilli bratwurst cooking over an open grill brought back happy memories of a deployment to Germany.

Just before she reached the halfway point of her circular tour, she came across Rainey standing engrossed in front of a stall. The name 'Beauty of the World' was emblazoned on a large banner over it and cosmetics of all kinds were displayed in rows and pretty patterns. She saw Rainey lifting up a lipstick.

'Ah, that is end of range, madam. We bought a lot of the products before the company went out of business. What you see here is all we have left.' The woman had a strong Eastern European accent but she spoke excellent English.

'My friend had one of their lipsticks and I loved the shade. It was called Salome, I think,' Gawn heard Rainey tell the woman.

'I know Salome but we don't have any of it left, just the ones you can see here. Sorry.' The woman turned back to arranging her display.

'Did you sell any Salome here?' Gawn asked, joining them. She held up her ID.

The vendor looked up, surprised. 'Everything we have for sale here is legal and safe, officer. They are well-known brands, end of lines or older products. We have all the correct customs papers. Everything is legal here.' She spread out her hands sweeping them over the displayed goods in a wide gesture.

'You're not being accused of anything. We just want to find out where someone could have got hold of some Salome lipstick in Belfast,' Gawn assured her.

The woman hesitated.

'You're not in any trouble at the minute but you will be if you withhold information from us. We're not worried about customs violations or counterfeit goods or anything like that. We only want to trace who might have been able to get hold of a Salome lipstick in Belfast,' Gawn said.

'I'm sure we're not the only place.'

'You're the only one we've found and, you've just told us, the company's out of business,' Rainey said.

The woman looked from Rainey to Gawn. She seemed to make up her mind.

'We offered some free samples of our products to some of the staff in your City Hall just after the market opened. It was a goodwill gesture.'

'Was there any Salome lipstick given out?' Gawn asked.

'We only had one left.'

'And it was given out?' Gawn pressed her. When the woman nodded her yes, Gawn added, 'I don't suppose you remember who got it.'

'I do. Your Lady Mayoress, I think you call her. I remember she joked how the colour matched her robes.'

Chapter 44

Her red robes.

The two policewomen were side by side looking up at a larger-than-life photograph of Alanna Lawson standing proudly in the vivid red robes of her civic office. They had left the market and were inside City Hall now. A tour guide was lecturing a group of eager tourists, explaining about the former custom of having a portrait painted for each new mayor. Nowadays they had a photograph taken instead – more cost-effective and quicker, she explained.

'What does it mean,' Rainey asked, 'that she got the lipstick?'

'I don't know. Maybe nothing. Our man couldn't have brought it with him from Poland or somewhere. Could he? There couldn't have been another one out there.' Despite what she had just said, she sounded uncertain. 'But, if it was the one Nixon found, how did it get from our Lord Mayor to an alley in East Belfast, possibly dropped by a pervert? I guess the only way we'll find out is by asking Mrs Lawson what happened to the one she was given.'

'You suspect her husband could be involved in this, don't you?' Rainey asked.

'I don't know. He knows about the Street Pastors but if it was him who was with Carla, why would he have got it wrong and called himself a Street Angel? A double bluff? And then there's always Mrs Lawson's driver as well, of course. Dave. Could he be the Davey?'

Gawn seemed to make a decision.

'I'll see if I can get to speak to her. I'll push for today even though it is Saturday. It needs to be today if he's going to attack tonight. In the meantime, you get some of the team started on a fuller background check. All the significant men in her life including her husband and her driver. Especially her husband and her driver.'

'What about women, boss?' Rainey asked.

Gawn noticed that Rainey had just started referring to her as 'boss', as the others all did. This was new.

'You think we could be looking for a woman?' Gawn remembered what O'Brien had suggested. She had told no one else about that. Even Maxwell. But Rainey had come up with it herself. She had good instincts. Or maybe her uncle had suggested it to her too, Gawn realised.

'I've been thinking about that. There's no evidence any of the women were raped, even Orla Maguire. Donna Nixon wasn't sure exactly what happened to her. She might have been raped or she might not. And we've no physical evidence of rape with any of them. They were drugged, assaulted and drawn on. It's a bitchy sort of act. But it could be a woman doing it. Wouldn't the victims be more likely to trust another woman and drop their guard with her? And she could be drugging them because she doesn't have the physical strength to subdue them.'

'But what about you being attacked? That was a man, wasn't it?'

'Copycat,' the quick response came back at Gawn.

Gawn still wasn't convinced. She didn't want to think Emoji Man could be a woman. But she knew women had been involved in heinous crimes. She wasn't going to overlook any possibility.

And what if they should be looking for a man and a woman working together? The mayor and her husband or driver?

Chapter 45

'Alanna Lawson. She's been on the city council for five years but she only became Lord Mayor last month when her predecessor took ill and had to stand down. She was a social worker. She's married and they have two children – a boy of three, and a baby girl.

'And she's a bit of a trendsetter. She caused a fuss breastfeeding during a council meeting in October. A few of the other councillors walked out. And, as the person I was speaking to said, although she looks as if butter wouldn't melt, she's regarded as a ball-breaker with women as well as men. She takes no prisoners, my source said.'

Erin McKeown was detailing what she had discovered. The board behind her was no longer blank. Alongside the numbered pieces of white paper, now with writing on them about the victim's experience, there were crime scene photos from the Orla Maguire investigation and a street plan of Belfast, a photograph of Lawson in her mayoral robes now and a headshot of her husband and timelines for some of the attacks. The board was filling up.

As Gawn listened to the young officer, she wondered how people would describe her. Being passionate about your work, wanting to get things done, not tolerating shoddy work from others, what was wrong with that? She supposed she was regarded as a ball-breaker too.

'No photo of Dave, the driver yet?' Gawn asked.

'Not yet. I'm still trying to get one.'

'I'm seeing Mrs Lawson at three. Her PA said she would fit me in. There's a school public speaking competition being held in City Hall today. She'll be there to present the prizes,' Gawn told them. 'What about the men in her life?' She directed her question back to McKeown.

'Her husband has no criminal record. He's even an elder in his church and involved in youth activities as well as the Street Pastors.'

'Any others?'

'Her father. But he's confined to a wheelchair. She also has a brother but he lives in Glasgow.'

'We can probably leave the father. For now, anyway. Just to be on the safe side, check if the brother has been over to Belfast in the last few weeks. He could take a quick flight across for the weekend. It's only, what? A forty-minute flight? And it might explain why the attacks only take place at weekends if he's not here during the week.'

McKeown nodded and returned to her desk. They could hear her fingers clicking over her keyboard as she made a start to finding the answer to Gawn's question.

'Who was looking at the City Hall staff?'

'Me, ma'am,' Grant said.

'Well?'

'There's a lot of staff but only three working directly for the Mayor's Office and they're all women.'

Gawn noticed Rainey looking pointedly at her.

'Did you check them, Jamie?'

'They're women.' He was surprised by her question.

'Check them anyway and any husbands or partners,' she ordered. 'Anyone pop out at you so far?'

'Only the mayor's driver,' he responded.

Gawn thought of Nixon's tale of being chauffeured back to her office and the friendly driver with the wealth of funny stories. The driver called Dave or maybe Davey, the same name as the Street Angel.

'What about him?' Gawn asked.

'I've had a bit of trouble finding out much about him at all. He's only been working there a few months. He just seems to have popped up in Belfast out of nowhere.'

'Could he have changed his name?' Rainey asked.

'I'm working on it.'

'Keep at it, Jamie. You might get something useful from the DVLA – at least a photograph of him from his licence application,' Gawn said.

'I'll not get anything at the weekend, ma'am. They're shut and so is HR at City Hall,' he said.

'Well first thing on Monday then, and I'll ask Mrs Lawson about him when I see her.'

Chapter 46

Gawn had been inside City Hall before, at formal events when she'd been representing the PSNI. She had never done one of the guided tours but she knew the building well from the outside. Everyone who lived in Belfast did. Its central position dominated the city although it was now hemmed in by shops and hotels and offices reducing some of its former prominence. But the Baroque Revival building made of Portland stone still managed to look impressive.

A reclining marble figure greeted visitors at the main entrance, but the mayor's PA had told her to come by the back gate, not through the market and main front door. During December, when the market was in operation, and for several weeks afterwards when the clearing up was taking place, all visitors had to use the back entrance. There was parking in the courtyard there too and she could go through the doorway straight up the back stairs and into the Rotunda.

There were a few visitors about, clutching tourist maps and cameras. Tours finished early on a Saturday afternoon so this was probably the last group to go through.

Gawn approached a friendly-looking woman at the reception desk and was directed up the Grand Staircase to the Mayor's Parlour. She could feel the history the place exuded as she followed the red carpet up the wide marble steps. Lord Pirrie, of *Titanic* fame, had had a hand in the fitting out of the building. Gawn had read the guidebook online. She never liked to go anywhere unprepared. She knew it was renowned for its plasterwork and hand-carved woodwork, the skills of the men who had worked on the *Titanic* put to a different use. The marble stairway and balustrades reminded Gawn of the imposing staircase on the doomed ship down which those famous first-class passengers had gone to their fate in the icy waters.

As she climbed the stairs, Gawn could imagine herself in some Italian palace rather than wintry Belfast. On a sunny day the Rotunda would be flooded with light bouncing off the white marble surfaces and black and white checkerboard floor. This was a favourite spot for photographs after civic wedding ceremonies and she could understand why. Today the grey sky meant most of the light was coming from a huge brass and bronze chandelier suspended twenty metres above ground floor level. She was impressed as she looked up and saw the scale of the central dome above her head, reminiscent of a mini St Paul's Cathedral. It even had a whispering gallery too.

When she reached the Mayor's Parlour the sight that met her eyes surprised her. She had expected an office but instead it was almost homely inside. The word 'parlour' was not misused at all. There was even a mahogany fireplace with a fire burning in the grate, a wooden-framed mirror hanging over it, and plush armchairs either side ready to welcome visitors. Gawn could feel her feet sinking into the deep blue patterned carpet. There was an almost overwhelming smell of furniture polish mixed with baby powder.

The mayor was seated at a long walnut dining table, her face reflected in its highly polished surface. Papers and an empty cup of something were sitting in front of her but she was busy feeding a baby. A tartan towel was slung casually over her shoulder to provide some privacy but the child's chubby legs protruded from under it and sucking sounds could be heard along with occasional squeaks of annoyance.

'Superintendent Girvin? I won't try to get up.'

Lawson smiled and Gawn's overwhelming impression was of a friendly, welcoming woman, a little younger than herself. 'Normal' was the word she would have used to describe her. There was no power-dressing outfit, just an elegant silk blouse and navy skirt, simple and timeless. She wasn't wearing any jewellery other than a thin silver chain with a cross and her wedding ring, Gawn noticed. She had only the lightest touch of make-up which served to emphasise her naturally pretty face and wide blue eyes. Only when she donned the heavy red robes of her office would she be impressive. Maybe then, she would become the ball-breaker McKeown had described. She certainly didn't seem like that now.

'Chloe isn't always very cooperative with my work.' She smiled and looked down at the squirming bundle as she explained. 'I'm trying to get away from demand feeding but I thought, to forestall some emergency during the event today, I'd better make sure she was fed and watered. My husband's coming after his rugby match to help but I don't want him to have to deal with a screaming infant in front of all the schoolchildren and guests.'

She was speaking as if Gawn would know all about small babies and demand feeding; as if they both belonged to the same sisterhood of mothers. To Gawn that was an alien world, a world she was very uncertain about. Sebastian was so keen to be a father but she still had doubts about what sort of mother she would be.

'I don't want to keep you back, Madam Mayor, but I'm investigating a spate of serious crimes against women in central Belfast,' Gawn began.

'Alanna, please. And you don't need to explain to me, Superintendent. I've read all about them and I saw you on TV. How can I help?'

How much should she tell her? She didn't want to say they suspected their culprit might be using City Hall and the market to target his victims. If her husband or driver or some man she was associated with was involved, she didn't want them to realise they were homing in on them.

'We're interested in a lipstick.'

Gawn saw the look of amusement that crossed the woman's face.

'A lipstick?'

'Yes. An unusual one. Eastern European and it's not on sale anymore. The company went out of business.'

'How can I help?' the mayor asked again.

Her look of bewilderment had persisted. If she was involved in some way and she and her partner had realised the lipstick had been lost during the attack on Kylie Renfrew, then she was making a good job of feigning complete surprise.

Suddenly her expression changed.

'Lipstick. Yes. I was given a few make-up samples from one of the market stalls. I remember now. We were doing a walkabout for the press just after the market opened and I tried some of the food stalls for the photographers and I was given two wee woollen hats for the children, I remember, and some make-up for myself. Yes. I remember the make-up now.'

'Do you still have the lipstick?'

Gawn didn't think she could have, of course, but she had to ask.

Lawson buttoned up her blouse. She hoisted the baby over her shoulder and walked across to Gawn.

'Could you hold her a minute, please? I'll have a look for you.'

It all happened so quickly and was so unexpected that Gawn found herself holding the child before she even realised.

'Just put her over your shoulder. She needs to be winded or she'll be murder.'

Gawn did what she was told. She felt the child's tiny body against hers, wriggling. The baby's skin was soft against her cheek and she inhaled the smell of baby powder that took her back to her own childhood days. Then a loud burp sounded in her ear.

'The joys of motherhood, eh, Superintendent?' Lawson laughed unapologetically. This was life to her. She managed to balance her career and her family. Gawn wondered if she could ever do that.

The mayor had been rifling through the drawers of an antique bureau while Gawn stood watching her and patting the baby's back, as she had seen other women do. Lawson pulled out two Scandinavian-style woollen hats and then continued to delve inside, pushing papers and other items aside as she searched. Eventually she turned round triumphantly. She held up a tube of cream and a small bottle of nail polish in her hand.

'The lipstick should be here too. They were together. I remember putting the things I was given into my handbag and then setting them out on the table here before I put them away in the desk. They should all be here but the lipstick doesn't seem to be. Maybe it got jammed down behind something or maybe it could have rolled off the table without me noticing and got tidied away somehow. Look, I don't have time to search anymore just now. My husband will be here any minute and the competition will be starting.'

She moved across and took the baby from Gawn's arms as she spoke.

'All I can say is that I'll have a good look for it on Monday. Sorry.'

She seemed genuinely apologetic.

Of course, Gawn had not expected her to be able to produce the lipstick. But she had hoped for a better explanation or some idea of how it could have ended up where it did.

'Who was with you when you were going round the market that day?'

'There was a whole group of us. The press people obviously, some admin staff, the High Sheriff and his wife, my husband brought Chloe and Arthur, our son, and my driver was there too.'

'Your driver?'

Chapter 47

Events moved very quickly after that.

When Gawn got back to her office she had just poured herself a cup of coffee and was about to phone Maxwell, when he pre-empted her. He rang and told her O'Brien had been looking for her and she was to report to him immediately.

She was surprised to find Rainey with O'Brien when she walked into his office. The ACC offered no explanation for her presence and Rainey just looked embarrassed. Gawn was stunned at what O'Brien said next. He informed her that he wanted them to mount an operation at the Christmas market to catch their man. Tonight. She had no problem with that. She had already decided she would have the whole team there looking out for him.

'I hear you think Emoji Man has been using the market to target his victims. And I hear he has contacted your journalist friend threatening another attack tonight.'

There was only one person who could have told him all this. Rainey was looking at the carpet, not raising her head to meet her eye.

'I want you to get him this evening. Set a trap for him.'

Set a trap? Something like that would take days of planning. It wasn't the sort of thing you could set up in an hour or two.

'Tonight? But it's just a theory about the market, sir,' Gawn said.

'You need to be doing something.'

She didn't need him to tell her that.

'Your theory's all you have, Superintendent. The press is baying for action. Use one of your female officers as a target. Inspector Rainey tells me you have an idea of the type of woman he prefers. There must be some young woman in the ranks who fits the bill. Find her and get her to volunteer.'

'By tonight?'

She was incredulous. It was already nearly four o'clock. They would only have an hour or two at most before they would need to have everyone in place. It was a crazy demand. Irresponsible.

'I can't just order one of my officers to make herself a target,' she replied but she was already thinking how Jo Hill could easily be made to look like the victims and in a red top she could be almost perfect.

'You can and you will. This can't go on. We need to put an end to it. Tonight's the perfect opportunity when you know he's going to be out looking for a victim,' O'Brien insisted.

'But even if he does what he told Nixon and attacks tonight, how can we know he'll strike at the market? He could decide to go somewhere else. He might already have a target picked out. We could be wasting our time.'

But O'Brien wouldn't take no for an answer.

'Then we'll do it again tomorrow and the night after and every night until we get him or the market closes. If it doesn't work, then at least we can demonstrate we did everything we could.'

Then she realised. He was covering himself. That was what he was doing. Of course. No doubt he did want to catch Emoji Man. Of course he did. It would look good on his CV when he went for promotion. And at any post-arrest press conference, she was sure she would not be wheeled out to face the journalists. No. Then it would be O'Brien front and centre, taking the plaudits. Unless they didn't get him. In which case she'd be the scapegoat.

Chapter 48

Operation Christmas Market. That was the name O'Brien had suggested. Now she felt rather like she had at the briefings before major operations in Afghanistan. And the faces before her were like those she had seen on those occasions. In the glare from the unforgiving overhead florescent lights, she could read both excitement and nervousness in equal measure.

All the men and women of the task force and others she had gathered up were in the operations room. It was packed. People were perched on desks or leaning against walls. There was an air of expectation. Gawn looked around before speaking. Much against her will she was briefing the task force but her voice betrayed none of the ambivalence she was feeling. They were so underprepared. They still had no idea what their perp even looked like.

She had spoken to Wilkinson and explained her misgivings about setting a trap and using Hill as a target but the ACC hadn't been prepared to step in to try to stop O'Brien. In fact, Gawn suspected she would be logging the information away to use against him in the future. Perhaps, if it all went pear-shaped, she would support Gawn's assertions that it had been done against her better judgement. Perhaps and perhaps not.

Emoji Man – even Gawn had begun thinking of him as this now – had not struck last night, at least as far as they knew. He might be hunting for a victim tonight, as his phone call had threatened, but he could be playing with them, wasting their time and she wasn't one hundred percent sure the Christmas market was his only hunting ground. They couldn't cover every part of Belfast. She had had to make a calculated decision. The plan was to saturate the Christmas market with plain clothes officers and Jo Hill, suitably dressed in red, would parade around making herself as conspicuous as possible.

O'Brien had told her Rainey had suggested using Hill and the young officer had jumped at the opportunity when Gawn put the idea to her. Gawn couldn't blame either of them.

Rainey had apologised and explained O'Brien had asked her directly for an update and she had had to tell him everything. Gawn wasn't sure whether she believed her or not. Maybe she had been spying on them all along. Maybe she had gone running to him with what they knew and suspected. But, if he had confronted her directly, Rainey would have had no option but to tell him. She understood that, although she had never been in the habit of telling senior officers everything. There were some things it was better for them not to know until afterwards. That's what she'd always found.

And she couldn't blame Hill either. The young officer did fit the general description of their victims but she was concerned that Rainey might have pressured her for her own career. Now Hill seemed slightly less sure of herself and Gawn noticed looks passing between her and Jack Dee. He looked in a foul mood.

'Jack, you'll lead the team on the ground in the market. Jo will check in with you every fifteen minutes.'

Dee and Hill nodded their understanding. He would be in charge of keeping her safe.

'Sandy, you'll be moving between all the rest of the teams in the city centre and Inspector Rainey will coordinate with you both. At the first sign of something happening anywhere, we move in.'

Trimble and Rainey both nodded.

Rainey had wanted to be in the thick of it. It had been her idea and she had suggested Hill too after all. That had been her argument but Gawn had been implacable. Rainey was still nursing an injured arm. She'd be a liability in the crowd. And Gawn didn't want her in sight in case the perp recognised her. She was going to keep out of view too for the same reason.

'I've already spoken to the City Hall people. They're happy for me to use an office on the ground floor at the front of the building where I can keep an eye on things,' Rainey told her, barely managing to conceal her disappointment that Dee would be in charge in the market.

The door opened behind her and Gawn looked round to see ACC O'Brien standing there.

'Just checking everything's ready,' he said.

'More or less, sir. They're still getting all the radio equipment sorted,' Gawn assured him, trying to sound more confident than she felt.

'Let's hope you get him.'

'We will,' Gawn said, more to encourage her team than because she really believed it herself. She had her fingers crossed behind her back just as she remembered doing as a small child when all she had was hope.

Chapter 49

'We've lost Hill. She hasn't checked in. I can't see her anywhere.'

Gawn leaned forward, listening to the voice on the radio. Dee was almost shouting to make himself heard against a cacophony of background sounds. The noise of shouts and yells and raucous laughter and a rendering of *Silent Night* from a school choir standing proudly on a platform at the front of City Hall made it difficult to make out his words. A crowd had gathered listening to the children. Gawn was watching the scene on a bank of monitors inside the PSNI command vehicle, parked in a side street parallel to the ornate municipal building.

City Hall grounds were host to a Christmas market. The narrow walkways between the colourful stalls were thronged. It was busy. Very busy. Little family groups, the children bouncing with anticipation of Christmas and already on a sugar rush from all the sweet treats on sale, were blocking Dee's way. The weather was unusually mild tonight for December. There were no flurries of snow, no chilly wind to keep people at home. The popular local TV weatherman had promised there'd be no rain, so half the population of Belfast seemed to be having a night out. And they'd all come here, it seemed.

It was almost gridlock. Dee was trying to move forward but Gawn could see how difficult it was for him to make any progress. A queue of children and their parents at the vintage helter-skelter was completely blocking one route. Shoppers laden with bulky packages hampered him at every turn. They cast angry glances at him as he barged past with a quick 'Sorry'. Some stalls had gathered customers around them queueing for crêpes or bratwurst. They were oblivious to the increasingly frantic plainclothes policeman.

Dee was elbowing his way through now. Gawn could hear his ragged breathing. He sounded panicked. Her own heart was racing. She had sometimes suspected there was something going on between Dee and Hill although they were careful to be discreet on duty. He would feel the responsibility of leading the surveillance team keeping her safe tonight.

The beer tent was the most popular meeting place in Belfast at this time of year. It was almost bulging at the seams. Everyone inside was caught up in the sense of celebration, an excuse for a good blowout, if anyone needed one. It was Saturday night, nearly Christmas. It would be one of the busiest nights of the season.

When she had first heard Dee's words, Gawn had to fight the urge to rush out to help. Instead, she took a deep breath before responding. She made her voice sound as calm and confident as she could. It wouldn't help anyone if she revealed her anxiety too.

'She's got to be around there somewhere. It'll be another problem with the equipment. Does no one have eyes on her?'

Responses came. All negative. With each one her sense of dread increased. She hadn't been happy about tonight. There hadn't been enough time to prepare. They'd been rushed. There were so many things that could go wrong and now it seemed something had. She had agreed only because of the pressure from O'Brien, the near hysteria in the press and the eagerness of Jo Hill to volunteer.

'Where'd you see her last?' Gawn asked.

'She was near the wee kids' roundabout, heading to the beer tent,' Dee replied.

'Did anyone see her go inside?'

'Yes, ma'am. I did. About ten minutes ago.' Grant's excited voice sounded even more youthful than usual.

'And she didn't come out?'

'Not past me,' Grant said.

'And she's definitely not inside now? Has anybody checked?'

There was an interminable wait until Collins spoke, his anxiety making his County Antrim roots more pronounced than usual.

'I've just been inside, ma'am. I checked as best I could. The place is heaving but I cudnae spot her anywhere. I don't think she's in there but I cudnae be sure. It would take the whole team to check.'

He sounded worried. Panic was contagious, she knew.

Gawn realised she couldn't send them charging in. That would start a mini riot. Some of the merrymakers would have passed from the happy hour stage to something more belligerent given half a provocation. And a group of men rushing in and asking questions would be likely to trigger an altercation.

'She can't have disappeared. She'll turn up somewhere. She must be inside. Keep looking, Mike. Help him, Jamie,' Gawn ordered, aware her voice was growing sharper. She wasn't angry with them. She was angry with herself for agreeing to this evening's operation. They'd had so little time and now they were paying the penalty or at least Jo Hill might be.

McKeown spoke from the control desk behind her. Gawn turned her head sharply at the young woman's worried tone.

'Her phone's showing up outside the beer tent. Round the back.'

'Get round to the back of the beer tent!' Gawn commanded.

Seconds passed.

'Her phone's here.' It was Grant. 'It was just lying on the grass. And her earpiece and mic are with it.'

Why had Hill abandoned her equipment? There'd been a problem getting everything working properly in the time they'd had. Gawn had wanted to wait then but O'Brien wouldn't listen. Hill wouldn't just have dropped everything.

McKeown spoke again from behind her. Gawn turned her head sharply at the young woman's tone.

'Look!' She was pointing to one of the screens showing the view from the bus lane cameras at the back of the building.

They could see a male figure, his arm around a female who looked as if she'd been a little too indulgent in the beer tent. They were standing at the kerb waiting to cross the road. The male was dressed in dark clothes, a hood pulled up hiding his face from view. The female was in a short black skirt. The hood of her anorak was pulled up, making it impossible to confirm whether this was Hill.

'Can you zoom in, Erin?'

'That's a feed from the bus lane cameras, ma'am. I don't have control of it. I can contact them and ask but it'll take time.'

'Don't bother. It is her, isn't it?'

'It could be. It looks like what she was wearing.'

'They're almost out of view. Jack, leave one man at the beer tent just in case she turns up there. The rest of you get round to the back of the building. Erin's spotted Jo with a man crossing towards Linenhall Street.'

Gawn would have liked to jump out and run there herself. She was closer than they were. But she knew she needed to stay where she could monitor everything.

Suddenly she remembered Rainey. Where was she? She hadn't reported in either.

'Inspector Rainey, sitrep,' Gawn barked.

No reply. Was she in some sort of blackspot or had her comms failed too? Gawn didn't have time to worry about that now.

She could hear the sound of panting over their microphones as Dee and the others ran past a row of waiting pink Translink buses lined up by the side of City

Hall. Some inquisitive passengers were watching the running figures while others were oblivious to what was happening, their attention focused on their Christmas shopping.

'I'm at the corner of Donegall Square West. I can't see anyone crossing towards May Street,' Dee shouted.

Gawn and McKeown had lost sight of the two figures when they had passed out of range of the first camera. Now they were waiting to see if they showed up again on the next one.

'Where to now? Which way should we go?' Dee asked. 'There's a lot of people about. Did they head towards Bedford Street?'

'No. The other way. Get across the road. They were heading away from City Hall. Look down Linenhall Street,' Gawn said.

'There!' McKeown pointed at one of the screens. From a traffic camera at the junction with Donegall Square East they had a view of the man half-carrying the other figure now as they moved further along towards May Street. He was hurrying and he glanced over his shoulder from time to time.

'Jack, they're heading down to May Street; towards the markets.'

He didn't reply but she could hear his breathing shorten as he started to run again. Soon Dee, Grant and Logan appeared in their view as they ran along the street and then stopped.

'You two, go down there. I'll check Adelaide Street.' Dee sounded breathless.

All Gawn could do was wait. Long seconds passed. Linenhall Street was mostly business premises and government offices. There wouldn't be much foot traffic at night. There were barriers and temporary fencing too for some road-widening scheme she remembered from the recce she had carried out on foot, walking the whole area around City Hall before she had allowed Hill to go into the market.

'No sign of them here,' Grant reported.

'Nothing,' Logan agreed.

'I don't see anyone in Adelaide Street either,' Dee reported.

As he spoke, Gawn could hear the siren of an emergency vehicle in the distance. It grew louder as it passed the three detectives, lights flashing.

'Keep going. Check Alfred Street,' she commanded.

'Could they have got this far without us seeing them?' Dee asked.

'Just do it!'

They did. But there was no sign of a man carrying a semi-comatose woman. There was a rowdy group heading out of a hotel halfway down the street. To Dee's left a church was cloaked in darkness. Tall trees fronted the site, their sturdy trunks providing handy cover for anyone wanting to hide. Someone could be in the grounds. Dee rattled the high gates, but they were unyielding, padlocked shut.

'Nothing, ma'am.'

Gawn could hear the despair in his voice. She knew he would be imagining all kinds of things. He had been at too many crime scenes not to know what could be happening to Hill and not to bear an overwhelming sense of responsibility. Gawn felt it too but she needed them to focus.

'I'll send backup. Erin, we need to get all the CCTV from these streets asap. There should be plenty on the government buildings and the hotels. Jack, you and the others, get back to the market. Begin questioning everyone in the beer tent and see if anyone noticed anything. I don't care if they complain. Start with where Jo's phone and mic were found. That must be where she was grabbed. And, Billy, find Inspector Rainey. Her earpiece must have stopped working. She mightn't know what's happening.'

She'd had a bad feeling about tonight from the very beginning. As soon as O'Brien had insisted they go ahead even though they weren't ready, she'd dreaded what could happen and now it seemed her fears had been all too real. Hill had disappeared and where the hell was Rainey?

Chapter 50

'Jesus!'

'What is it, Billy?'

'It's Rainey, ma'am. Inspector Rainey,' he corrected himself.

Logan was an experienced officer with over twenty years' service. He'd seen everything during that time. What had he found that had shocked him?

'She's here. On the floor.'

'Is she alive?'

'Yes.'

'I've called the paramedics, ma'am. They should be there any minute. They already had a crew on standby for the market,' McKeown informed her.

Gawn listened as they arrived and worked with Rainey. Logan kept her informed about what was happening. The inspector was semi-conscious. Her pulse and breathing were steady, he told her. Her blood pressure was OK too.

'Any idea what happened to her?' She heard Logan questioning the paramedics.

'Could be anything, mate, but if I had to guess I'd say drugs. Maybe she's a user who nipped in here for a quick fix.'

'She's a police officer,' Gawn heard Logan say.

'You go in the ambulance with the inspector, Billy. We need to know what drug was used on her asap,' Gawn said.

'Ma'am, I have a confession to make. There's something you should know.'

Logan's voice had dropped to almost a whisper.

'What is it, Billy?'

'Inspector Rainey's skirt was pulled up and her–' he hesitated '–she had no pants on and there was a drawing on her stomach. I covered her up, ma'am.' He hurried on, 'I know I shouldn't have interfered with evidence but I couldn't just leave her lying there like that for everyone to see. Anyone could have walked in. It didn't seem right to leave her like that but I didn't touch the drawing, ma'am.'

It took Gawn several seconds before she could respond. Her mouth was dry.

'No one else hears about this, Billy. Understand?'

'Yes, ma'am.'

'No one.'

Emoji Man had found his victim alright. But if he'd attacked Rainey, where was Hill?

Gawn needed to turn her attention back now to the search for the detective constable. But she couldn't get Sam Rainey out of her head. The whole situation was a mess and O'Brien would blame her. It would be her mess, not his, even though he was the one who had insisted they set this trap tonight. He hadn't listened to any of her concerns. And now his niece and one of her officers were paying the penalty.

The two figures spotted on camera leaving the scene seemed to have just disappeared. They could find no sign of them. For the next two hours they searched everywhere. They spoke to everyone on the streets around City Hall, gradually widening the search area. Locked doors had been shaken, to make sure no one was hiding inside darkened shops and office buildings; and homeless street-sleepers had had their doorway slumbers rudely interrupted. A team had gone into the beer tent, closed down sales and questioned everyone there.

Nothing. There was nothing to show for all their efforts.

Just after midnight Gawn sent Dee home. He resisted her order at first, but he was distressed and she knew his mood would infect the others. She needed to keep a clear head. He needed to take a break. They needed to work on without him.

The Christmas market was long closed. The colourful twinkling lights festooning the stalls were extinguished leaving only the tinkling sound as they jingled in the wind. The beer tent was dark and silent. Few people remained on the streets. Only the massive Christmas tree, still lit, reminding them of the season of joy and goodwill, stood impassive, seeming to mock all their efforts. A small huddle of reporters who'd responded to media posts about something happening at City Hall had gathered round the gate. She'd seen some of the tweets and the speculation already and had had to run the gauntlet of their questions when she'd stepped out of the van.

Unwillingly, she called off the search. It would begin again at first light.

Chapter 51

Gawn didn't go home. There would be no point. She wouldn't sleep. Instead she made her way to the hospital. With everything that had been happening over the last few hours as they'd searched for Hill, she'd had little time to spare to think of Rainey's condition. Emoji Man must have drugged her but how had he even known she was there and how had he gained access to City Hall? The front door had been locked to prevent casual visitors wandering into the building from the market. The only entrance open was at the rear but a security man was stationed there signing everyone in and out. He would need to be interviewed, if he hadn't been already.

Lights were blazing around the entrance to the hospital which only made the car park and corridors appear even darker and gloomier. There was a lone man sitting behind the reception desk in the foyer, reading a magazine. He didn't even look up as she passed.

The clicking of Gawn's stiletto heels echoed through the eerily empty corridors, so different to their daytime bustle, as she made her way to the elevators up to the wards. The side clinics were dark and unmanned. With each step her nervousness increased. She didn't know what she would face; what condition Rainey would be in. She felt so guilty. She should have insisted the inspector stayed well away from the operation. It was her fault – again – that the woman had been injured.

The ward was in semi-darkness. Gawn could hear the usual moaning and whispering she associated with hospital wards at night. Nurses moved almost silently between the beds as if floating, answering calls for help or offering reassurance. Gawn was directed to a side room. She could hear the murmur of voices as she stood outside the door.

She took a deep breath and poked her head into the room. A woman, who couldn't be anyone other than Rainey's mother, was sitting at the bedside holding her daughter's hand. The family resemblance was unmissable. A man was sitting beside the bed too, his back to her, and she thought it must be Rainey's father until the figure glanced over his shoulder and she realised it was Aidan O'Brien. There was nothing intimidating about him now. He had lost his authority; become more ordinary, less daunting. His eyes were blotchy. He looked vulnerable, she thought to herself and the thought surprised her.

'Superintendent,' he said. His voice sounded tired. She realised he had been crying. 'Pat.' He tapped the woman beside him on the arm. 'This is Superintendent Girvin. Samantha's been working with her.'

The woman looked up. She looked exhausted. She managed a weak smile before turning back to her daughter.

'How is she, sir?'

Rainey stirred in the bed and her eyes opened briefly at the sound of Gawn's voice.

'She's going to be alright. So they say.'

He didn't sound convinced.

'Physically anyway. They just want to keep her under observation until the drugs clear out of her system and they're sure she has no adverse reactions. She should be fine by the morning. That's what they've told us. She was lucky apparently.' The bitterness in his voice was unmistakeable.

O'Brien signalled to her then to accompany him out into the corridor. Once through the heavy ward doors, he stuck his hands deep into his trouser pockets and hung his head as if his shoes were the most interesting sight in the world. He looked like a recalcitrant schoolboy caught red-handed scrumping for apples. He couldn't seem to look up or make eye contact with her.

'I suppose you blame me for this cock-up,' he said.

Gawn didn't respond. What could she say? Of course, she did. Although she blamed herself as well.

'My sister does, you know. She blames me. You know what the bastard did to Sam, don't you?'

'Not the details, sir, but I know there was a drawing like the other women.'

'So now everyone knows.'

'No, sir. My people can be discreet. Only one of my officers knows about it and I've already told him he mustn't tell anyone else.'

'And you think he won't?' His voice was disbelieving.

'I trust my team, sir. He won't.'

That didn't mean it wouldn't eventually come out, of course. Someone at the hospital, maybe some friend of

Rainey's family who was confided in, would let it slip and, of course, if there was a court case, it would all come out then.

'No one will hear about it from us.'

She had begun walking away when O'Brien spoke again. His voice was so low, she almost didn't hear him.

'Get him, Gawn. Please.'

Chapter 52

Sunday

By Sunday morning, before even the most fervent churchgoers were thinking of setting out for their places of worship, McKeown had already begun scouring through the CCTV footage she had cajoled from business owners around City Hall. Gawn knew the sergeant must have started early, perhaps not having gone home at all but returning to her desk when they had been stood down for the night. The shops wouldn't be open until lunchtime in line with the Sunday Trading Act but McKeown would have been telephoning keyholders, speaking to anyone she could get hold of, seeking their cooperation. She and Jo Hill were good friends.

By the time Gawn walked in, McKeown was already working her way through the first recordings she had sourced, aided by Walter Pepper who wasn't even supposed to be on duty today. Her eyes and the slight nod of her head as she looked up at Gawn passing on her way to Maxwell's office showed she had found nothing yet to show how Hill had been spirited away.

And the detective hadn't just 'turned up' as they had all hoped. No females had been found, dead or alive, anywhere in the Greater Belfast area overnight. Gawn had ordered all reports be sent directly to her.

After leaving the hospital, she had spent most of what was left of the night at her desk, fuelling herself with strong black coffee until she succumbed to exhaustion and snatched a nap in an uncomfortable armchair in the corner of her office. She had showered and changed this morning into the spare set of clothes she kept in her locker so now she was looking, but not feeling, just as she did every other morning.

There had been no sightings of anyone matching Hill's description anywhere. The two men she had dispatched to watch Hill's home in the hope the rapist would follow his normal pattern and leave her somewhere nearby had had nothing to report.

Was it good news or bad that there was no sign of her? The other victims had all been dumped within a few hours. They had not been held overnight except for Orla Maguire but she didn't want to think about that case and its outcome. Was he holding Hill somewhere? But why the change? Or was it simply that they hadn't found her yet? Could she be lying somewhere unconscious? She wasn't allowing herself to consider the alternative – that Hill could be dead.

The phone rang on Logan's desk. Everyone in the room seemed to freeze at the sound. The veteran detective looked even more dishevelled than usual this morning. His eyes were heavy and black-ringed. He looked as if he had been on a bender, but Gawn knew he had stayed at the hospital with Rainey until her mother had arrived and then returned to the market to help in the search and was back at his desk by 8am. His movements were slow as if he was half asleep. He must be exhausted. They all were, functioning on nervous energy now.

He lifted the phone.

'Yes. Right. Where?'

His voice gave nothing away. The call could be about anything but somehow Gawn didn't think it was. Logan paused and listened to the response on the other end of the phone. The room had gone deathly silent. Every face was turned in his direction. Everyone was listening, waiting for his next words.

'Which hospital?'

Logan replaced the receiver.

'Jo?' Gawn asked.

'Yes. A couple of joggers found her under a bench on the Ormeau Embankment.'

'How bad?' she asked, afraid of what she was going to hear.

'Unconscious. She's been beaten up.'

'Which hospital, Billy?'

'The Ulster.'

'Let Jack know,' she ordered.

Chapter 53

Gawn hated hospitals, the sounds and smells, the pervading sense of fear and distress in spite of the bright lights and cheery pictures on the walls. She had spent a long time in different hospitals and a rehabilitation centre after her injury in Afghanistan. Nothing could disguise the fact that it was a place where lives were changed forever.

As she expected, Jack Dee had beaten her to it. He was sitting on his haunches against the wall in the corridor outside the A&E department, his jacket collar turned up against the cold. He cut a disconsolate figure, his elbows on his knees and his head bent forward, covered by his hands. He looked as if he had been there all night. He needed a shave and he was wearing the same shirt and suit as yesterday. Gawn suspected he had never even tried to get any sleep, maybe never even gone home, and she was aware of a slight whiff of whisky off him. Passers-by probably thought he was a drunk taken to A&E after a night out.

He jumped up when he saw her and straightened his tie.

'How is she, Jack?'

'I haven't been able to see her yet, ma'am. They won't tell me anything and they won't let me in. Maybe they'll tell you. Her husband's with her,' he called after her as she moved towards the automatic doors.

This was a complication. She'd almost forgotten Hill was married. She had known of course but Hill seldom talked about her home life and Gawn was not one to pry into her officers' private lives unless it impacted their work.

'I'll see what I can find out and I'll let you know. In the meantime, get some fresh air and get yourself a cup of strong coffee. Or make that two or three cups. I don't want to have to send you home.' She looked at him meaningfully.

It was Sunday morning but Gawn knew the A&E department would be busy dealing with the aftermath of overindulgence and fights from Saturday night as well as the daily routine of car crashes, drug overdoses and accidents. She stepped up to the reception area where a harassed-looking woman was sitting behind a glass screen. She was concentrating on filling in a sheet lying on the desk in front of her. She lifted her head and looked up.

'Good morning.' Gawn held her ID up to the glass screen. 'I'm looking for information about a young woman who was brought in within the last hour or so. She'd been attacked. Her name's Hill, Josephine Hill. She's one of my officers.' Gawn smiled trying to elicit some female solidarity.

'Yes. Josephine Hill.' The receptionist called up information on her screen. 'She's been triaged. She's in a side ward until we can get a bed for her in the main building.'

'Is she conscious? Can I speak to her?'

'I'll get someone to check for you.'

A nurse appeared soon after and led her into a corridor.

'Mrs Hill is in here. You can see her but only for a couple of minutes. That's all. She needs to rest.'

The nurse drew aside a curtain and Gawn hesitated before moving forward. There were only thin curtains dividing the room off into sections and offering some semblance of privacy. But they had no effect on the noise. She heard moaning and retching and a belligerent drunk berating someone in a foul-mouthed rant.

Gawn stepped into the cubicle. Jo Hill lay on a narrow bed. She looked like a life-size porcelain doll. Her face was swollen, one eye puffy and half-closed. There was a purple bruise already formed over her left cheek and congealed blood under her nose. She seemed asleep but, as Gawn moved closer to the bed, Hill must have sensed movement for she opened her one good eye.

A bulky dark-haired man was sitting beside the bed. He made no attempt to stand up and barely gave Gawn a look. He was resting his hands, clenched tightly into fists, on top of the bedcover, not holding his wife's hand even though it was out of the covers and within inches of his own.

'Boss,' Hill greeted her in a barely audible whisper.

'How are you doing, Jo?'

'How the hell do you think she's doing?' The man's voice, unexpectedly loud and angry, surprised her but his tone was matched by the expression on his face when she turned to look directly at him. 'She could have been killed.'

He spat the words out at her, specks of saliva flying into the air and he stood up so he was facing her across the bed. He was squat and had the build of someone who worked out regularly. His outfit of black suit and heavy overcoat reminded her of a bouncer at one of the city centre clubs. His voice had been almost a snarl and his expression could have been threatening under different circumstances.

'Robert,' Hill tried to speak but her husband would not be interrupted. He grasped her hand in his and Gawn saw her wince as his dark-skinned paw closed tightly over the almost translucent white skin of her fingers.

'What the hell were you thinking of setting my wife up as a fucking target for some psycho?'

Gawn was aware there would be listening ears all around them. She could have explained that Hill had volunteered. They couldn't use one of the male detectives. It had to be a female and there was only Hill or McKeown available at such short notice and McKeown was too tall and dark-haired. To bring someone else in would have taken time. Time they didn't have. And Hill had been keen to do it. But she wasn't going to start excusing her decisions to Robert Hill or explaining operational matters to a civilian. If her decision had been wrong, no doubt it would be pointed out to her. But none of that was important now. What was important was that Hill would recover and that they caught the man who had done this to her. Quickly.

Gawn turned away from Robert Hill, pointedly ignoring his comments, and looked at his wife as she explained, 'I'm going to put a guard with you, Jo. I don't think our man'll come back but I'm not going to take any chances.'

She heard Hill's husband snort. 'Bit late for that.'

'When you feel able to tell us what happened then you can speak to the detective. I thought Jack could do it, unless you'd prefer a woman. I could send for Erin.'

Gawn's and Hill's eyes locked for a second. Gawn could read thanks in those eyes.

Chapter 54

Dee was on guard by Hill's bedside. Gawn had spoken to him before she left, as much to check he was in a fit state to be on duty, as to issue instructions. He wasn't to try to question Hill, just be there if she wanted to talk. And on no account was he to engage with Robert Hill. She didn't want a brawl breaking out in the hospital. She guessed Hill's husband didn't know about his wife and Dee but then perhaps she was wrong about it all. Perhaps she was assuming they were in a relationship. It might be nothing more than camaraderie. Strong friendships could be forged between colleagues over long nights spent on stakeouts and in dangerous situations. Perhaps it was no more than that and she had read more into it.

'How is Jo, ma'am?' McKeown asked when she got back.

'She looks a mess. He gave her a good hammering for whatever reason.'

'Could he have worked out that it was a trap?'

'I don't see how, Erin. Unless she identified herself and tried to arrest him but I don't know why she would have done that. All she needed to do was cause a fuss and they'd have been with her within seconds. Well, a minute or two,' she corrected herself remembering the crowds around City Hall.

'Maybe she was drugged before she realised what was happening to her and she couldn't let anyone know,' McKeown said, feeling guilty that she had not been able to save her friend.

'That's the most likely thing, I suppose. But she was on high alert. I'm surprised he was able to drug her. We need to get a proper medical update to know exactly what injuries she has and what drug was used on her and if he used the same on Inspector Rainey.

'Can you chase that up please, Jamie? And, Erin, go to the hospital and question Jo. I don't need to tell you to take it easy with her. She seemed calm when I saw her but she was full of painkillers and the realisation of what nearly happened to her will have kicked in by now. At least I'm not having to send you to Dr Norris for information,' Gawn couldn't stop herself adding. She heard McKeown's sharp intake of breath and wished she hadn't voiced her thought.

As McKeown moved off, Maxwell walked in.

'I heard about Jo. How is she?'

'She took quite a beating.'

Maxwell's face crinkled in concern but when he spoke his voice betrayed nothing. They must all keep it professional, they both realised. Gawn was concerned her people would react emotionally because one of their own had been hurt. What they actually needed to do was to look at things dispassionately.

'That's a bit of a change, isn't it? Orla Maguire seems to have been an accident. Beating someone up – well, that's deliberate.'

'Yes. Very. And it wasn't just a punch or two either, Paul.'

'He's escalating,' Maxwell said.

'That's what we thought would happen, isn't it? Our man's got a taste for the power he can exert over his victims. And from the headlines in the newspaper and from people being so afraid. And it's clear he's enjoying that power. That's what rape is all about, isn't it?'

'So next step, rape and murder?' Maxwell suggested. 'Jo and Sam were lucky.'

Gawn sucked in her cheeks.

'I doubt either of them are feeling too lucky just at the minute, Paul.'

Collins rushed into the room.

'Ma'am, we've got another one.'

'Another what?' Gawn asked.

'Another victim.'

'Another one!' Maxwell said.

Maxwell's face showed his disbelief at what was happening.

'He said he was going to show us how clever he was, didn't he, Paul? Where was she found?' Gawn asked, turning back to face Collins.

'Woodstock Road.'

'Near her home?'

'Couple of hundred yards away.'

'Where is she now?'

'She wouldn't go to hospital so she's at home. But she had been drawn on, ma'am.'

'Who found her?' Gawn was shooting out her questions at high speed as she grabbed her jacket and made for the door.

'A lady walking her dog.'

'I want to have a word with the victim myself. Mike, get me everything on this attack.' She paused halfway to the door, turned round and asked, 'Did you want to see me for something, Paul?'

'No. I was on my way to a meeting with Wilkinson when I heard about Jo.'

'Right. Catch up later then.'

He watched her as she hurried along the corridor. He had some news for her that he knew she would want to hear but it could wait.

Chapter 55

This area of East Belfast had once been familiar to Gawn. The clanging trolley buses had once plied their trade down this road – many years before her time of course – and she had listened to tales from her grandmother of cattle being herded at a run towards the Sand Quay. The thought of encountering a rampaging herd of cows had formed part of her childhood nightmares.

Gawn had grown up not so far away, gone to primary school here and played in these streets as a small child. Halcombe Street. Her mind went back in time as she read the street sign. Another of her childhood friends had lived nearby too and their little gang had spent hours playing in and out of the back-to-back terraced houses. But she had lost touch with them after her family moved away and they had gone to different schools.

As she scanned the narrow street now, nothing was familiar. The little Victorian terraces were gone, replaced by rows of modern angular red-brick houses. The older buildings had been part of the industrial growth of the area and stood as a reminder of the heyday of the shipyards and the Sirocco Works and the Belfast Rope Works. Belfast had been a manufacturing powerbase then and streets like these had provided homes for the workforce.

Now only the gates of the primary school, which turned the street into a cul-de-sac, remained the same. She remembered their peeling paint, the creaky noise as they closed, and how she and her gang of friends had played in the grounds of the school until the caretaker came to chase them away and lock up each afternoon.

That morning the gates were lying open but the fluttering police tape shut them off to any casual passer-by, its flapping noise like birds' wings. And this area of Belfast had once been famous for birds. The nightly murmuration over the Lagan had more or less disappeared in recent years, an unintended consequence of the introduction of new lighting.

A couple of women were standing out in the street watching the comings and goings. A forensics tent had been erected close to the railings and Gawn could see two white-suited figures moving in and out of it. A uniformed constable was manning the perimeter tape and nodded as she approached.

She paused and leant against the railings to don foot coverings and gloves, then walked carefully over the stepping plates to the opening of the tent. Inside Damien Lyons was crouched over, writing on a clipboard. He glanced up.

'Good morning, Superintendent.'

It still sounded strange to hear herself addressed as superintendent. She was looking forward to going back to being plain chief inspector as soon as possible, when all this was over and their perp was safely locked away.

'I didn't expect to see you. I thought this was Inspector Graham's case,' Lyons said.

'It is but I suspect it's linked to mine. I wanted to see where the girl was left for myself. How did he get her over the railings?'

'He didn't.'

She raised her eyebrow at him but asked nothing.

'He came prepared. He must know the area. He'd selected where he was going to dump her. He opened a pedestrian gate round the side with bolt cutters.'

'And then carried her here? Where does she live in relation to where he left her?'

'Just across the road there. You can see the house from here.' He nodded in the direction of the main road. 'I guess he didn't want to risk someone on the main road seeing him,' Lyons suggested.

There wasn't much more for Gawn to see so she had already begun to remove her shoe coverings as a car pulled up and a man stepped out.

'Superintendent Girvin!' he called to her. She saw the expression on his face. He was trying hard to disguise his annoyance.

'Inspector Graham. Matthew, isn't it?' Gawn was getting used to the polite dance she was having to take part in to keep everyone happy. She walked across and, having removed the blue forensics gloves now too, offered him her hand. 'We've never met. But you obviously know me.' She tried a slight smile hoping to ease his mood. 'I was just having a quick look at your crime scene. I hope you don't mind.'

She was being conciliatory. It was his case but if it was Emoji Man who had attacked this girl, her team would be taking it over. And he would realise that but she didn't want to make any more enemies than she had to. She already had plenty.

'You'll know, of course, that this bears all the characteristics of the man the task force is after.'

He nodded.

'Have you questioned the victim yet?' Gawn asked.

'A PC spoke to her when she was found but I'm just on my way there now.'

'Perhaps I could tag along?' Gawn said.

'I was going to suggest it,' Graham said. 'We can leave the cars here and walk.'

'What's her name?'

'Kim Cray.'

Chapter 56

The young woman was huddled in a slightly disreputable-looking grey oodie, pulled down over her knees so that it almost reached her ankles and encased her completely like an Egyptian mummy. The hood was pulled up even though she was indoors and within inches of a blazing fire. Her blond fringe straggled out from under the edge of it, framing her pale face and blank eyes.

Mrs Cray had ushered the two detectives into the little front room fussing around her daughter and resting a comforting hand on the girl's shoulder.

'Hi, Kim. My name's Matt and this is Superintendent Girvin. We're investigating what happened to you. How are you feeling? Do you feel able to talk to us?'

The inspector's manner was friendly, his words softly spoken. Gawn caught Mrs Cray nodding at her daughter from the corner of her eye and squeezing her shoulder in encouragement.

'What do you want to know?' the girl asked in a small voice. She was probably about the same age as Carla, Gawn thought.

'What's the last thing you can remember last night?' Graham asked.

'Waiting for a bus.'

'Where was that?'

'Lanyon Place. Near the Waterfront. The 6A.'

Gawn wasn't familiar with the bus routes in Belfast. Her puzzled look drew a question from the inspector.

'You were going up towards Forestside?' he asked, giving Gawn the clue that the bus route ran from the city centre past a popular shopping complex on the outskirts of South Belfast. 'What time was that?'

'After nine o'clock, I think. I'd been shopping in town.'

'She'd been looking for a present but they hadn't got what she was looking for in any of the shops. She thought she might get it in Forestside. It was special late-night shopping for Christmas, you see. Some of the shops were staying open until midnight,' Mrs Cray explained, almost chattering, keen to help when it seemed her daughter could say no more.

'What happened when you were waiting there?' Graham asked, turning very pointedly to Kim, wanting to hear directly from her.

His voice was soothing. He smiled encouragingly at her as he spoke and she responded with a weak smile but she shook her head. Her voice, when she did speak, had the monotone pitch of someone in shock.

'Don't remember.'

'Were there other people waiting at the bus stop, Kim?' Gawn asked.

'Don't think so,' the young woman replied, looking up at the new questioner.

'And what's the next thing you remember after that?' she asked.

'Waking up in the field at the school. Some woman found me. I ran home. Well, staggered.' She almost laughed but the sound that came out of her mouth was more of a strangled cry. 'I must have looked drunk.'

'And you remember nothing else?' Gawn asked.

'No.'

* * *

'Your Emoji Man seems to have perfected spiking his victims,' Graham said as they stood outside the Crays' front door. 'She'll probably never remember anything more.' He took a packet of chewing gum out of his pocket and offered her a stick.

'No. Thanks.'

He popped a piece into his mouth before saying, 'She refused to let them examine her, you know. She wouldn't have a rape kit done. We probably wouldn't even have heard about it if her mother hadn't phoned. It was Mrs Cray who reported the drawing on her daughter's stomach.'

'Did you get any photos of the drawing or a sample of what he used to do it?' Gawn asked.

Graham nodded his head. 'Afraid not. She'd already had a bath before her mother contacted the station.'

'Pity. He's been lucky that his victims seem to be more worried about what other people will think than what he's done to them. But he's not *my* Emoji Man, Inspector,' she corrected him sharply, annoyed that this seemed another dead end for evidence.

'Right. But he seems to have his abductions down to a fine art. You have to give him that. Except this time he might have pushed his luck a bit. There's a stack of CCTV cameras around Lanyon Place and Oxford Street between the bus lanes and the courthouse and you have the approximate time Cray was taken. It should be easy to find her waiting at the bus stop and see what happens to her next.'

He was right.

Chapter 57

The man looked... pathetic. That was the only word Gawn could think of to describe him. Could this really be Emoji Man?

Gawn and Maxwell were observing a dejected Jimmy Sutton sitting fidgeting at a table in the interview room next door. As soon as Gawn had got back from talking to Kim Cray, the inspector had appeared in her office and told her his good news.

'They've matched the fingerprint from Orla Maguire's necklace. It belongs to a Jimmy Sutton. He has a record. We've picked him up. Want to come with me to interview him?'

Of course she'd wanted to.

'Do you really think that's our man?' Gawn asked. She remembered O'Brien's comments about an attractive male who would be able to charm women into his car.

'His fingerprint was on her necklace,' Maxwell responded, but he didn't sound so confident now.

'You can't seriously believe Orla Maguire was excited about going out to meet him, can you? Does he even own a car?'

'A 2009 Ford.'

'Not a Mercedes?'

'No, not a Mercedes,' he agreed.

She glanced down at a folder in her hand.

'Burglary, breaking and entering, receiving stolen property,' she read aloud. 'Not exactly Mr Big or Casanova, is he?'

'According to the local boys he's been warned for lurking around watching girls at the university campus. They know him and they suspect he's been trying a bit of upskirting in Abbey Centre recently too. They'd warned him off.'

Sutton was scratching his ear and then they watched as he picked his nose. He examined what he had extracted before wiping it under the edge of the table.

'Dirty bugger. Let's get in there before we need to have the whole place fumigated for health and safety,' Maxwell said and hurried out.

Sutton looked up at them with frightened eyes when he heard the door swing open and they walked in. He ran his hand over the stubble on his chin and emitted a short nervous cough.

'You're in a spot of trouble, Jimmy. Serious trouble. Unless you help us,' Maxwell began without preamble, sitting down opposite him.

'Anything to help the police. I'm on the straight and narrow now, sir. I'm getting too old for all that other stuff.'

His mouth smiled, his eyes didn't.

'How did you meet Orla Maguire?' Gawn asked suddenly.

The name meant something to him, she was sure. She'd seen the telltale twitch at the side of his eye as he jerked his head round in response to her question.

'I've never met anyone called Orla Maguire. I didn't know her,' he spluttered.

'But you know she's dead now, Jimmy, don't you?' she pressed.

'But I didn't kill her. She was already,' he stopped. 'Fuck!'

His head went down.

'She was already dead when you saw her. Is that what you were going to say, Jimmy?' Gawn asked.

He looked up and nodded at her. He looked so defeated, she was almost sorry for him. But not quite. He mightn't be their quarry – she was sure he wasn't – but he had crossed paths with their victim somewhere to leave his fingerprint on her necklace and she thought it was in the park. She hoped it was in the park. If so, he might have seen something or someone.

'When did you meet her, Jimmy?' Maxwell asked.

'I didn't meet her... I found her. She was just lying there in the grass. She was already dead.'

'What time was that?' the inspector persisted.

'About four in the morning. I was on my way back from Belfast. Along the cycle path.'

'I'm not going to ask what you were up to or where you'd been. I'm only concerned about what you saw; who you saw,' Gawn added hopefully.

'Only the wee girl. I nearly ran over her. She was just lying there.'

'There was no one else around?' Maxwell asked.

'No. I hadn't seen anybody all the way from Belfast.'

Gawn noticed an almost imperceptible pause.

'You saw someone,' she persisted.

'No. I didn't see anybody. But I thought I heard somebody or something.'

'Like what?' Gawn asked.

'Like oars in the water.'

Gawn wondered if Maxwell had considered that the body might have been dumped from a boat.

'You touched her necklace,' Gawn said.

He nodded.

'You were going to steal it,' she added.

He didn't respond.

Suddenly Gawn banged her hand down hard on the table. Sutton and Maxwell both jumped.

'What else did you take from her?'

'Nothing. It was only a cheap badge. It was lying on the grass. It wasn't worth nothing,' he spluttered.

'Do you still have it?'

Sutton put his hand into his pocket and drew out a small round badge. Gawn extracted a blue forensics glove from her jacket pocket and used it to lift the badge from his hand. It had some sort of Latin inscription on it and three wavy lines in the centre.

The two detectives looked at it and then at each other. Nothing to help them; probably just something dropped by a visitor to the park, their look seemed to say.

Chapter 58

So now they knew Orla Maguire had been dumped by 4am at the latest. But that didn't really help them much. They were also considering if the body might have been brought to the site by sea. That was new. It couldn't have been a large boat or it would have been spotted, and Sutton's assertion that he had heard oars made it likely it didn't have an engine or at least it hadn't used one. It might have been a rowing boat. But how far would anyone risk rowing? He'd probably only come a short distance. Gawn had suggested to Maxwell he set someone to checking for nearby spots where a rowing boat could be launched.

The badge Sutton had given them was sitting on Maxwell's desk in an evidence bag, labelled but waiting for now, ready to be sent to the lab first thing in the morning. Gawn had had hopes when he'd admitted to taking something else from the scene that it would provide a clue to the attacker's identity. She had been disappointed when he had produced the badge. Perhaps they would be able to get fingerprints from it. It might still be helpful but she wasn't getting her hopes up.

'Gosh, that brings back memories,' Walter Pepper said. He had come into the office bearing two cups. 'Coffee for you, ma'am, and tea for you, Inspector,' he said putting mugs down in front of them on the desk and glancing over at the evidence bag.

Gawn snatched up the bag.

'What memories, Walter?'

'From my misspent youth, ma'am. I was a member of the rowing club in my school.'

'And this badge is something to do with your school?' she asked.

'No, not my school, ma'am. May I?'

He held out his hand and Gawn placed the evidence bag into his palm. He read the inscription on the badge. '*Fortis Fortuna Adiuvat*. Fortune favours the strong. That was the motto of our arch rivals. They always seemed just that little bit better than us. They beat us every year.'

'Who were they? A local school?' Maxwell asked.

'No. It was a rowing club from a boarding school down south.'

'Can you remember the name?' It was Gawn's turn to ask.

'Something or other college. Meldrum or Melville. Mel something.'

* * *

'Maldane College,' McKeown said.

'Never heard of it,' Maxwell responded.

'It was a small private boarding school for boys in County Wicklow. It closed down about thirty years ago. There was some sort of a scandal.'

'Scandal?' Maxwell queried.

'Yes, sir. I'm trying to access some of the local newspapers from the time to find out exactly what it was but it's probably the usual.'

'Is there anyone you can contact to find out about the rowing club there? It would be good to get a list of former members,' Gawn said.

'I'll keep trying.'

'Thanks, Erin. Good work.'

Gawn had lifted a printout which McKeown had set down on Maxwell's desk along with her notes.

'I've seen this building somewhere before.'

'Is that the school?' Maxwell asked.

'Yes. She must have got the picture from the internet. It's some pupils, a rugby team or something, but it's the house in the background. I've seen it before.'

'Do you think you've been there?' he asked.

'I don't think so. I went down to Dublin once or twice when I was on the school hockey team but I would have remembered the name, I think, and I've never heard of Maldane College. Anyway it was a boys' school so we wouldn't have been playing hockey against them. Maybe it just looks a bit like Sebastian's old school. Big old buildings like a mansion. They all look much the same.'

Chapter 59

It looked like a council of war. It was a council of war.

The team was gathered in the ops room around the huge central table. They had been there nearly thirty minutes, just waiting. There had been little chatter, just the odd comment and some worried looks exchanged. They knew Gawn had been called to a debrief of Operation Christmas Market with Wilkinson and O'Brien and now they were waiting for her return. Anxiety was in the air. No one knew what was going to happen next. Perhaps she would be replaced.

When the door opened, every head turned and everyone stood to attention. Gawn walked in and positioned herself at the head of the table before speaking. Her face was inscrutable but she looked pale. They waited anxiously, anticipating an explosion. Instead, she took several deep breaths and then spoke quietly.

'Sit down all of you, for goodness' sake. You look as if you're all about to be shot. What happened last night is down to me. No one else. I'm not passing the buck to anyone. But I'd love to know how the hell our perp managed to abduct two women and attack another. Not one but two, right under our noses.'

She wasn't shouting. If anything, her voice was more controlled and quieter than usual. She sat down. Maxwell, who knew her well, noticed her bite her lip, a sign that she was worried.

'We know when Jo was taken. Sometime between her last check-in and when Jamie found her phone. That's a window of less than fifteen minutes. I spoke to Kim Cray, the other victim from last night, and it seems she was taken when you were all rushing around trying to find Jo.'

'You think he took advantage of us trying to find Jo to grab someone else?' Grant asked.

'That would mean he knew about our surveillance operation. Which he must have, of course, to know where Inspector Rainey was and to attack her. But how is that even possible? Who else knew, outside the team, what was going down last night?' Gawn asked.

'The traffic control people knew we were patching into their camera feeds,' McKeown suggested.

'But they didn't know the details of why we were doing it,' Gawn responded.

'A few of the people in City Hall knew. We'd had to have access to set up all our equipment and Inspector Rainey was in talking to someone from the mayor's office,' Erskine, their IT expert, said.

Gawn didn't respond to his comment. She had been watching Erin McKeown's face.

'Have you something to say, Erin?'

'I've worked with Jo for a long time. We all know her. She's my best friend. But Inspector Rainey doesn't know her.'

'What's this got to do with Inspector Rainey?' Gawn asked.

'When I was with Jo, the inspector came down from her ward to visit her while she was waiting to be discharged. She told me that if Jo wasn't one of our own and she'd just been asked to interview her cold, she'd have been suspicious.'

'Of Jo?' Maxwell asked.

'She said Jo came across as being… less than truthful, she said; as if she was hiding something,' McKeown explained. When no one said anything, she added, 'She said it was only a gut reaction. She'd no hard evidence, but Jo hadn't been very forthcoming. To her anyway.'

'Maybe she can't remember very much. She was drugged, after all,' Maxwell said.

'I'm glad Jack's not here,' Grant whispered out of the side of his mouth to Logan but loud enough that they all heard.

'But that's just it, sir,' McKeown said. 'I spoke to one of her doctors. They didn't find any drugs in her system. She'd been beaten unconscious, not drugged.'

'She wasn't found until this morning. That would have been over twelve hours. Maybe the drug had worked through her,' Maxwell suggested.

'I put that to the doctor, sir. He said he would have expected to find some trace. But they didn't find any. Just cuts and bruises from where she'd been beaten and tied up, and a concussion from the punch that knocked her out.'

Looks were exchanged. No one was quite sure what this could mean.

'She was bloody beaten.' Logan sounded belligerent. 'She didn't do that to herself.'

'Yes, Billy. Take it easy. No one's saying that. She didn't beat herself up. We know that. But maybe Jo knows more than she's saying and, if she is, I think I know what that means,' Gawn said. 'I'll speak to her myself.'

Her determined tone suggested that was to be an end to any discussion of what had happened to Hill.

'Are we any closer to identifying how Cray was taken? Was she drugged?' Maxwell asked, changing the subject.

'She remembers having coffee near the Jaffe Memorial Fountain and then going across to Lanyon Place to wait for the bus. Has anyone started looking at CCTV in that area yet?' Gawn asked.

'I have,' Pepper answered. He had worked closely with Jo Hill since Gawn had convinced him to come out of retirement to work for her and he had come to regard Hill as a sort of surrogate daughter. Although he was not officially on duty, he had come in to help. 'That's her there.'

Everyone turned to look at the CCTV footage on a screen on the wall. They watched as a dark car pulled up and a woman moved across from the bus stop and spoke to whoever was inside before opening the door and getting into the car. It had driven away then.

'Are you sure that's our victim?' Gawn asked.

'Yes, ma'am. I followed her on the cameras from the café.'

'She doesn't seem drugged. She got in willingly,' Maxwell said.

'Can we get the number plate?' Gawn asked.

'It's obscured. Covered in mud or something.'

'What about the make?'

'It's a big saloon. Expensive. I think it's a Mercedes,' Pepper replied.

Gawn nodded.

'That fits with victim five. She was picked up by what she thought was a Mercedes. Cray looks happy enough to get into the car,' Gawn said, thinking of O'Brien's comment about how plausible the predator would be. 'Someone needs to have another word with that young woman. She might have remembered something more by now. She spoke to our man. She should be able to identify him. Can you contact Matt Graham and see if he has anything more for us?' Gawn asked Maxwell.

'I'll ring him. But what's that on the back window?' Maxwell said. 'Can you zoom in a bit, Walter?'

When Pepper tried, the picture went out of focus and it was impossible to make anything out. It was just a blur.

'I can take a look at it and see if there's anything I can do with it; try to clean it up a bit,' Erskine said.

'Thanks, Gary. Billy, you and Jamie go to that café in Victoria Square. Talk to the staff. See if any of the baristas remember Cray and if they noticed anyone following her or acting strangely.'

Logan twisted his mouth and Gawn noticed.

'Have you something to say, Billy?'

'Half the population acts strangely, ma'am. All kinds of weirdos hang about the city centre. How is anyone expected to identify the invisible man? No one notices him. No one sees anything. He managed to spirit Jo away and then stash her somewhere so he could grab this other one. And he'd already got inside City Hall and attacked Inspector Rainey,' Billy responded.

'What if he didn't?' Maxwell spoke tentatively.

'Didn't what?' Gawn asked.

'Grab two women,' he replied and their eyes locked.

'You're not suggesting we have a copycat, are you?'

'There's been so much in the papers with all the details now that it wouldn't be surprising, would it?'

The colour drained from Gawn's face. A copycat would complicate matters even more.

Chapter 60

Grant's eyes were bright with excitement. He could barely contain himself, like a puppy who has just mastered a trick and is waiting for a pat on the head from his mistress.

'Say that again, Jamie,' Gawn ordered.

'Robert Hill has been working at the Christmas market since it opened. He was there last night.'

'Doing what?'

'He's a manager in Nancy's Kitchen and they have the contract for the beer tent,' he responded.

'And he was working there on Saturday?'

'Yes.'

'All evening?'

'He's responsible for banking the takings across the street in the night safe so he was there until closing and one of our guys remembers questioning him after Jo disappeared,' Grant replied.

'Get on to someone from the bank, Jamie. See what time Hill banked the money in the night safe. And, Jamie…'

'Yes, ma'am?'

'…don't let them fob you off until tomorrow. We need the information today.'

'Right, ma'am.' Grant hurried off.

'Could this be what Hill was hiding, ma'am?' Rainey asked. Gawn hadn't noticed the other woman coming into the room. She was standing behind her.

'What are you doing here, Sam?'

She remembered Maxwell's comment about Rainey being the poor man's Gawn Girvin and thought the inspector didn't just look like her.

'They only kept me until the midazolam had worked through my system. They needed the bed and I didn't need to spend another minute lying around twiddling my thumbs doing nothing while this man seems to be able to grab women whenever and wherever he feels like it. I need to be here, ma'am. I feel responsible.'

Rainey spoke and her voice and her eyes challenged Gawn to argue with her. Gawn understood. She decided not to accept the challenge. Not here and not now, anyway. None of the others knew that the suggestion for both Saturday night's operation and Hill's involvement had come from Rainey. They would assume it was Gawn's idea or maybe the ACC's. She didn't think there was any point telling them otherwise but that wouldn't stop Rainey feeling it was all her fault.

'I don't suppose you remember anything about being drugged?' Gawn asked.

'No. But I checked with the CSIs. They think the midazolam was in water. Someone had left a carafe and I must have drunk some of it. I don't remember but my fingerprints were on it and on a glass so I must have.'

Gawn looked puzzled.

'That's a bit of a departure,' she said.

'Yes. I spoke to the doctors. Midazolam can be injected like it was with the other victims but it can be delivered through a nasal spray or ingested as well. I can only assume he used this method with me because he knew I was a police officer and I'd resist if he attacked me and tried to needle spike me. Once I was out of it, he must have been watching and come in.' She stopped abruptly.

Gawn had noticed Rainey's discomfort and changed the subject.

'I don't know why Jo would think she needed to hide that her husband was working in the market. She probably just thought it wasn't relevant to our investigation,' Gawn said, looking at Rainey.

'I thought you didn't like coincidences,' Rainey said.

'I don't.'

Even as she spoke Gawn was picturing Robert Hill's massive hand enveloping his wife's in a tight grip, tight enough to make her wince.

'It's interesting that he was in the vicinity but does it mean anything? Robert Hill's our Emoji Man? I don't think so. He's only marginally more likely than Sutton on the charm scale. What evidence do we have? He was there on Saturday night? So were hundreds of other men. Does he drive a Mercedes? And wouldn't someone have noticed if he slipped away and grabbed Cray when he was supposed to be working? Someone needs to check where

Hill was on the evenings when the other women were attacked,' Gawn suggested.

'I'll sort it,' Maxwell said.

'Perhaps you and I should go and have a word with Jo, Sam. Let's see if we can get her by herself. If her husband is there, you can take him aside and ask him a few questions while I talk to her,' Gawn said, already halfway out the door.

But once out in the corridor and away from the others, Gawn stopped and turned around to face Rainey. She hadn't wanted to confront her in the ops room in front of everyone.

'I don't think you should be here, Sam. You spent a night in hospital. You were drugged and assaulted. You can't just appear as if nothing happened. You need to follow return to work protocols and check in with Occupational Health. You should go home now. Maybe you feel you're alright, but you couldn't possibly be. Not after what you've been through. Let the rest of us get on with this.'

'The midazolam was no worse than a minor anaesthetic to get a tooth extracted. That's what the doctors said. I'm fine. He didn't hurt me, just…' There was a minute pause before she added, 'drew on me. Please, ma'am. I need to be here. I need to help,' Rainey pleaded.

Gawn said nothing.

'ACC O'Brien knows I'm here and if you don't let me help, I'll just go after Emoji Man myself. I can't sit at home and do nothing while he's out there.'

Gawn believed her. She saw the determined line of her jaw, the steely look in her eyes. Gawn thought Rainey would do exactly what she said. It would be what she would do if their roles were reversed. Better to keep her with her, watch her, stop her rushing off to do something stupid. It was risky, against every rule in the book, but she agreed. But she would keep her close.

'OK. Let's go.'

Chapter 61

Robert Hill wasn't at the hospital. Jo Hill was sitting up in bed sipping something through a straw with Dee beside her. He had just said something which had made her smile, or at least try to. Gawn couldn't help noticing the speedy withdrawal of his hand where his fingers had been touching Hill's when he saw them walking into the ward.

'Right, Jack, take a break. We'll be here talking to Jo for a while. Time to grab yourself something from the cafeteria or a quick cigarette.'

'He's given them up. Didn't you know, ma'am?' Hill said and looked up at him. Her voice sounded strange. She was trying to speak without moving her lips too much. It made her sound like someone practising ventriloquism.

'No. I hadn't realised. Well done, Jack. But take a break anyway.'

Gawn shooed him away. Reluctantly, Dee moved off. Gawn and Rainey sat down either side of the bed.

'You're looking a lot better than you did the last time I saw you,' Gawn said. 'I told Jack not to bother you with any questions and I know Erin talked to you already but we need to know if you've remembered anything else. It's really time-critical now.'

'It all happened so quickly, ma'am. I should have been more on my guard. I thought I was being careful but I mustn't have been.'

'You were grabbed?'

'I don't remember.'

'You were inside the beer tent?' Gawn asked.

'I remember being inside. It was very busy. And I remember pushing through the crowd to try to get myself a drink and find somewhere I could sit and make sure everyone could see me.'

Hill moistened her lips with her tongue. She was looking anxiously from one woman to the other. Gawn realised it wouldn't be surprising if she was anxious. She had been through an ordeal and Gawn was asking her to relive it. But she wondered if that was all it was.

'Then what?' Gawn asked.

'I got my drink and carried it to a bench. I remember that. But that's all I can remember.'

'You were grabbed in front of everyone?'

'I must have been. He must have injected me with something in the crowd when I was pushing past. But I don't remember. Or maybe he slipped something into my drink. Next thing I do remember there was a paramedic standing over me and I was in an ambulance.'

No one they had questioned had seen anyone manhandling a woman. One or two had mentioned noticing a pretty blonde in a bright red anorak but she hadn't seemed distressed, they said, and she was on her own two feet when they'd seen her.

Gawn's mobile buzzed. The screen showed it was Grant.

'Hill banked the money just before midnight, ma'am, according to the timestamp on the night safe.'

It had probably taken that long to get everything cleared away and they hadn't finished questioning people until after eleven. So he had been there long after his wife had disappeared. He had been questioned too but she wondered why he hadn't told anyone who he was or that the missing woman was his wife. Had he really not known who they were looking for?

'And Inspector Maxwell asked me to check his whereabouts on a couple of the other dates. He's in the clear, ma'am. He has solid alibis.'

'OK. Thanks, Jamie.' She turned back to the bed. 'What happened to your phone and mic, Jo?'

'My phone and mic?' Hill looked surprised at the question.

'Yes. We found them. On the grass,' Gawn said.

'He must have taken them and thrown them away after he grabbed me,' Hill said. But her eyes didn't meet Gawn's. She was lying. Gawn knew it now.

'Was it Robert who did this to you? We know he was there, Jo,' Gawn asked gently.

Rainey drew in her breath sharply at the question.

For a second it seemed Hill was going to deny it.

Gawn's voice was quiet and she leaned forward so she was nearer to Hill. 'Emoji Man attacked two other women on Saturday night, Jo.' She didn't tell her that one of them was Rainey. 'He's getting greedy. Three in one night. We can't afford to waste time. We need to get him.'

Gawn caught a flicker in Hill's eyes again. If Rainey hadn't voiced her suspicions, would she have noticed anything? Maybe or maybe not. She hadn't told her that her tox screen had come back negative. She hadn't been drugged but she had been beaten up. Should she wait or should she push her further?

'Jo, we can't afford to waste time chasing after false leads. Emoji Man is dangerous. I don't need to tell you that. If there's anything, anything at all you can tell me to help the investigation, please, now's the time.'

Gawn looked straight at Hill. And waited. At first it seemed the woman was going to stay silent and then a tear started to trickle down her face. Just one silent tear. Then more tears welled up in her eyes. And she swiped her arm across her face to wipe them away.

'It was,' she sobbed quietly.

'Your husband did this to you?' Rainey asked.

'It was my fault. He's a good man, Inspector. He's been a good husband but things haven't been working between us for a while. He found out I'd been seeing someone else and he went a bit crazy. Then he saw me at the market last night. He thought I was there to meet my new man when

I'd told him I was on duty. He asked me to come outside so we could talk.' She paused, looked down at the bedcover and then looked up at Gawn. Her voice was nearly a whisper. 'I turned off my mic so we could talk for a minute. I thought it would only be for a minute or two and then I could go back inside but we argued in his van. He hit me and that's all I remember.'

* * *

'Her husband did that to her and she says it was her fault? She wasn't going to say anything? She was going to cover for him?' Rainey said.

The two policewomen were standing in the corridor outside the ward. They had left Hill alone preparing herself for Dee's return and what she would tell him.

'He's her husband, Sam. And she was in an impossible position. By the time she came round in hospital and realised what was happening, we'd already started the search for her attacker assuming she was another of Emoji Man's victims. She never told us that. We just assumed it was him.

'And wives get battered every night of the week and husbands too. Just ask Tilly. It happens and nine times out of ten they don't even call us and very few press charges. If Hill had battered her at home, she'd probably have told us she fell down stairs or walked into a door or something and we'd probably have accepted her explanation.'

'Do you think she'll press charges now?'

'I doubt it. That would mean official interviews and a court case and everything coming out about Jack. She'd be worried about her own career but even more about his. I think she'd prefer to let it die down. But I'm sure, given time to think, she would have told us it wasn't Emoji Man who attacked her without having to be asked. She's a good police officer. She wouldn't want to stuff up the investigation.'

'Are you going to report this?' Rainey asked.

'Report what? I was visiting a friend in hospital. It wasn't an official interview. Jo Hill's a good officer with a promising career. It would do nobody any good to ruin it. And she hasn't withheld any information about Emoji Man. She can't tell us anything about him. She doesn't know anything. But at least now we can concentrate on how he got to you and Cray.'

Gawn couldn't help wondering what Rainey would do with this new information. Would she run to her uncle or could she trust her now?

'So, who were they all chasing at the back of City Hall?' Rainey asked.

'Probably some drunk girl being helped home by her boyfriend, I guess. And all the time poor Jo was unconscious in Robert Hill's van parked right in front of us.'

'But Emoji Man was there, boss. He attacked me,' Rainey said.

'Yes. He was. And that begs the question, how did he get inside the building? I want to speak to the security man on the back gate myself.'

Chapter 62

Monday

It was just before 8am. Traffic in central Belfast was already building up. The buses were disgorging their passengers at stops all round City Hall. Pedestrians were hurrying by on their way to schools and shops and offices.

Liam Roberts was sitting in his little office at the back entrance to City Hall reading a copy of the morning newspaper when Gawn drew her car up to the gateway. He walked stiffly out, rubbing his back. The office was warm and cosy. It was wet and cold outside. He was due to finish his shift at eight. He had hoped to have a cup of tea in peace and then hand over to the day man.

'Do you have business here today, madam?' he asked and managed a polite smile although he was tired. It had been a long shift. There'd been all the excitement of the men searching for some missing girl on Saturday night but it hadn't involved him. They'd barely spoken to him, just asked if he'd seen anyone acting suspiciously.

'Yes. With you, if you're Liam Roberts,' Gawn said. She had already checked which watchman had been there on Saturday evening. Two constables had spoken to Roberts, but only briefly and they hadn't checked the visitors' log.

When she had driven through the archway and parked in one of the spaces by the side of an ornate fountain, she joined him in his tiny room. It was stuffy and very hot. She wondered how he could manage to stay awake all night.

'Cup of tea?' he offered and held up a stained teapot.

'No. But thanks. You were here on Saturday night, Mr Roberts?' she began, keen to get down to business.

'I thought it might be about that. You know a couple of your boys asked me if I'd seen anything but I didn't. It was a quare fuss though, wasn't it? A wee girl grabbed. Terrible. What's the world coming to?' Roberts said and took a slurp of his tea.

'I need to see the log from Saturday.'

He lifted a heavy ledger down from a shelf and turned over several pages before handing it to her.

The page was blank.

'There's nothing here.'

'That's right.'

She turned back a page and could see several signatures, including her own, from earlier in the day.

'No one was in City Hall on Saturday night?'

There had been the public speaking competition. There had been an audience for that.

'Oh, there were people alright. There was some do on in the Banqueting Hall. But they were nearly all away by the time I took over at eight. At this entrance we only log the cars, not every person coming in and out on foot. The ones at the event hadn't been told they could park inside the courtyard so there were only a few cars inside and we don't log the cars that have passes. Only visitors' cars.'

'Who has a pass?' she asked.

'A few of the senior staff have parking spaces here but none of them were in. Not on a Saturday night.' He half-laughed at the idea. 'And the official car, of course.'

'The mayor's car?'

'Yes,' he said.

'Was it here on Saturday night?'

'Aye. It was. I remember because I had a good old chat with Dave over a brew while he was waiting for the mayor.'

Chapter 63

'We've got him,' Maxwell almost shouted. He was jubilant.

Gawn had been standing looking at the map of Belfast and hoping for some inspiration when he walked in brandishing a piece of paper. Everything seemed to be pointing to David Milton, the mayor's chauffeur, as the Davey they were looking for. She was certain he was involved. She needed to interview him but she would have to tread carefully.

She swung round at the sound of Maxwell's voice.

'Mark pulled DNA from the badge and a partial too. It was Orla Maguire's DNA on the pin. And the fingerprint—' He didn't get a chance to finish.

'Please, tell me he got enough to match it with someone on our database.'

He didn't say anything, just nodded with a wide grin on his face.

'Who?' she asked.

'David Sykes.'

'Who the hell's David Sykes?'

'He's ex-army. It's his print. He's done time in prison. He served three years for attacking an off-duty redcap in Leeds. That's why his fingerprints were on record. He put her in a coma. When he was released, he disappeared off the grid but after that David Milton turned up and got the job driving the mayor. Look.'

As he'd been speaking, Maxwell was pinning up a new picture on the board.

'Here's his photo I got from army records. It's about ten years out of date.'

The man was in uniform. There was nothing distinctive about the face. He didn't look like a monster.

'You're sure that's Milton?'

'Yes, I showed it to Nixon. She said he looked younger but she was sure it's him. I didn't want to send anyone down to City Hall flashing it around in case Milton got word of our interest.'

'He must have had the proper documents to get that job. They wouldn't just have appointed him without checking,' Gawn said.

'I have Erin on with HR in City Hall now. I'm sure they did check but you know yourself if you pay enough you can get false documents.'

'What about a CR check? They would have done that,' Gawn said.

'It's in the works but there's a backlog,' Erin McKeown joined in the conversation from the doorway. 'And his referees must have been good so they went ahead and gave him the job.'

'Who were his referees?' Maxwell asked.

'One was an elderly lady from Portsmouth. He was supposed to have been driving for her when he was in prison. They have to get back to me with his other referee. They'd misplaced part of his application.'

'Maybe Kim Cray will be able to recognise Sykes or Milton or whatever he's calling himself,' Gawn said. 'Did you speak to Graham as I asked?'

'Yes. He interviewed Cray again but she still claims she can't remember speaking into the car. If it was midazolam he used on her, well, it's a memory inhibitor so it's not surprising she doesn't remember but, maybe if she sees a photograph of Milton, it might jog her memory.'

'Let's ask Milton where he was on Saturday night and see what he has to say for himself. Bring him in, Paul.'

Chapter 64

Milton was sitting in the interview room. He was dressed in a dark grey business suit. He looked quite attractive in a rugged sort of way, Gawn thought to herself. She knew that type appealed to some women. He was glancing around, taking in his surroundings, relaxed about being there it seemed.

'Mr Milton, or should that be Mr Sykes?' Gawn began as she and Rainey walked in. She had decided to bring Rainey with her to interview him. If he was Emoji Man then he had a problem with female authority figures. They could use that. And he might give himself away when he saw Rainey. If he had attacked her, he might be worried she could identify him.

Milton sat up straighter at the sight of the two women. His face clouded over momentarily but there was no look of recognition, just a truculent twist to his mouth. Gawn placed a folder on the desk between them and sat down. Sykes' eyes flicked from one to the other. Gawn was struggling to take her eyes off him. There was a black spot in the sclera of his left eye. It was distinctive. It hadn't been there in his army photograph. She had to make a conscious effort to look away. She didn't want him to realise it meant something to her.

'So, I changed my name. So what?' He shrugged. 'It's not against the law to call yourself something else.'

He was almost smirking and Gawn had the impression he had expected to be interviewed and had all his answers ready.

'It is if it's to deceive or defraud. You used a false name to get your job at City Hall.'

'I'm a good driver. But they'd never have given me a job if they'd known I'd been in prison. No one will. I've tried being straight with employers and it got me nowhere.' A touch of anger sounded in his voice. 'And I'm doing a good job here. Ask anyone. Ask Mrs Lawson,' he added.

'We will. Don't worry. And we'll be talking to your referees as well.'

'Mullholland?' Sykes asked.

Gawn felt Rainey react. She tensed her hands under the desk too but hoped she had revealed nothing in her face. Surely it couldn't be the same Mullholland, the MLA, he meant? They had no connection between Sykes and Mullholland; no suggestion the two men knew each other. Until now. And no connection between Mullholland and their investigation either except his call to O'Brien to complain.

'Joshua Mullholland?' Gawn asked.

'Yes.'

'How do you know him?'

'I don't. He's on the board of a charity for the rehabilitation of ex-servicemen. They put me in touch with him. I phoned him and he said I could use his name for a reference. That's all. I've never met him. I just spoke to him on the phone.'

Gawn decided to leave that line of questioning. For now. She could come back to it later. After she'd checked with Mullholland. The MLA probably had associations with lots of different charities. But it was careless of him to allow his name to be used like that.

His name popping up in the investigation was odd after he had intervened on behalf of the school. Odder still that the page with Mullholland's name on it as referee was missing from City Hall records. They would need to warn him to be more careful about allowing his name to be used. If he had. Maybe Sykes had simply lied on the form. After all he had lied about his background. And he worked in City Hall now. He would have access to all the offices. He could have removed the form to cover his tracks if there was ever any query about it.

'I'm not concerned about your deception on your application. I want to know your whereabouts on Saturday night, Davey.'

Gawn saw a tell, a slight movement by the side of Sykes' mouth when she had called him Davey. He recovered quickly.

'Dave. I'm Dave or David. No one calls me Davey. What do you want to know about Saturday night for?'

'Just answer the question, Davey,' Gawn said.

He flicked her an angry look, then paused as if to show he was thinking carefully. 'I was working on Saturday. I picked Mrs Lawson up from home and took her to City Hall. She had an event on Saturday evening, some school thing. Then I waited around to take her and her family home afterwards.'

'What time would that have been?' Rainey asked.

'She was finished about eight o'clock.'

'What did you do then?' Gawn asked.

'I took them home and then Mr Lawson invited me to eat supper with them. I hadn't had anything to eat since lunchtime and they were sending out for pizza. They invited me to stay. Then afterwards Mrs Lawson went to bed and Mr Lawson and I played poker for a while. Until about midnight.'

He sat back in his chair. He seemed confident of what he had told them. It would be easy enough to check. He would know that. The fact that Taylor Lawson was his alibi didn't fill Gawn with confidence. It meant Sykes would be Lawson's alibi too and they could have slipped out together once Mrs Lawson was asleep or one could be covering for the other. There might be not one, but two Emoji Men.

Chapter 65

'Well?'

Gawn looked at Rainey.

She and Maxwell had been talking while Rainey had gone to phone Alanna Lawson. Gawn had already phoned Jenny Norris and asked her about the spot in Sykes' eye. The pathologist had said her best guess without examining him was that it was a nevus, a coloured mole. Sometimes they were present from birth but they could develop at any time which is what must have happened with Sykes. It was usually nothing serious but distinctive enough to get him noticed; distinctive enough that women would be able to recognise him unless he disguised it in some way. By wearing sunglasses, Gawn had suggested.

'Mrs Lawson confirms his story,' Rainey said. 'She says Milton's great company. He's travelled all over the world and has lots of good stories to tell. He's had meals with them before. On Saturday he stayed and ate with them but she doesn't know exactly when he left because she went to bed before ten o'clock. You'd have to ask her husband, she said.'

'So it couldn't have been him, either of them, Sykes or Lawson, on the CCTV picking up Kim Cray around nine o'clock. Unless all three of them are involved.' Gawn looked at Maxwell. 'I was so sure we had him,' she said.

'So was I,' Maxwell responded.

Gawn didn't share her thought that Alanna Lawson might just about have had time to slip out while the two men were playing poker and abduct Cray.

'OK. Let's see how he explains his fingerprint on the badge then,' Gawn announced and stood up, trying to recover her enthusiasm for the interview. So far, it seemed, Sykes had all the answers.

Gawn threw the evidence bag onto the table in front of the chauffeur. He looked at it but made no move to pick it up. Instead he very pointedly looked away.

'Ever seen this badge before, Davey?' Gawn asked.

'I told you. I'm Dave not Davey.'

'The badge?' She pushed the bag closer to him, glad he seemed to be getting annoyed at her use of his name.

'No.'

'Sure? Because your fingerprints are on it.'

His eyes flickered for a second. He picked the bag up then, almost as if it might burn him. He brought it closer to his face and examined it carefully.

'Oh, yeh, I have. Yeh, of course. I found it in the Rotunda at City Hall. A couple of weeks ago. I remember now. Someone must have dropped it,' he explained and smiled up at her.

'And what did you do with it?' Gawn asked.

'Blimey, I can't remember that. It was weeks ago. I probably gave it in to reception or, wait a minute, Taylor was with me. I gave it to him and he said he'd check if anyone was looking for it.'

'Taylor Lawson?'

'Yeh.'

Sykes sat back in his chair, a satisfied look on his face.

Was this Sykes trying to throw suspicion onto someone else or did it show Lawson was involved in some way? He knew all about the Street Pastors. He had easy access to City Hall. But he'd been with Sykes on Saturday night. They both had alibis albeit just each other. One of them could have slipped out and the other was covering for him now. Or what about Mrs Lawson? Could she and her husband be working together? Could she have slipped out and grabbed Kim Cray? A girl would be more likely to get into a car with a woman driving, wouldn't she? Gawn was thinking the unthinkable.

* * *

'You let him go?' Maxwell said. Gawn, Rainey and Maxwell were in his office. She was updating him on how they had got on questioning Sykes.

'Pending further enquiries. You know the drill, Paul. We hadn't anything to hold him on. Any decent solicitor would have had him out in two minutes flat if we'd tried to hold him for giving a false name on his job application. We can't prove he touched the badge at the park. He could have found it and handed it in at City Hall as he says and saying he gave it to Taylor Lawson really muddies the water, doesn't it? Sykes' fingerprints don't match the ones we found on the lipstick from the alleyway either. And he has an alibi for Saturday.'

'But an alibi that depends on the Lawsons,' Rainey reminded her.

'So you think they're all in it together, Sam? A conspiracy? Maybe the fingerprints on the lipstick belong to Lawson. I haven't met him yet. Let's rectify that.'

Chapter 66

Alanna and Taylor Lawson lived in a pleasant avenue of detached 1940s houses in the leafy suburb of Belmont. As she drove along the Holywood Road on her way to facing this man for the first time, Gawn couldn't help thinking that it was not too far away from where Kylie Renfrew had been attacked. Was that significant?

The house had a neat front garden but not much in the way of flowers or shrubs. Instead, there was a lawn, well-maintained and some practical paving, the kind of thing one might expect for a busy couple with a young family who wouldn't have much spare time to spend gardening.

When Rainey pushed the doorbell, it set off an immediate howling from inside the house. If the bell hadn't alerted the inhabitants, then the dog certainly would have.

'Just a minute. I'll be with you in a jiffy,' a man's harassed voice sounded through the speaker on the video doorbell. He could obviously see and hear them.

They waited without speaking, conscious they could be overheard, and eventually the door was opened.

Gawn almost didn't recognise Lawson from the photograph on the board in the ops room. His picture hadn't done him justice. He was more handsome in person. His hair looked as if it hadn't been brushed, curly strands falling down over his forehead like a child's. It was a cute look which would appeal to some women. He was flushed and slightly breathless, whatever he had been doing.

'Mr Lawson? I'm Superintendent Girvin and this is Inspector Rainey. From the PSNI.'

She held up her ID. He didn't even glance at it.

'Yes. Yes. I recognise you from the TV. I'm sorry. My wife's not here. She had a meeting up at Stormont this morning.'

'It's not your wife we wanted to speak to.'

He looked perplexed at this announcement and a little uncomfortable.

'Me?'

Gawn nodded.

'Right. You'd better come in then. Anything I can do to help the police.'

Gawn was instantly reminded of Sutton's response to their questions.

'I've just been taking the opportunity of having the house to myself to learn my lines. I'm into am-dram, you see,' he explained with a smile. 'Alanna told me you were investigating this rapist. I heard about the kerfuffle on Saturday night of course.'

Gawn thought it was a strange word to use to describe what had happened. However, they had managed to keep any mention of Hill's abduction and the attack on Rainey out of the press and Cray's attack had been discovered after the morning editions so he might only know that there'd been an incident at the market without knowing any details. That was if he wasn't involved in it, of course.

Lawson gestured for them to go into the front room. It was used as an office or study. One wall was filled with bookshelves and they were sagging under the weight of all the books. Papers were scattered over the desk.

'Sorry for the mess. I don't get a lot of free time.'

'We're checking everyone's whereabouts on Saturday evening, sir,' she said, keen to hear what he had to say.

'Saturday? Oh well, that's easy. I played rugby in the afternoon. For the Thirds.' He smiled and Gawn had to admit it was a charming smile. This man would be able to charm a woman, unlike Sutton. 'It was an away match in Ballyclare. Then I joined my wife for a public speaking competition in City Hall so I could look after the weans. And then when it was over, her driver brought us home and he stayed for supper. When he left, we went to bed. It was late.'

'You didn't play poker at all?' Gawn asked and watched his expression.

'Oh, yes. You're right. I'd forgotten. Alanna was tired. She went to bed and Dave and I played a couple of hands.'

His brow had creased. He must be puzzled how she knew that detail but Gawn pressed ahead.

'Was it usual for your wife's chauffeur to eat with you?'

'Not exactly usual, no, but it's happened a couple of times before. He's a good guy. We had a good laugh.'

'I see. Thank you, sir.'

Gawn put a lot of meaning into the phrase, 'I see'. She meant to. They left him, looking puzzled, as they drove away.

Chapter 67

Tuesday

A more up-to-date photograph of David Sykes, taken from his driving licence, had joined the others on the noticeboard. Rainey was just pinning a press photo of Mullholland up beside it when Gawn walked in, carrying her morning coffee.

'Has Billy got the information on our MLA I asked for yet?'

She wanted to know more about Mullholland. Would he really have given a total stranger a reference or was there some connection between him and the chauffeur?

'I want it before I speak to him again. And I think I'll need to have something a bit more than allowing his name to be used for a reference before O'Brien will let me talk to him.'

'He still had a few calls to make, ma'am,' Collins told her. He was sitting alongside Walter Pepper watching a computer screen very closely.

'Ma'am, Gary's managed to clean this image up. Do you want to have a look at it now?' Collins asked.

Both Gawn and Rainey walked across to look at the screen. They stood behind the two men.

'You can make out the last number of the registration now. It's a six,' Pepper said and pointed to the image.

'Does that match the mayor's car?' Gawn asked.

'No,' Collins answered.

'He's managed to enlarge the area with the sticker too. You can just about make it out. Look. It's for the Street Pastors charity,' Rainey said and she couldn't keep the excitement out of her voice.

'So we have another dark Mercedes with a Street Pastors sticker. But we don't have another suspect with a Mercedes, do we?' Gawn said and her voice betrayed her disappointment.

'Yes, we do, ma'am.'

It was Logan. He had come into the room unseen while they were all focusing on the screen.

'Mr Mullholland drives a black Mercedes.'

Gawn's head jerked up at his words.

'What else have you found out about him, Billy?'

They listened carefully as Logan reported what he had discovered.

Mullholland had been born in Belfast, he told them, but his parents had divorced when he was only eight and he had moved to County Wicklow with his mother and her new husband. At the mention of Wicklow, Gawn had tensed slightly.

'He studied at Trinity College and then moved back north and set up in business. He published a magazine and ran some sort of PR agency as far as I could find out. Then he entered politics. Six years ago.'

Logan seemed to have finished his report and looked up to hear what she wanted him to do next. He waited while she was thinking.

Mullholland was a well-known public figure. Gawn knew she would need to tread very carefully before she could suggest he was involved in their case in any way, even only by allowing his name to be used. And she remembered the photograph of Mullholland and O'Brien on his office wall. Were they good friends?

'Wicklow. Did you find out what school he went to in Wicklow, Billy?' she asked.

'It was a boarding school, ma'am. Maldane College.'

A knowing look passed between Gawn and Rainey.

'Funny you should ask about that, ma'am. In a newspaper report I came across there was mention of his name in association with a court case concerning the school. It was only very sketchy so I had a wee word with the local guards. One of the older sergeants remembered the case from when he was just starting out. It was the talk of the place but of course it was all hushed up. As things were at that time.

'Mullholland and some other boys were witnesses against a couple who were employed as house parents. The pair were convicted of child cruelty and abuse.

'I didn't get all the details, ma'am, but it sounds like they were real sadists. The boys were physically and sexually assaulted on a regular basis. They went too far when they left some poor wee soul miles away from the school to find his own way back. That's how it all came out. He was found wandering barefoot in his pyjamas near a railway line.

'The couple were clever enough to involve the older boys in what they were doing to keep them quiet, the sergeant told me. The big boys weren't going to tell anybody what was going on because they'd been terrorising the younger boys too. None of the older boys were identified by name in court. Except Mullholland. His mother was the prosecuting barrister and she chose to allow him to be named and questioned.'

'That would have been tough. Your mother putting you through that,' Pepper said.

'He didn't seem to have a very good relationship with her. Not surprising really, eh? I found an obituary for her in *The Times* from earlier this year. She only died a couple of months back.'

As he had been speaking, Logan had pinned a coloured photograph of a woman on the board, her grey hair pulled back into an austere bun, her face serious, her dark eyes staring out coldly. She was wearing the traditional red robes of a High Court judge.

'This is his mother. Lady Justice Riverton. She divorced husband number two and moved to London. Married again and ended up a judge. There was a comment in the article to the effect she and her only son were estranged and he didn't attend her memorial service in the Temple Church.'

Gawn thought of O'Brien's suggestion that their culprit would have experienced some change in his life and that he had difficulty relating to female authority figures. It all fitted. She'd thought Sykes was their man but now it seemed Mullholland could be Emoji Man.

Accusing a major public figure of involvement in a series of sex attacks was almost unthinkable. It would be the sort of sensational fodder that would fill the papers all over the UK for weeks, months even, if a trial dragged on. If they accused him and they were wrong or some clever barrister managed to get him off on some technicality it would end all their careers. She would have to be very certain before she did anything.

'I think I'll have a word with the ACC now,' Gawn said. Her voice was very controlled, disguising her feelings.

'You might want to tell him that Mr Mullholland is Joshua *David* Mullholland, ma'am,' Logan said and smiled.

David. She couldn't help but smile back at him.

Chapter 68

Gawn was preparing herself to tackle O'Brien. If he was a personal friend of Mullholland's, as the golfing photograph seemed to suggest, she wasn't sure how he would react to her belief that the MLA was involved; not just that but that Mullholland was Emoji Man and that he had set Sykes up to take the blame. Would he think she had enough evidence? He would want to be extra careful. Arresting an MLA was a minefield. Even bringing one in for questioning was a big ask. That promising career of his could be down the toilet in a minute. His hopes of being chief constable would disappear. She didn't care about any of that for herself. She just wanted to find Emoji Man and stop him.

She was just about to leave her office when the door knocked and Maxwell walked in.

'I'm just on my way to see O'Brien. Can it wait, Paul?'

'I think you might want to share what I have to tell you with him,' Maxwell said. 'Orla Maguire's phone service provider just got back to us. At last. She had calls to and from a burner phone in the couple of days before her death including on the day she disappeared. That must have been Emoji Man setting up their meeting.

'Of course, it's been turned off ever since and we've no way to trace it but just before she made the very first one, she dialled a landline. It was a twenty second call. Just enough time for someone to give her a mobile number and tell her to use that instead. We were able to trace that call.'

He paused enjoying his moment.

'It's the number for Runway, a PR and modelling agency; the one Mullholland set up. He still has shares in it and he's on the board of directors. And you'll be interested to hear the Dockers' Doughnuts delivery – the big order they rushed to before bringing the box here – was to the Runway offices. I checked with them. Mullholland was at that leaving do and he was the one who suggested ordering the doughnuts. He even okayed the expenditure on the business card. Anyway, they told me Orla Maguire had been trying to get in touch with Mullholland about some modelling work he had promised her. He had left a mobile number for them to give her if she rang.'

'Got him!' Gawn said and banged her fist down on the desk.

A direct link between Mullholland and their dead girl; something else for him to have to explain when she got him into an interview room.

'And,' Maxwell said and paused again.

'There's more?' she asked.

'Guess where David Sykes went to school.'

'Maldane College,' she said.

'Got it in one, boss.'

* * *

She didn't quite run to O'Brien's office but she was confident now she would be able to convince him they needed to bring the two men in. Mullholland must have been happy to get Sykes a driving job. If anyone ever suggested Mullholland had some connection to the assaults, suspicion would fall on Sykes instead. He was the one with a police record. He was the one with a history of violence against women. But she suspected it had been more than that. They might have been in cahoots all along, with Mullholland using Sykes to cover for him so he always had an alibi for when the women were assaulted. Sykes would have been happy to follow Mullholland's lead. He would feel he owed him a favour for getting him the job.

She rounded the corner and saw O'Brien and Chief Superintendent McDonald standing together. They were deep in conversation. They weren't quite touching and yet there was something in their body language which hinted at an intimacy. O'Brien looked up, saw her coming and almost jumped away from McDonald.

'Sir, could I have a word please?' Gawn asked. 'It's urgent.'

'Of course. Come in.'

He opened his office door and walked through ahead of her.

'Just a minute, Superintendent.' McDonald called her back. 'I've remembered something about the taxi that picked me up.' She kept her voice low. 'There was a sticker on the back window.'

'Do you know what it was?' Gawn asked.

'Yes. I just realised this afternoon when I saw another one of them. It brought the memory back of what I'd seen. It was for a charity called Street Pastors. I don't know if that helps at all but I was coming to tell you.'

'Thank you, ma'am.' Then as an afterthought, Gawn asked, 'Have you ever met JD Mullholland, the MLA, ma'am?'

McDonald pulled a face.

'Oh yes. We had a bit of a clash a couple of weeks back. I don't know how his poor wife puts up with him. He's a real misogynist.'

'Where was this, ma'am?'

'At City Hall. I was at an event the mayor had invited me to. The two of them were locking horns and I backed her up, I'm afraid. Not very diplomatic of me but he never made an issue of it. That surprised me. I was expecting him to complain to the chief about me.'

He hadn't needed to. He had got his revenge another way.

Chapter 69

O'Brien had okayed it. Reluctantly at first, but even he couldn't overlook the evidence they had amassed. She had taken him through it all and she had stressed they needed to act quickly. He was getting bolder. Women were at risk. Tonight. Finally, O'Brien had agreed.

Mullholland's detached home in Jordanstown overlooking Belfast Lough yielded nothing but his slightly hysterical wife who was in no fit state to answer questions about her husband's activities or more importantly his current whereabouts. She was already displaying a cut lip courtesy of Mullholland. She had gone to pieces when an armed police unit had arrived at her front door. They had found nothing incriminating so far but reported that Mullholland had a boathouse at the end of his garden where he could launch a cruiser, which he normally kept in Carrickfergus Marina, and a small rowing boat directly into the lough. When she heard that, Gawn immediately thought of Maguire's body transported by sea and Rainey's attacker disappearing so quickly and easily at the harbour.

Sykes' tiny flat over a chip shop in South Belfast didn't take much searching. There was nowhere for anyone to hide in its three tiny rooms but the search team was going through it now, trying to find some clue as to where he might have gone.

Mullholland's constituency office had been raided too. They had got the keys from his wife. All they had found so far were some magazines in his desk drawer. They were mildly pornographic, top-shelf fodder from local newsagents. And they were of grown, well-developed women as Grant had reported to Gawn.

'He must like them big and busty, ma'am,' he'd added.

'I don't care what he likes, I want to know where he is,' Gawn had snapped back.

She had an almost permanent ache in her stomach now. She knew the sensation well. She had had it before. It happened when a case was coming to a climax, when she was closing in on her prey but when things could still go spectacularly wrong. That was how she felt now. She was sure they had identified their Emoji Man, or rather men, but they still needed to find them before they snatched another woman.

Gawn was in Maxwell's office. She had wanted to go with the search teams but he had convinced her she needed to stay and coordinate everything. He had stayed with her. She was pacing the room waiting for news.

'Sod this, Paul. This is exactly why I never wanted to be a superintendent. It's out there on the street that real policing gets done. That's where we get results, not sitting behind a desk thinking up strategy and policy and being careful to tick every box.'

'I think we probably need both.'

She was about to berate him for his attempt to be conciliatory and even-handed when an urgent knock sounded on the door and it was thrown open. It was Erin McKeown, a breathless Erin McKeown.

'There's been a call from the mayor.'

'Oh great. She's probably heard about us questioning her driver and her husband and wants to complain,' Gawn said.

'No. She doesn't. She didn't say much. She couldn't. She was cut off. But she managed to tell the call handler that she'd been abducted before the line went dead.'

Gawn and Maxwell jumped up.

'When did the call come in?' Gawn asked.

'A few minutes ago.'

'Can they trace it?'

'They've started working on it. If it's been turned off they won't be able to tell us where it is now but they can find which tower the call pinged off and that should help, boss.'

It did.

Chapter 70

City Hall was in near darkness. It was easy to imagine figures hidden in the nooks and behind the display cases in the empty corridors, silent but for the howling of the wind echoing through the halls. The darkness was menacing, adding to the tension. Everyone was on high alert.

There were no crowds milling around outside. The market had closed hours ago. The tourists were safely tucked up in bed. Only an occasional passing car or taxi showed there were still some people awake in the city.

The ornate lamps lining the way to the portico, designed more to be decorative than effective, provided weak circles of light on the pathway. Gawn had ordered the interior lights be kept off. They had found Liam Roberts unconscious in the back doorway. He was on his way to hospital, a silent ambulance having picked him up.

There had been some weak light showing on the upper floor when they had first arrived. But it had been turned off. Someone was there or at least they had been. Mullholland's car was sitting in the courtyard alongside the mayor's official car. There was no other vehicle there but he and Sykes could already have made their escape, in Sykes' Renault. Its registration had been circulated. Patrols were on the lookout for it.

They needed to search the building. Carefully and quietly. If they were still here, Alanna Lawson's life might depend on it. If she was still alive. They might find themselves searching for a dead body as well as their two suspects.

Gawn didn't want to warn the two men or scare them into action and she was worried about attracting attention too. Blazing lights would signal something was happening. Someone would notice and film on their phone or tweet. Social media and citizen journalism were an ever-growing challenge for policing. She didn't want an audience. This needed to be done quickly and quietly under cover of darkness.

It was lighter inside the building than Gawn had anticipated when the cameras came online and she got her first view of the interior. The high windows were allowing moonlight to find a way in, their stained glass forming colourful patterns on the floor but creating darker corners too. The white marble statue of Frederick Chichester, Earl of Belfast, on his deathbed looked almost real in the gloom. With only a little imagination, Gawn could picture him rising to join in their search.

She could hear footsteps echoing on the checkerboard tiles even though they were all trying to move as quietly as possible. The wide staircase came into view as Rainey moved forward, the red-carpeted treads and white marble balustrades illuminated from above by shafts of moonlight shining through the upper windows in the domed roof.

Someone coughed and the noise echoed through the silent corridors radiating from the central atrium where the team was gathered. Their quarry was in here somewhere. At least one of the men knew the building well. They didn't.

The searchers were divided into three teams. Each lead officer was wearing a body-mounted camera connected to McKeown's monitors. The screens were displaying the feed from these and the building's security system too. If she couldn't actually be inside with them, at least Gawn could see what they were seeing.

Dee was leading Bronze team. They were to search through the ground floor offices and exhibition spaces. Trimble was in charge of Silver team, working through the basement with its plant room and dusty storage areas. Rainey's Gold team was to search upstairs in the main council chamber, the Lord Mayor's Parlour and the ornate Banqueting Hall. Gawn had thought long before allowing Rainey to even be there but she was the most senior officer on the team apart from Maxwell and herself and she deserved the closure of facing her attackers.

Gawn, Maxwell and McKeown were monitoring everything from the command vehicle parked on double yellow lines right beside the building. There was no need for them to be inconspicuous tonight. Their quarry would probably be expecting them after Lawson's phone call.

An ARU was hanging back, awaiting orders. Gawn had no reason to think Mullholland or Sykes had guns but she was going to take no chances. They had them cornered, she hoped. But the men had Lawson and they would be desperate.

Police cars filled the councillors' numbered parking spaces around the central fountain, its waters still sprouting into the air, the cheery noise incongruous in the tense atmosphere. Grant had joked with the po-faced armed men of the ARU that he hoped it wouldn't go for their bladder. He wouldn't want them pissing themselves. Someone might think they were scared. No one had laughed. Not even Grant.

The ARU's unmarked black SUVs were stationed near the disabled access ramp leading to the back door. They had found the back entrance to the building unlocked. This must have been how Mullholland and Sykes had got in and how they intended to get out. But there would be no exit into the back courtyard tonight. This ended here. Gawn was determined.

Just as she was about to give the order to start searching, O'Brien's voice came over her personal earpiece rather than the open radio where everyone could hear.

'Superintendent, they've found Taylor Lawson. He was in Coleraine visiting his parents. His son was with him but the baby is with Mrs Lawson tonight.'

He didn't say anything else. He didn't need to. Gawn had heard it in his voice. Her stomach had done a flip at his words.

'They didn't find her in the house?' she asked.

'Negative. It's been searched. She's either with her mother or...' He didn't finish the sentence.

'Understood, sir.'

'Ready, ma'am,' Rainey reported.

None of the others had heard O'Brien's message. Only Gawn knew their search had just moved up a notch.

'Green light,' Gawn said.

Her voice was calm. She knew what they had to do. They knew what they had to do. Now she just had to trust them to do it.

All she could do was watch and pray.

Chapter 71

The search was slow. Slower even than it had seemed when she had been watching Dee trying to make his way through the crowds searching for Hill. There were no crowds tonight of course to block their way, but the darkness and all the nooks and crannies of the building meant they were having to be extra careful. Gawn and Maxwell had accessed architectural drawings of the building and identified possible hiding places but it would be so easy to miss someone in the shadows, someone who knew the building as well as Sykes did. They had heard how he had spent hours hanging around, exploring its history while waiting to drive the mayor to official engagements. And he spent time in the basement working on his hobby. He was a keen photographer and he had set up a darkroom, with the mayor's permission, where he developed his pictures.

The search teams were working in silence. Occasionally footsteps could be heard. Someone had blundered against a table and almost knocked over a vase. The hissed curse, although barely above a whisper, sounded loud in the silence. A helicopter flew overhead. Gawn heard the beat of its rotor blades and imagined she could feel its downdraft. She guessed it was the air ambulance on a mercy mission. It was nothing to do with them. She hoped it wouldn't spook their quarry.

Long minutes passed. Gawn's eyes were following the screens, afraid to look away. Her whole body was tense.

'Here!' It was Logan's voice, barely more than a whisper.

He was with Trimble in the basement. She could see on Trimble's body camera Logan pointing to a small bottle lying on the floor. He picked it up and held it up to the camera, shining his torch directly onto it. Gawn read the label.

Body paint. Colour: Ravishing Red.

'No sign of the two men? Or Lawson?' Gawn asked.

'No, ma'am,' Trimble answered, 'but they must have stored their stuff down here.'

'Stuff?' she asked.

'Quite the little home from home.'

He was walking around the room, the camera following his movements. She could make out a saggy old armchair, a small TV and an unmade camp bed in the light of their torches.

'Sykes must have stayed down here,' Trimble said as he opened the door of an old wardrobe. 'Hell's bells!'

He didn't need to say anything else. Gawn could see for herself the pile of women's underwear. Trimble opened the door fully and passed his torch over the inside revealing photographs of women in various states of undress, most with the smiley face on their abdomen. She recognised Donna Nixon in one of them.

'He must have taken pictures while the women were unconscious and then developed them down here,' Trimble said.

'As soon as we get the two of them, we'll need a forensics team in there. Leave someone there now in case they come back and the rest of you keep searching,' Gawn ordered.

Chapter 72

'Stay back. Don't try to come in.'

A loud voice, a man's voice, which sounded like Mullholland's and yet didn't, cut through the silence. The suddenness and unexpectedness of the noise shocked Gawn. It had been so quiet, like the subdued reverence of a cathedral.

It was higher-pitched than Mullholland's normal voice when he was making a speech in Stormont or parrying some journalist's question on TV. It had lost all the smooth assurance of the meeting Gawn had had with him in his office. Was that only Thursday? It seemed a lifetime ago.

'You've nowhere to go, Mullholland. Give yourself up. We have the building surrounded. There's no way out for you.'

'You'll let us walk out of here or we'll kill the bitch and her baby.'

As if on cue, a child's wail rose through the stillness. It was frighteningly loud, magnified by the silence all around. Baby Chloe was in there with her mother. There was no doubt. Gawn could make out three dark figures on the Banqueting Hall security camera which McKeown had just accessed. Two seemed to be supporting the third and that third was clutching something to her.

'The mayor's baby's here.' Gawn heard Rainey's surprised voice.

'Get the lights on,' Gawn ordered. 'Now!'

There was a sudden blaze of light, the screen flaring for a second showing the scene inside the room. Gawn could see the two men with Lawson slumped between them. She was clinging to her daughter.

Gawn had sent for a hostage negotiator as soon as she'd realised they were inside and were holding Lawson but she could see and hear for herself how jumpy Mullholland was. She didn't know how long they could afford to wait without acting.

'I want everyone out of the building. Now. We walk out to my car. No one comes near us or I'll kill the bitch and her brat,' Mullholland shouted. Gawn saw him brandishing a long knife at the woman and child.

He walked across the room and began dragging Lawson behind him by the arm. He positioned himself directly in front of one of the security cameras. He was holding the sobbing woman with one hand, clutching her by her hair so that her face was in full view of the camera. Her terror was clear to see. She was desperately shielding Chloe from him. Gawn saw a flash of light from his other hand. It was the knife and he brought it within inches of Lawson's throat. Mullholland knew he was being watched. He wanted them to see the danger the mayor was in.

'You have five minutes to clear everyone out of the building or I'll throw the child out the window.'

Gawn could hear the woman's plaintive, 'No. Please,' and see her vain attempt to break free of Mullholland's grip. He let go of her hair suddenly and she fell to her knees, covering her daughter with her body and sobbing.

'Let me know as soon as the negotiator gets here, Paul,' Gawn said to Maxwell beside her. Then she spoke into the radio. 'All teams move out. Now!'

Chapter 73

Gawn grabbed a radio handset and opened the van door. She was out in the street almost before she had finished issuing her orders. She ran along the footpath following the line of the building until she reached the gate and then cut across the grass, running over the open space beside the empty market towards the main entrance. She was aware of the crunching sound of her feet on the gravel pathway and her own breathing as she ran.

The whole building was flooded with light now. It was streaming from every window like a beacon. It would attract watchers soon. And the press.

Gawn could see officers pouring out of the front door like a stream of black ants. They parted to let her pass.

'Sam, keep a couple of your people inside with you but make sure you're well out of sight.'

'Understood, boss.'

Only a few stragglers were still passing through the Rotunda as she reached the bottom of the stairway.

'Hurry!' Gawn hissed at them.

She took the stairs two at a time, the carpet deadening any sound of her steps now.

No one was outside the Banqueting Hall now. At least, no one was in sight. She hoped Rainey and at least one or two others were safely secreted somewhere nearby.

'Everyone's out. I'm the only one here now, Mullholland. You can come out,' Gawn shouted at the carved wooden door.

'Superintendent Girvin?' It was Mullholland's voice.

'Yes. It's me.'

'How do I know you're not only saying that they've all gone? You'll storm the door as soon as we unlock it,' he said.

She could hear fear in his voice. Frightened men did crazy things. She had seen that before.

'We're not going to take any chances with two lives. I know you're armed. I know you're holding the mayor and her daughter. All I want is Alanna and Chloe out safely. If that means letting you walk out, then that's what'll happen. You have my word.'

There was a pause which seemed to go on forever.

'Get your people to connect the CCTV from the building to my phone so I can see what's happening outside the door. They can do that, can't they?'

Gawn was sure they probably could. She just wasn't sure how long it would take and if she could use it as a stalling tactic to gain them some time until the negotiator arrived.

'I'll check. Don't do anything stupid, Mullholland. I'll get back to you.'

'Be quick, Superintendent.'

Gawn spoke quietly into her personal mic.

'Did you hear that, Erin, what he wants done?'

'Yes, ma'am.'

'Is it possible? Can you do it?'

'Oh, yes. We already have his mobile number. He just needs to turn his phone back on. We have control of the cameras. We can text him a link to access the feed from the upper atrium.'

'Right, listen.'

Gawn dropped her voice to a whisper and issued commands to her sergeant and then to Rainey.

'How long will it take?' she asked.

'A few minutes,' McKeown replied.

'No sign of the negotiator yet?'

'No, boss. He's been held up. Something to do with an accident on the motorway.'

'OK. Don't rush,' Gawn ordered.

Chapter 74

'I'm getting tired of waiting, Superintendent Girvin.' There was a singsong cadence to Mullholland's voice which was unnerving. He was unravelling.

Another long five minutes passed. Maxwell told her the negotiator was about twenty minutes out now. He kept her updated on what was happening inside the room too. Mullholland and Sykes were getting more agitated, he told her. The MLA was pacing up and down muttering to himself. He was like a caged animal. Gawn knew she couldn't keep them waiting too much longer.

'Ready, ma'am,' McKeown's voice informed her in her earpiece. Gawn could hear the tension in the young woman's voice. Much would depend on her being able to do what Gawn had asked of her. Timing was crucial. If her idea didn't work, Lawson or her baby or both of them could pay with their lives.

'Standing by,' Rainey said. Her voice was firm but Gawn knew she must be scared. She knew she was.

'Turn your phone on, Mullholland. We've sent a text. It has a link to the CCTV feed of the camera out here. You should be able to see everything now,' Gawn shouted.

A few seconds passed.

'OK. I've got it. I can see you.' His voice sounded slightly more calm now. Then he spoke again. 'Take off your stab vest. Now lay down your radio and put your gun on the floor.'

Slowly Gawn did as she was told, trying to use up precious seconds until the negotiator would arrive.

'Kick the gun away.'

The Glock skittered across the shiny stone floor, spinning like a child's toy until it bounced off one of the marble pillars.

'Now take off your jacket.'

Gawn complied. He noticed her microphone attached to her collar.

'You're wearing a mic.' He was angry. 'I told you, no tricks.'

'No tricks. I promise. Look.' She ripped the microphone off her shirt, and the earpiece, and threw them down too.

'Now take your shirt off.'

'Come on, I'm not armed. I've ditched my mic. I don't have anything else. You can see that.'

'Just do it!' he screamed at her. 'No hidden weapons or any more microphones or cameras. I need to see, otherwise…' He left the sentence unfinished.

Did he really think she had something hidden under her tailored shirt? She couldn't risk arguing with him. She needed to keep him calm.

Slowly Gawn unbuttoned her blouse and removed it, aware of watching eyes. She let it drop to the floor beside her like a stripper performing for an audience. Mullholland was her audience and she wanted to keep him happy.

She was standing shivering now in just the black plunge bra from a sexy lingerie set which Sebastian had brought her as a present. She had worn it for him today. She was aware of the ugly white scar which ran down her abdomen. Normally she kept it well hidden.

'Put your arms out and turn around slowly.'

She did as he ordered, aware all the time of those watching eyes, not just his but the officers who would be monitoring everything. She was also aware of the goosebumps on her skin. Her teeth would be chattering soon. It was cold and getting colder by the minute as she stood there.

She wondered if he really was worried that she had a hidden weapon or if this was his way of publicly humiliating her as he had enjoyed humiliating his victims by drawing on them and photographing their bodies. He was enjoying the power he had over her now. For one second she considered what she would do if he ordered her to strip completely. If that was what he demanded, it would buy the Lawsons more time until the negotiator arrived but... She left the thought unfinished.

'Look I'm standing here freezing my tits off.'

She tried to sound as upset as she could, almost on the verge of tears. She wanted to give him his vicarious victory. Let him think he was getting to her and she was humiliated in front of her fellow officers; a woman brought down to size by a man; by him.

'We have the car ready for you, Mullholland. Let's get on with this and stop wasting time,' she shouted at the door, trying to sound angry now when all she really felt was frightened for Lawson and her baby.

'OK. You can put your shirt back on.'

Mullholland obviously watched crime dramas on TV. He knew about some of the tricks they could use. She hoped not all. She put her shirt on glad to get some protection from the chill and the watching eyes.

'Now move forward slowly,' Mullholland commanded.

As Gawn stepped forward, she heard the key turn in the lock and the door opened just a crack. She could see an eye looking out at her. It was Sykes. She recognised the telltale mole.

She was close enough now to reach out and touch the heavy oak door but she didn't. She waited for Mullholland's order. After a few seconds, the door was slowly opened a little more from inside and she had a view into part of the room. She saw Lawson sitting on the floor hugging a sleeping Chloe to her. The mayor looked up and Gawn could read the terror in her eyes.

'Come in.'

Mullholland's voice sounded almost friendly; almost welcoming. She could imagine him smiling although she couldn't see him yet. No doubt he was contemplating what he could do to her when he got her inside. She remembered the message with the doughnuts.

Slowly Gawn moved forward again and pushed gently at the door. She didn't want to make any sudden movements. It opened just enough to let her walk through.

As soon as she took one step forward she was grabbed by the hair and the door was slammed shut with a loud bang which reverberated through the empty corridors, followed by a click as it was locked. Mullholland was in front of her beside Lawson, still clutching the knife and hovering over the frightened woman. It was Sykes with his arm around Gawn's neck in a chokehold and something sharp pressed into her back. She guessed it was a syringe or maybe another knife.

'Search her,' Mullholland ordered.

'For God's sake, you saw I don't have a weapon.'

In spite of her protest, Sykes spun her around again and slammed her hard into the door, her head hitting the hard wooden surface with a thud.

'Oops! Sorry,' Sykes mocked her.

She was momentarily stunned as a pain shot through her temple. Sykes was pressing one hand firmly against her back between her shoulder blades to hold her in position. He began to pat her down with the other hand.

'Make sure she hasn't got a gun at her ankle,' Mullholland ordered. He really did watch those TV cop shows, she thought.

Sykes' hand moved up her trouser legs. More slowly than she liked. Then he ran his hand under her shirt and slowly over her breasts. She gritted her teeth.

'Nothing, Davey. She's not armed.'

Sykes dragged her round again so she was facing him.

'Enjoy that did you, Superintendent, cos Davvveey did.' He drawled the name out and leered at her. She could feel his breath on her face. 'Just a pity there's no time for doughnuts tonight.' He laughed and she knew exactly what he meant. 'Not so bossy now, eh, bitch?'

'Very wise, Superintendent. I'm glad you decided to do as I asked. Now get over there beside the other bitch,' Mullholland commanded.

A rough push in the centre of her back propelled her towards Lawson. She landed on her hands and knees beside the mayor and her baby.

The two men withdrew across the room into a far corner. Gawn noticed Sykes was careful to put the door key in his pocket. There would be no chance of making a run for it while they were distracted. They were talking but Gawn couldn't make out what they were saying. She tried to look encouragingly at Lawson. There was no point in telling her everything was going to be alright. She was an intelligent woman. She would know the dire situation they were in but she patted her arm to offer some comfort. The men had finished and were walking back towards the doorway.

'We're going out now.' Mullholland nodded towards the door. 'I trust you've done what I told you, Superintendent, and not tried anything silly. No tricks.' He glanced down at his phone screen again and seemed satisfied with what he saw. 'I don't expect to see anyone out there when I open the door. If I do, this will be the mayor's last municipal duty.'

He laughed. Mullholland's eyes were almost glazed. Maybe referring to Emoji Man as a maniac, as the papers had done, wasn't so far wrong.

'Now. Move!'

Gawn tried to put her arm around Lawson's shoulder to protect her but Sykes pulled her back. Mullholland grabbed Lawson's arm and yanked her forwards. Sykes unlocked the door and then stood behind Gawn waiting for Mullholland's command.

'Open it. Slowly,' Mullholland ordered Gawn.

She reached out. She saw her hand was shaking and knew Mullholland would have seen it too and enjoyed it. She turned the handle. It opened easily. Now she could see part of the empty hallway in front of them. Their way to the stairs was clear.

'Good girl, Superintendent,' Mullholland said, checking their escape route from behind her.

He was looking straight ahead out into the atrium. Gawn knew the next few seconds would be critical. He mustn't look down at his phone again now. She took one step out of the room and saw something, someone, just a brief movement in her peripheral vision tight in at the side of the doorway. She moved forward manoeuvring herself between Lawson and the men and shielding whoever was waiting for them from view. She had one hand on Chloe. Just then the baby woke and let out a cry.

'Shut her up or I'll throw her over!' Mullholland darted forward and grabbed the child. He wrenched her from her mother's arms.

Gawn lost her hold on the baby. He took a step towards the balustrade with Chloe dangling from his hand like a puppet. Lawson was crying hysterically, begging for her daughter's life. Both women realised he might drop the child onto the hard floor of the reception area far below.

'Now!'

Gawn's voice was stunningly loud. Instantly the lights went out and they were plunged into darkness, not total, but it would take seconds for their eyes to adjust. Gawn had lunged at Mullholland as she shouted, marking his position before the lights went out, and made a grab for where the baby had been. Then everything was confusion. There was the sound of running feet and shouts and grunts and a yell followed by a heavy thud.

As suddenly and unexpectedly as the lights had gone out, they came back on. Mullholland was nowhere to be seen. Sykes was flat on his face on the ground, his hands behind his back and two armed officers standing over him while another was handcuffing him. Rainey was with Lawson comforting her. Gawn realised she was still holding Chloe tightly in her arms, her hand around the baby's head shielding her. Chloe was wailing and Gawn was relieved when her mother rushed across and took her.

'Are you OK, boss?' Rainey asked.

'Yes. I'm OK. Where's Mullholland? He didn't get away, did he?'

Rainey didn't speak, just tipped her head in the direction of the stairs. Gawn leaned over the balustrade and saw Mullholland's twisted body lying on the floor far below. The paramedics were already there but she could see from the steadily expanding pool of dark liquid forming around his head that he was in a bad way. Maybe even dead.

Chapter 75

Wednesday

Gawn looked at him, trying very hard not to let her feeling of disgust show. Sykes was sitting directly across the table from her, almost within touching distance in a room that suddenly felt far too small to hold both of them. He looked as if he hadn't a care in the world, his chair pushed back to give him more room to spread out, his legs splayed, his hands resting across his stomach. He seemed in total control of himself. Gawn was sure he would want to control the interview as well. She was glad Maxwell was by her side.

'Are you ready to talk to us, Mr Sykes?'

She had decided not to antagonise him by calling him Davey, as she had at their previous interview. Then she had been trying to rattle him, get him to give himself away. Now she knew, from her years of experience in rooms just like this one, that he was ready to talk. He would probably boast of what they had done and how clever they had been.

Sykes' solicitor had said very little other than to introduce himself as Ronald Baxter. He leant across and whispered something in his client's ear. The man shook his head. Perhaps Baxter thought his client should keep quiet but Sykes wanted to show them how clever he had been. She could read it in his eyes.

'Sorry about your head, Superintendent. I hope it's not too sore,' Sykes said looking at the bruise on her temple where he had slammed her against the door. His expression showed no sign of him being sorry.

'Now, what do you want to know?' he asked as if he was in control of the interview, not her.

'Why you helped Mullholland abduct the women and assault them.'

'Helped Mullholland?' His voice rose. He bristled at her question, his nostrils flaring in disdain. And then she knew. She had been right. Sykes had not been doing Mullholland's bidding. It was Sykes who had been Emoji Man. Mullholland had been his helper.

'I didn't help him. He couldn't have organised what we did. Look what happened when he tried. Davey was always the weak link. Always. In everything. You know what happened at Maldane, don't you? It was so easy for our house parents to get him to do what they wanted. You've no idea what he did for them. And so easy for me to play the innocent caught up in it all. Just another poor victim.'

Gawn nodded. 'We don't need details about the school now. We want to know what happened here in Belfast.'

He didn't even miss a beat. He was ready to talk.

'When I turned up here, it was just so easy for me. Too easy really.' Sykes almost sniggered. 'I only had to suggest I might tell a few people about what he had got up to at school, what he had done to the other boys. Maybe I would tell some journalist or other. Sell my story to them. Mr Respectable. He would have done anything I asked to stop me talking.

'He got me the job in City Hall. He said it would be useful for me to have the car. And he paid the rent on a place for me. He said he wanted to give me a new start. He thought that would be enough to pay me off.'

Sykes' mouth turned up in a sneer.

'It wasn't. I wanted some fun in my life after prison but then one night a stupid bitch took one look at my eye and told me it turned her off. I decided to take what I wanted but I couldn't go back to prison again so dear Davey covered for me. That was the start of it all. Our little game.'

Sykes laughed. Gawn realised there was at least one woman they hadn't found yet who Sykes had raped.

'At first, I just took my chance whenever it came along but, then I started planning my fun. I knew I could always have an alibi, you see. Sometimes I got Davey to grab a woman for me when I was working so I had lots of witnesses if anybody asked any questions. Which they never did. You lot hadn't a clue.

'Then he had the bright idea to grab some wee girl himself. Down an alleyway. He couldn't even manage that. She was drunk but he still almost got caught. But he'd tried to draw on her.'

Gawn realised he was talking about Kylie Renfrew.

'I liked that idea. It was the only good thing he'd ever come up with. It showed we could do what we wanted, you see. They didn't know what we'd done; what we could have done, and we wanted them to know. We wanted to brand them. They were ours. We wanted them to realise we could take their body any time we felt like it. We owned them. They would never feel safe again. Davey enjoyed the drawing bit. He could be quite artistic, you know. Stupid, but artistic.'

Sykes laughed and the sound chilled Gawn. She could still feel his hands all over her body when he had searched her for weapons. Thinking of it now made her feel sick.

'They would have to live with that, wondering what had happened. Wondering if it could happen sometime again.'

He laughed and this time it went on for a long time. Neither of the detectives spoke. They didn't need to. Sykes was enjoying himself. He wasn't going to stop.

Chapter 76

Sykes' whole face was lit up as he boasted of what he had been doing. All Gawn and Maxwell had to do was play the attentive audience.

'And then we started targeting some women. We decided to use Davey's connections with the modelling agency to find girls like Maguire and that Cray girl. Silly wee airheads with big ideas and firm young bodies.'

Sykes paused and allowed his eyes to move downwards from Gawn's face. She knew he was remembering his hands all over her body and she remembered his fingers pausing momentarily to trace the line of her scar on her abdomen.

'And all the time we had perfect alibis, you see. When I saw someone I wanted, Davey could grab her and I could be somewhere well away with a stack of witnesses. Then I could take over and do the business.

'It was all perfect. Perfect,' he repeated, 'until he got besotted with that friggin' Maguire girl. He was always, always the weak link. He wanted more than a few minutes with her; more than just to put his mark on her. He brought her to City Hall for a photo shoot. That's what he told her. He thought he loved her. Loved her!' The disdain in his voice was clear.

'He tried to bone her but he couldn't manage that even though she was half out of it on midazolam. The poor bastard couldn't do the job at all. And then when she came round and saw what he was doing she tried to get away. He pushed her too hard.' Sykes laughed, the sound reverberating round the small room.

Now they knew. It was Mullholland who had killed Orla Maguire. If they could believe Sykes. But could they? He was a manipulator. He could be saving himself a murder or manslaughter charge by blaming Mullholland.

'Was it Mullholland who drugged Donna Nixon too?' Gawn asked. She wanted to be able to tell the journalist, to give her some closure. She owed her that at the very least for identifying there was a sexual predator.

'No. That was me,' Sykes said proudly. 'I listened to her stupid chatter in the back of the car. She was so sure of herself. Miss Modern Woman. Me Fuckin' Too. Huh! So dismissive about men. She thought she knew it all but I taught her a lesson.

'I heard her making her arrangements with her friend. It was easy for me to follow her later and pick her up in the car. I offered her a lift from outside Spud's and she thanked me. Thanked me! I knew she'd never remember anything about it by the time the drug had worked on her. I'd made sure to give her plenty, not like Davey. He had one come round before he even got started.'

Carla, of course, Gawn realised.

'And Chief Superintendent McDonald?'

Gawn felt Maxwell react to McDonald's name. He hadn't known she was one of their victims. But the chief superintendent had come forward now.

'She was Davey's idea. She'd stood up to him, you see. In public. At some event in City Hall. So did Lawson. That's why he wanted to do the pair of them. He wanted to cut them down to size; show them who was boss.'

'But you didn't rape your victims. We know that. Maybe Mullholland wasn't the only one who couldn't always get it up,' Gawn said. She wanted to be sure if the women had been raped or not.

She enjoyed the flash of anger that crossed his face.

'Who says I didn't rape them? You haven't found them all,' he taunted her. 'When I wanted to, I gave them my best. You can be sure of that.' He laughed as if at some huge joke. 'You'd have got the same last night if we'd had time.'

'What about the doughnuts? Was that your idea?' she asked.

'No. Mullholland wanted you put in your place. He said you needed being taught a lesson and I was the man to do it. He came up with the idea. I hope you put our little gift to good use, Superintendent.'

He laughed again but then bared his teeth in a snarl.

'I would have made a better job of it. Perhaps I still will someday.'

Gawn couldn't help a shiver going down her spine. He was mad. Here he was confessing, threatening her, proud of it all. But she realised they were going to have to go further back now, right back to the time Sykes had moved to Belfast to check all the rape and sexual assault reports again. There were more victims out there, some who may not even realise what had happened to them.

Sykes was enjoying himself. He was happy to give them all the details. But Gawn had heard enough. She needed to get out of that room. The thought of what he'd wanted to do to her was too much. And Sykes was proud of what he had done. There was no remorse. She could feel her breathing becoming more difficult. Her chest felt tight. The walls seemed to be getting nearer, closing in on her. Not a panic attack. Please God, no. Not here. Not in front of him. She mustn't give him that victory.

In the end it was Baxter who suggested they take a break. He looked as if had been struggling with his client's revelations as well. He had grown steadily paler during the interview. Gawn was happy to agree. She brought the interview to a speedy end.

As she reached the door, she turned round and looked at Sykes.

'You do know I was in the army too, don't you, Sykes?'

She could see from his reaction that he didn't.

'I was a redcap.'

That was all she said but the look of fury on his face was her reward.

Now she needed to speak to Donna Nixon and the governor at HM Prison Maghaberry. Urgently.

'Paul, I have a few phone calls and arrangements to make and I want to get my report written. I'm supposed to be on leave, you know.'

They were standing in the corridor outside the interview room. She was leaning against the wall, fearful her legs might let her down.

'Yes, I know, boss. Are you alright?' There was concern in his voice.

'I will be. Don't worry, Paul. A few days away from this place, away from that monster, and some good wine and time with Sebastian and I'll be fine.' Her voice grew firmer and she said, 'When Baxter gives you the nod they're ready to start again, take Sandy in with you and get the rest of the story. All the details.'

'Not Erin? It would be good experience for her.'

'It probably would be but I don't want to put her through that. I think Sykes would enjoy talking with Erin there too much, making her listen. I think that was what he was doing with me. He was feeding off the fact that he could relive some of his power by going over it all with a woman in the room.'

Chapter 77

Gawn sat for a long time just thinking, just concentrating on her breathing. Breathe in, exhale, slowly, slowly, breathe in again until she had it under control. She waited until her hands had stopped shaking and her legs felt like she had control of them again too. She was glad to be away from Sykes' leering looks. And his eye. There was no trace of the matey chauffeur with his funny stories this morning, just a psychopath who enjoyed thinking of what he had done.

She worked at her report. It was hard to concentrate and she had just finished when the phone rang and she was summoned to Wilkinson's office.

'Have you seen this?'

ACC Anne Wilkinson pushed a copy of the local newspaper across the desk towards Gawn. It was a déjà vu moment and she was carried back to the wet Monday morning just over a week ago when she had been called to this same office. And asked this same question. A lot had happened since then. And some of it Gawn would never be able to forget.

Gawn glanced down and saw a photograph of herself on the front page of the newspaper, carrying a sleeping Chloe out of the main door of City Hall. She remembered the sensation of the child's little hands clutching her neck, the sound of her contented breathing in her ear. A headline proclaimed the arrest of the monster Emoji Men who had been preying on the women of Belfast and invited readers to turn inside to the six pages of details and interviews with some of the victims.

Jonah Lunn had certainly gone to town on the coverage, including a teaser for an exclusive feature on David Sykes, complete with an interview in their Sunday edition. Nixon was getting her exclusive, the one Gawn had promised her; the one she had negotiated with Sykes last night in the back of a police car before he had been taken away from City Hall. He had been happy to be promised his moment of fame.

Neither of the senior officers commented on it but she was sure they had noticed. He could have been interviewed previously, before he was arrested, before he was even a suspect, but they all knew he hadn't been. It was a price they were prepared to pay.

'You take a good photo, Gawn,' O'Brien said and smiled at her. His eyes were twinkling and she noticed his long lashes again. His presence in Wilkinson's office had been a surprise.

She didn't know how to respond to his comment. She had been blinded by the camera flashes as she'd exited the building hours before. TV crews had already set up in the street outside and their lights had been stunningly bright. It had looked like a scene from some Bruce Willis action movie with flashing emergency service vehicle lights and white-clad CSIs. Armed officers in tactical gear were patrolling the grounds and even the PSNI helicopter had been hovering overhead, its searchlight picking out the building and the grounds. And it had had that surreal feeling for her too like watching a Hollywood movie, only finding herself starring in it instead.

'We got them. That's the main thing. And the mayor and her daughter are OK.'

'Mostly thanks to you,' Wilkinson said.

Gawn didn't want praise. She hoped that wasn't why she had been summoned there. She'd finished her report and Maxwell and Trimble were interviewing Sykes. She wasn't even supposed to be on duty today. Her leave should have started last night. She'd booked the time off months ago for Sebastian's visit home. He was waiting for her there now. He had been waiting for her early that morning when she had arrived home exhausted but elated and fallen into his arms and cried for a long time while he just held her.

'That was a clever trick, Gawn,' O'Brien said. 'Quick thinking. My niece was telling me all about it. We had lunch together and she was still buzzing about the whole thing.' He smiled at her.

So, he was acknowledging their relationship. At last.

'What exactly did you do?' Wilkinson asked. 'I haven't heard the details. I've spent most of the morning with the press office people and the chief and some folk from the PPS. The chief's pleased at how it all turned out, by the way. The best result we could have hoped for.'

Gawn was sure he was. They had their men: Sykes in custody and Mullholland in intensive care under guard. He was on life support and the prognosis was not good.

Both Alanna Lawson and Chloe were fine. The baby would remember nothing of her ordeal. But it would be a very different story for her mother. Gawn could imagine there would be nightmares for a long time to come and hoped she would get the mental health support she would need.

'I used a trick from my husband's TV show, ma'am.'

She'd never admitted to Sebastian before that she watched his programme. When she had told him last night, she'd seen how pleased he was. It felt like a link with him each week when he wasn't around, she'd admitted.

'The cops in the show fooled bank robbers who were holding hostages by freezing the CCTV feed of the front of the building so they were getting an out-of-date picture while the cops were able to get into position to grab them when they came out. I didn't even know if that was possible, or Sebastian had just made it up because it suited his plot. Hats off to our people, ma'am. Especially Sergeant McKeown and PC Erskine. They were able to pull it off. They deserve the praise, not me.'

'I wish I could have seen it. But there was some sort of a glitch with the City Hall security system, apparently. Some of the footage was lost. And the body cameras didn't pick up much when the lights went out. Let's just hope we don't need it for a court case. If we have to admit we've lost it, there'll be more conspiracy theories,' Wilkinson said with a sigh.

'Oh, I think it's unlikely there'll be any court case, Anne. Not a contested one anyway,' O'Brien said. 'Sykes is singing like Pavarotti for Maxwell. I was down watching part of the interview. He's proud of what they did. It seems Mullholland got a taste for exerting his power over the younger boys while they were at school together.

'Then when Sykes turned up in Belfast, they formed a team again. They both resented female authority figures after their experiences at school, and Sykes in the army and Mullholland with his mother. When she died, he felt cheated according to Sykes that he'd never had the chance to get his revenge on her. So when Sykes suggested their "little game", as he's calling it, Mullholland was only too happy to follow his lead. Sykes is proud to admit it was all his idea although personally I think one was as bad as the other. They're both twisted bastards.

'Ferguson's team has collected enough evidence already, fingerprints and trace from Orla Maguire and her suitcase, and photographs and underwear from the other victims too, enough to convict Sykes ten times over. As for Mullholland, he'll never make it to court,' O'Brien said.

Gawn made sure her face gave nothing away although she saw O'Brien looking at her carefully and thought he knew more than he was saying. She wondered exactly what his niece had told him. Erin McKeown had taken her aside and confessed to having made a terrible mistake. She'd pushed the wrong button so the cameras hadn't been recording for the minutes outside the Banqueting Hall.

But Gawn knew McKeown was too careful an officer to have made a simple mistake like that. No one would ever see what Mullholland had made her do or what had happened to him. Had he jumped over the balustrade rather than face arrest and prison? Had he fallen trying to escape? Or had he been pushed? They'd never know, would they?

She wondered too if Rainey had told her uncle about Jo Hill. She hoped not. Gawn intended to visit Hill before she was released from hospital. She wanted to introduce her to Tilly. Whatever help she needed, Gawn was determined she would get it.

'I didn't know they'd found Orla Maguire's blood in City Hall or her case, sir,' Gawn said.

'Yes. Ferguson and his people are processing everything even as we speak. Sykes and Mullholland had tried to clean it up. They got most of it but you know how difficult it is to get rid of microscopic traces. And they found letters Mullholland had sent inviting Maguire and Cray to audition for his modelling agency and arranging to meet up with them.'

'That was why Cray got into the car and why Maguire was so excited. They thought they were going to be models,' Gawn said.

O'Brien nodded. 'Poor girls.'

'A press conference is set for 4pm, Gawn. With the press on our side for a change, the chief constable thought it would be a good idea to make sure they get their facts straight in time for the TV evening news.' Wilkinson smiled. 'You'll be there.' She was not issuing an invitation.

O'Brien was looking straight at her, maybe straight through her, Gawn thought. He knew how she felt about press conferences.

'I'd prefer not to be involved. I'm supposed to be on leave, ma'am.' Gawn tried to make sure her voice did not sound too plaintive.

'Yes, I know that, but it would look very strange if the leader of the task force wasn't there. They'd ask questions and make up their own answers. More bloody conspiracy theories,' Wilkinson added with a wry smile.

'It's an order not a request, Superintendent,' O'Brien added firmly but his expression was sympathetic.

'About that,' Gawn said. 'The task force will be stood down now, won't it? I won't be an acting superintendent any longer.'

'You sound pleased,' Wilkinson said, looking surprised.

'She is pleased. Don't you know your own officers, Anne?' O'Brien asked. 'She doesn't like being behind a desk. Do you, Gawn?'

'It's not for me, sir. I think I always knew that but last night confirmed it for me. I couldn't just sit in the van and watch other people taking risks. That suits some people, I know, and we need them.'

She thought she'd better add that. She didn't want to offend either of the ACCs who spent their time behind desks.

'But I'm happy where I am, doing what I do. For now, at least.'

'The chief has big plans for you, you know,' Wilkinson informed her. 'There could be something very exciting in your future.'

'Yes, ma'am, I'm sure there will be.'

List of characters

Acting Detective Superintendent Gawn Girvin
DC 'Jack' Dee
DC Jo Hill
DC Jamie Grant
PC Mike Collins
DS Erin McKeown
Assistant Chief Constable Aidan O'Brien
Assistant Chief Constable Anne Wilkinson
Detective Chief Superintendent Reid
Donna Nixon – a journalist
DI Paul Maxwell
Paula – Donna's friend
Susan – Donna's friend
Jimmy Sutton – small-time crook
Orla Maguire – a victim
Jarlath Magennis – her boyfriend
DC Billy Logan
Dr Jenny Norris – pathologist
Mark Ferguson – Crime Scene Manager
DCI Megan Rowe – Rape Unit
Sgt Sandy Trimble
DI Samantha (Sam) Rainey
Kylie Renfrew – a victim
Shannon – her sister
Troy – her brother-in-law
PC Gary Erskine
Tilly – a social worker
Carla – a victim
Hermione – a victim
Chief Superintendent Susannah McDonald

Noel Christie – Director of Strategic Communications
Joshua Mullholland – Member of the Local Assembly
Fiona – Mullholland's wife
Ms Halstead – school principal
Sebastian Girvin-York – Gawn's husband
Alanna Lawson – Lord Mayor
Taylor Lawson – her husband
Mrs Dunmore – organiser of the Street Pastors
Chloe Lawson
Arthur Lawson
Walter Pepper – civilian investigator
Robert Hill – Jo's husband
Damien Lyons – CSI
DI Matt Graham
Kim Cray – a victim
Mrs Cray – her mother

If you enjoyed this book, please let others know by leaving a quick review on Amazon. Also, if you spot anything untoward in the paperback, get in touch. We strive for the best quality and appreciate reader feedback.

editor@thebookfolks.com

MORE IN THIS SERIES

All FREE with Kindle Unlimited and available in paperback.
Books 1 and 2 are now also available as audiobooks.

THE PERFUME KILLER (Book 1)

Stumped in a multiple murder investigation, with the only clue being a perfume bottle top left at a crime scene, DCI Gawn Girvin must wait for a serial killer to make a wrong move. Unless she puts herself in the firing line.

MURDER SKY HIGH (Book 2)

When a plane passenger fails to reach his destination alive, Belfast police detective Gawn Girvin is tasked with understanding how he died. But determining who killed him begs the bigger question of why, and answering this leads the police to a dangerous encounter with a deadly foe.

A FORCE TO BE RECKONED WITH (Book 3)

Investigating a cold case about a missing person, DCI Gawn Girvin stumbles upon another unsolved crime. A murder. But that is just the start of her problems. The clues point to powerful people who will stop at nothing to protect themselves, and some look like they're dangerously close to home.

KILLING THE VIBE (Book 4)

After a man's body is found with strange markings on his back, DCI Girvin and her team try to establish his identity. Convinced they are dealing with a personally motivated crime, the trail leads them to a group of people involved in a pop band during their youth. Will the killer face the music or get off scot-free?

THAT MUCH SHE KNEW (Book 5)

A woman is found murdered. The same night, pathologist Jenny Norris goes missing. Worried that her colleague might be implicated, DCI Gawn Girvin in secret investigates the connection between the women. But Jenny has left few clues to go on, and before long Girvin's solo tactics risk muddling the murder investigation and putting her in danger.

MURDER ON THE TABLE (Book 6)

A charity dinner event should be a light-hearted affair, but two people dying as the result of one is certainly likely to put a damper on proceedings. DCI Gawn Girvin is actually an attendee, and ready at the scene to help establish if murder was on the table. But the bigger question is why, and if Gawn can catch a wily killer.

OTHER TITLES OF INTEREST

YOUR COLD EYES by Denver Murphy

A serial killer is targeting women. He is dressing them up and discarding their bodies. Detectives become convinced that it is something about the way the victims look that is making them be selected. They need to find out just what that is, and why, to hunt down the killer.

Available free with Kindle Unlimited and in paperback!

EVIDENCE POOL by Ian Robinson

When a powerful Russian oligarch finds his assistant's
lifeless body in his London mansion's pool, he is quick to
claim diplomatic immunity and scurry into the panic room.
Detectives Nash and Moretti are convinced the killer is still
in the luxury residence, so they place the building on
lockdown. But it seems that all of the members of the
household, family and staff alike, have something to hide.

Available free with Kindle Unlimited and in paperback!

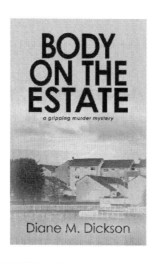

BODY ON THE ESTATE by Diane Dickson

DI Jordan Carr has left serious crimes in favour of more community policing, but his first case propels him abruptly back into a murder investigation. A woman has been killed in her home on a housing estate. The residents won't talk to the police, and when Carr heads to Blackpool following a lead, he receives abuse of another kind: racism. Justice for the victim is all that keeps him going.

Available free with Kindle Unlimited and in paperback!

www.thebookfolks.com

Printed by Amazon Italia Logistica S.r.l.
Torrazza Piemonte (TO), Italy